J. A. JACKSON

Lovers, Players & The Seducer

First edition

Editing by Rossi V. Jackson, Jr.

This book was professionally typeset on Reedsy.
Find out more at reedsy.com

"Hatred stirs up strife, but love covers all offenses."

—PROVERBS 10:12

Contents

<h1 style="text-align:center">Acknowledgement</h1>

I'd like to give out a big endless gratitude of thanks and appreciation for the wonderful support and editorial guidance of my editor the very knowledgeable Mr. Rossi V. Jackson.

I'd also like to say a special thanks to the incredible man in my life, my husband who believed in my writing and supported my dreams. Also, to my mother Dorothy Henson you blew the wind beneath my feet and made me enjoy learning, writing and living this life. God gave me you and you gave me unconditional love and support – Thank you.

Also, a special thanks to my sisters Kay, Shelia and Marie. I am so grateful to you for your support and love. And to my brothers Ray and Eric I thank you also.

To my readers and fans, I am forever grateful. Thank you.

For Rossi, Daddy & Mommy always...

Chapter 1

O akland, California February 2006

Traffic was light in the Oakland foothills, Nicholas La Cour thought as he drove his car up Skyline Boulevard. He checked his watch. It was a little past midnight. He glanced ahead, and his eyes caught the vibrant lights of the City of Oakland looming out before him. The chill of the night had a strong bite he thought, as he closed his sunroof.

A few minutes later the bright lights of the old familiar house loomed before him. Only a select few men were ever invited to the parties held here. His best friend Quinn Rolandis was one of them.
Nicholas found a place to park his car. A few minutes later he headed for the front door and felt the familiar churning feeling in the pit of his stomach before he rang the bell. The front door opened for him. "Jesus Christ girl, you don't have any clothes on!" he said, his eyes bulging. His mind wandered back to the time Quinn had taken him to a bachelor's party. He wondered if tonight was going to be one of those parties. He didn't have long to wait to find out.
"Lips, hips, or fingertips?" the young girl asked smiling up at him.
  "How old are you?"

"None of your damn business," Quinn's slurred voice coldly sliced the air. It was obvious Quinn was inebriated.

Nicholas looked back at Quinn. He was surrounded by women. He knew he wasn't ready to leave.

"Look Nicholas, get your butt in here. The party has started. Now that girl that answered the door gives a mean blow job." Quinn sluggishly chuckled. "Let her get you started."

Nicholas hesitated. He hated it when Quinn had been drinking too much. "Quinn, I thought I was just coming to pick you up. You said you were ready to go," he murmured under his breath. He was torn between looking at the naked woman beside him and looking back at Quinn. He shoved his hands in his pockets.

Quinn's laughter carried on the air.

Nicholas heaved out a sigh. "It's the middle of the work week, for crying out loud, Quinn! And I have an early appointment, remember? And its past midnight as it is."

Nicholas was in agony. He wished the naked girl standing in front of him would stop smiling at him. He swallowed hard and lowered his eyes.

The young girl bushed her naked body against him.

Quinn laughed. His eyes were red and bloodshot. "Nicholas my man, I can't believe you sometimes. Right now, you've got a beautiful naked woman standing in front of you ready to fulfill your every desire and you are standing here thinking about work."

With one hand Quinn took a big swallow from a bottle of bourbon. With his other hand he swatted the backside of a naked girl. "Nicholas man, you don't have your priorities in order! Tonight, I'm a bad boy. Tomorrow…Well we will just have to wait and see how good a boy I can be tomorrow. And then Friday will take care of itself."

The naked girl giggled loudly as she rubbed against Nicholas. She groped her own breasts as she giggled.

Quinn spoke without giving Nicholas his full attention. "Look here Nicholas. Right now, Luscious Lola is waiting for me.And you know

I can't resist Luscious Lola," he said with an effort to steady himself. "See what you can do with that naked girl in front of you. Go and have some fun," he said before heading back up the staircase.

The naked girl standing in front of Nicholas reached out and took his hand. He followed her like a child. She led him down a long corridor. Finally, they reached a door. She reached out and opened the door wide. Standing on the threshold she held her arm out wide beckoning Nicholas to enter.

Nicholas stood there taking in the room. A Jacuzzi tub sat in the middle of the room. Its soft hum purred like a kitten.

Nicholas slowly smiled.

The young woman closed the door.

Slowly the young woman ran her hand over Nicholas shoulders and removed his jacket. She dropped it to the floor. She ran her hands down his spine and under his polo shirt. In one swoop she pulled it over his head. In seconds she'd striped Nicholas naked.

Her hands reached out and slowly caressed his bare chest.

Nicholas smiled nervously. "It's chilly in here."

"Come, let's get in the Jacuzzi," the young girl said. "Then you'll relax, and I'll fulfill your every pleasure!"

Nicholas hesitated. "Hey look. I… I hope you don't think this is strange but is there an older girl around maybe? Say one that's at least eighteen" He hesitated. "And maybe one that hasn't screwed Quinn tonight?"

The young girl smiled. "Luscious is here tonight," she said. "Quinn prefers Luscious. By the way I'm twenty-one. I have a driver's license to prove it. I just look young. And no, I haven't screwed Quinn tonight. Blow job yes, screw no," the girl added.

Nicholas smiled. "Okay then let me start over. My name is Nicholas… And I'll have what Quinn didn't have. In fact, give me the works, but before you ride *Mr. Nicky* wrap him up in a condom."

Chapter 2

Summit Country Club Hills February

The overnight rainstorm was typical for February. Late that Thursday night Maëlle Moulard pulled her car into the driveway. She hoped it would stop raining before the concert tomorrow night. She was looking forward to the five old friends getting back together. She waited as the automatic garage door opener started. Slowly she pulled her car into the garage and parked alongside the sleek BMW.

A man's voice sliced the air. "Are you playing hard to get? Hurry up. I'll be in the bedroom."

"I'm coming lover," Maëlle said, as she got out of her car and quickly walked through the doorway where the man had stood.

Maëlle felt her stomach churn as she walked down the long quiet corridor. The house sat in at the very top of *Summit Country Club Hills* with a view of the mountains that was breathtaking. She opened the door to the bedroom.

Her lover was lying naked on the rug, propped up on his elbow in front of the fireplace.

She walked over and stood in front of him.

The man's eyes glowed with a hungry sensual passion. "Are you going to take off those clothes or do you want me to?"

Maëlle wasn't shy about taking off her clothes. Her green eyes held the man's as he watched her. She quickly removed her jeans and sweatshirt. She stood naked before him and purred. "You like?"

"Hmmmm no underwear, yes I like that," he said, as his eyes admired her leg.

He reached his cold hand out and gently stroked her ankle and then placed a kiss where his hand had been.

"Whew! You've learned a new trick Quinn," she moaned.

"And you're beautiful… I've been waiting for you for over an hour," he said.

All at once Quinn stopped what he was doing and seriously stared back at her. "Oh, and did you bring me a slice of chocolate cake to eat after," his lips curved into an inviting smile.

Maëlle squinted her eyes back at him. "Yeah Quinn, but you keep forgetting that I'm not your wife, or your maid, or your, bring me a slice of chocolate cake when you come, girl."

Quinn just ignored her. "Oh, why do you make me suffer waiting for you?" He hissed under his breath. "You drive me mad waiting to possess the magic secret of you," his lips curled up into a wicked grin, as he looked up at her. "Aren't you going to come closer? Why do you make me wait so? I can't stand it."

She looked down at him. His predatory eyes stared back at her. She stooped down on her knees in front of him. "Cut out the drama crap Quinn Rolandis. This is just sex, plain and simple."

He drew her close. He leaned in to nuzzle her neck. He could smell her skin. "You borrowed Lacey's perfume again didn't you Maëlle?"

She pulled away from his reach and studied him. His eyes betrayed him. She knew he was thinking of Lacey.

"I knew you liked it so much Quinn, that I begged her to give me a bottle for my birthday," she said hesitating. "Now if you're done smelling Lacey's perfume.I'll have to make you beg for it. That is if you want your itch scratched."

She leaned over and kissed him softly. "Now say please and mean it," she purred commandingly.

He flashed his most charming smile murmuring low. "Okay, please…!"

She kissed him hard. He tasted so good. Suddenly he pushed his tongue into her mouth.

She pulled his hair hard. "You've got the condom Quinn?"

"Oh, you know I do," he said, as his mouth took possession of hers. He devoured her with kisses. His tongue left her mouth and trailed down to her breasts.

Maëlle stopped abruptly and pulled away again.

Quinn shuddered. "What is it now?"

"This is just an empty hearted screw. You know that don't you? Don't go blabbing this to anyone. Tomorrow I'm giving up meaningless sex and going back to being a virgin," Maëlle hissed out.

"Me too," Quinn moaned between kisses. "This is just our little secret. Our agreement stands. No one is to ever know about this."

Maëlle pulled out of his embrace. Her affair with Quinn was their little secret. Quinn was where she went to escape. He gave her the attention she craved and as a bonus his wild animalistic sex drive matched her own.

Sometimes her life was beyond crazy.

"Don't ever tell Lacey and for God's sake you'd better not ever tell Nicholas," she murmured under her breath. "You hear me?"

Quinn shook his head. He'd agree to anything. But he wasn't worried about himself. He enjoyed having sex. He knew what he wanted. He thought about it. "I'd better be able to trust you," he said with an edge in his voice.

Maëlle smiled with her thoughts. All Quinn meant to her was a quickie and a chance to enjoy something she knew her best friend Lacey had never experienced. Every day she had to live with the fact that the only man she ever loved would forever be in love with her best friend. She long ago gave up thoughts of ever having Kienan

Egan as her man. The mighty Quinn was just something she could say she had that her best friend, Lacey La Cour, had never had, but wanted.

Her eyes sparked dangerously. "Look Quinn don't be so edgy. You're a fool if you think I'd ever want Lacey to know I've been with you."

Quinn was annoyed. He spat out the words vehemently. "Good! Then we understand each other."

Maëlle's voice was effortlessly cool, "So Quinn, are you still holding on to that secret dream of yours? You know the one that one day Lacey will be your girl?"

Quinn frowned. "Stop it Maëlle, you know I hate to play games. You and I both are suspicious and despicable people," his eyes lingered on her lips. He reached out a finger and ran it seductively across them. He hated the way she could make him feel. He felt weak. But he needed her. Slowly he inhaled savoring Lacey's perfume. He smiled back at Maëlle. He knew she knew he needed her to wear Lacey's perfume. He stared at her.

Maëlle held his eyes unflinching. She was impatient.She slowly caressed her hand down his hard chest and brought it to rest at his engorged member. She seductively looked up at him. "I know why I'm here Quinn. My body's starving. What about you Quinn? Do you have an appetite tonight?"

Quinn moaned as he kissed her. "You know I'm always hungry and up for some real hard

Chapter 3

San Jose, California
February 2006
21 years later

Lacey Kadira Catherine La Cour's soft gray eyes glowed in anticipation, waiting to catch another glimpse of the man. She felt a breath of cold air against her neck.

The San Jose Concert Area lights suddenly dimmed, and time seemed to stand still. She saw the man that she saw earlier.

Lacey tilted her head and adjusted her eyes to catch another glimpse of him. All of a sudden, the air felt strange around her. She listened and could have sworn that she heard the ticking sound that the hands of a clock make. Then she felt a cold wind against her neck. I must be hallucinating, she thought. She looked up and the man stood just by the isle, he refused to come closer.

The man glowed like a star against the midnight sky.

The man stood there and stared at her. The fathomless depths of the man's eyes caught hers and it seemed his face summoned a smile.

Her eyes grew as wide as saucers as she gasped as a shiver ran down her spine. Her thoughts raced. Was it really her father she thought, no it couldn't be, her father was dead?

"Please excuse me!" The shrill voice burst forth and drew her back to reality.

"What?" Lacey gasped startled and terrified by the voice. She looked up. It was the woman who had been sitting next to her earlier. She looked past the woman to see if the man was still there. He was gone.

The lady had walked past her during the concert too many times to count.

"I'm so sorry for squeezing past you like this again," the lady said before sitting down next to her. She then leaned over and whispered. "Your boyfriend has a profile that is really quite handsome. He looks like a god. I hope you don't mind my saying so?"

"Where did a woman like her go to school to learn to sound so convincing?" Lacey wondered.

Lacey Kadira Catherine La Cour didn't want to appear rude. She had experienced this sort of thing before. She opened her mouth to say something but thought better of it. The woman reminded her of her Aunt Delta.

Her Aunt Delta was also a slim, attractive woman well up in age, but didn't look like it.

Lacey let a refined sigh escape her lips.

Just at that moment the woman reached out a well-manicured hand. Her voice carried like a whisper on the wind. "By the way, my name is Josephine. Josephine Deville.

"Hi Josephine, Lacey said, with a vague nod. "My name is Lacey."

"Lacey, call me Auntie Josie, all my nieces do. You're a very beautiful young woman and I bet you get a lot of attention from the men."

Lacey gave a little nervous laugh as she felt her face flush. Her words failed her.

"You need to take care of business with that young man of yours," Auntie Josie said, as her lips curved upward into a catlike smile. "You've got to take a man like that by the balls and screw him hard if you want to secure him in matters of the heart. Many a beautiful woman has wondered why men stray. A woman's beautiful face and body may catch the man, but it is raw sexual talent in bed that will keep the man coming back for more. A man never forgets good sex. It always leaves a man spellbound," she said just above a whisper. "Take my advice to heart and fuck him hard."

"What! I cannot…" Lacey gasped frowning.

"Oh, dear there goes my bladder again," Auntie Josie said rising abruptly. "Well I'm off to the ladies' room again."

For a moment Lacey's gaze wavered as she stared after the woman called Auntie Josie. Something caught her eye. Again, for the second time that night she thought she was hallucinating.

She heaved forward with a loud sigh as her thoughts overwhelmed her. She thought she must have fallen asleep wide awake. The man she saw earlier looked like an angel.

"Something wrong Lacey?" Kienan Egan's gray eyes narrowed with deep concern.

Lacey turned her head and looked at him.

Kienan Egan, was broad-shouldered handsome with a gentle mild and kind disposition.

Slowly she shook her head no and smiled nervously back at him.

"Are you enjoying the concert?" He asked softly.

Spellbound, Lacey looked at him in astonishment. "Ah…The concert…It's great!"

Lacey felt like something was hovering behind her head. She was afraid to turn around.

Nervously, Lacey slowly breathed out smoothing back her hair. Her fingers pressed across the side of her cheek. Her cheeks felt cold. She felt like she'd seen a ghost.

She knew the man wasn't her father. Her father had died a few years ago. Her Grand mere Catherine often said the dead spent their time watching the living. She normally never gave that sort of thing any thought; the supernatural, ghosts and stuff.

It was funny, she smiled. Just last night she had dreamt about her father.

Lacey had adored her father. He was her number one hero, her rock; to her he was the ideal man, the ideal father. No man on earth could ever compare to him. No matter what, he'd always been there for her in times of crisis or peace. Once upon a time she thought Kienan would be her rock or rather her second rock. But just like she sat and watched her father being buried, she'd long ago buried her feelings for Kienan. She smiled softly, drifting with her thoughts.

"Excuse me, Lacey…Didn't you hear me?"

Lacey almost jumped out of her seat. She turned and threw her best friend Maëlle Moulard an ice-cold look.

"What's the matter with you? You look like you've seen a ghost or something," Maëlle sympathetically asked, as she took the empty seat next to her.

"Hey Kienan, where are we going to eat tonight?" Maëlle inquired.

Kienan nodded and smiled calmly. "I guess that's my cue to go and see what the guys feel like doing," he said, getting up and strolling off.

Maëlle stole a gaze in Kienan's direction. "He's so geeky and sexy at the same time. Aren't you glad you and Kienan got to sit together for tonight's concert Lacey?"

"Sure, I'm just so ecstatic about it," Lacey curtly said, as she tossed back a loose strand of hair. "Too bad we couldn't all get seats together."

Maëlle knew Lacey was still angry at Kienan for dumping her when he went off to college. Besides, she knew Lacey craved a hot relationship with guys she thought were way cooler than Kienan could ever be. Still Maëlle knew Kienan had done a lot of growing up since his days in college. "There's nothing wrong with a safe guy."

Lacey tossed back a loose strand of hair. "What? That's what I thought. You think I don't know you purposely put me right next to Kienan?"

Maëlle giggled out a smirk. "I am so full of surprises."

Lacey's eyes widened. "Well, what if I told you I had my sights set on Quinn. He's been looking really good to me lately," she said smiling faintly. "In fact, my sex life is so boring right now I'd follow Quinn to a hotel room in Las Vegas if he asked me to. Just as long as he can work the equipment God blessed him with."

"What if I told you Quinn and Nicholas both reek of whores right now?" Maëlle sighed. She felt ill-tempered as she peered back at her best friend, curiously. "You should be thanking your lucky stars that a man like Kienan wants you."

Lacey knew where this was going. Maëlle wanted to get married, really bad. What young woman didn't? "Don't jump on your high horse about marriage Maëlle, you'll ruin the evening."

"I'll have my say about marriage or anything else," Maëlle said throwing her a cursory glance. "Did you know that if Nicholas or Quinn ever married the only thing that would be consistent in their marriage would be that both of them would cheat on their wives? Neither one of them knows how to treat a woman. They never have, and they never will!"

Lacey shrugged and stood up. She walked and stood by the main isle. She was tired of Maëlle preaching sermons. She'd forgotten what a bully Maëlle could be, especially if she was mad at her brother Nicholas. She knew Nicholas and Maëlle had a history together, a history that often caused her a lot of pain.

Maëlle moved in close sensing the tension she was causing her best friend. She put her best forgive me, smile on her face. "Lacey, I'm sorry I've been so grouchy. Remember how the two of us promised each other we were not going to end up having people call us sluts, like that girl Tiara Blake, back in junior high."

Lacey never could stay mad at Maëlle for long. "Yeah, I remember. Maëlle, forget I said anything about Quinn. I was just joking. Besides, you know I've got to break things off with James Fairway.

"I'm so glad to hear that. I never liked James Fairway," Maëlle stated with mirth. "He is just so the non-existent boyfriend."

"I agree, and that's why I'm dumping him," Lacey winked back at her friend.

The two friends laughed simultaneously.

Seeing the two friends laughing Quinn walked over.

"Hey Lacey, there is a private party upstairs in the Sky Club. We're all going to head up there for a spell and then we can go and get something to eat," Quinn said, closing the gap between them.

From all outside appearances Quinn Rolandis was tall, and had a medium build, with a brown face. He loved dark suits and owned an array of different colored glasses.He'd always felt his black framed glasses suited his face better than his wired-rimmed glasses. Still he knew every pair of his glasses and contact lenses hid from his eyes his true feelings of discernment of human feelings.

Tongue tied Lacey stammered. "Thanks Quinn but I…We… Ah" she flushed and found it difficult to answer. She found it hard to look him straight in the eyes.

"Going to get something to eat was my idea Quinn. I'm the one that's hungry," Maëlle pointed out assuredly. She gave Quinn a disgusted look.

"You're always hungry Maëlle. Don't worry, we'll feed you. We won't let you starve," Quinn knowingly smirked out, with gleaming white teeth.

Maëlle stopped smiling. "That was so funny Quinn. Do tell us another joke and remind me to buy you a joke book for your birthday. Now stop trying to act like a good old church altar boy in front of Lacey. Quinn, because no matter what you do, you will always be a snake that wears glasses."

"Okay you two, cut out the friendly banter," Lacey interrupted.

Quinn didn't want to end up in an argument with Maëlle. It would defeat his mission to get Lacey's attention. "I didn't mean it to sound mean. I just meant that there is bound to be some appetizers' or something up in the Clubhouse."

Maëlle shook her head. "Go back and join the men Quinn, before I get angry and go in search of one of your old dumbass girlfriends. I'm sure there has to be a couple of them here tonight at the concert.

Lacey let out a giggle.

Quinn threw Maëlle an angry look that silenced her before he tilted his head and looked back at Lacey.

Lacey could feel his eyes penetrating like a laser beam as it bore back at her. Her laughter died in her throat.

Quinn's voice got a strange hoarse quality to it as he glanced up. "Lacey, it looks like I've been commanded to leave, but let me say, you look beautiful tonight as always. It is so refreshing to be in the presence of a lady," he said as his face seemed to light up with enthusiasm.

Maëlle's voice was strained as she breathed out."Oh brother!"

Quinn ignored her and kept his gaze leveled on Lacey. "Oh, and Lacey don't worry, I'm buying your dinner tonight. You can order whatever you like," he said, as his hand pulled her hand to his lips and kissed it.

The nearness of him affected Lacey greatly. There was something about Quinn. He had an air of danger and a wild side about him that made her heart skip a beat and she giggled.

"As for you Maëlle," Quinn turned and said. "Need I remind you that Nicholas would be more than happy to have you eat off his plate?"

"Tempting Quinn, but I think I'll pass," Maëlle condescendingly said. She couldn't help wondering if she was feeling jealousy watching Quinn lavish attention on Lacey.

A frown crossed Maëlle's face as she cleared her throat. She leaned in close and whispered. "Don't be a fool Quinn. Stop the lovey dovey act. People are watching," she motioned in a gesture only he could see.

Quinn quickly gazed where she nodded. His brows rose.

"Keep your head down Quinn," Maëlle muttered out a warning. "You don't want Kienan to acknowledge he saw you."

Quinn slowly rubbed his chin.

Lacey took a deep breath and grew silent as her eyes caught Kienan's as he marched over.

Kienan held a commanding stance as he walked over. His eyes

gave Quinn the once over and Lacey knew by the way Quinn quickly departed it wasn't a good thing.

Quinn may have been brash and boastful, but he wasn't a fool when it came to messing with Kienan or what he felt belonged to him. "Kienan old friend," Quinn uttered, cracking a smile trying to look cool.

He looked around and said. "I'll just go see what Nicholas is up to."

"Kienan," Maëlle stammered shaking her head. "I'm going to go catch up with Quinn."

Kienan watched her go and turned and gave his attention too Lacey. "So how is everything going for you tonight Lacey?"

Kienan's eyes didn't flinch. Words seemed to fail him as the two of them did the trite dance of politeness. And then he did a strange thing and licked his lips as his brow rose.

She stared back at him mentally remembering. A heavy wave of nostalgia hit her as she remembered how Kienan had been as a young boy. He'd always had an extremely handsome built-in geekiness that was irresistible to her. He was the boy next door. The one you always wanted to build your life with."

She cleared her throat hoping emotion didn't show on her face. "I'm fine," she said, determined never to be anybody's fool ever again.

Kienan's eyes didn't flinch. "I hope you aren't tired yet. We are going to head up to the Clubhouse for a while. That is if it is okay with you."

Lacey forced a smile. "Lead the way,' she said extending her hand.

Chapter 4

Revelation & The Clubhouse

When Lacey looked at the clock two hours had passed. Her mind had been racing since she arrived in the Clubhouse. She hadn't even noticed any of the action happening around her. For some reason her eyes kept focusing on the huge red disco ball hung high above the dance floor.

The club house was famous for the huge revolving disco ball that hung high above the dance floor. It was known for throwing out flashes of red, green and blinding white light, that caught the eye and mesmerized anyone who took a moment to focus on it.

Watching the bright lights her thoughts, wandered. She went back to that moment she held out her hand and let Kienan escort her. At the moment, her hand touched his she realized he still wanted her. She knew it was dangerous to be close to him again. Kienan may have had his bad points but he was still a good man. He was a hard worker and he was the kind of man a girl could think about having a life with.

She let her eyes wonder over to where her brother sat. Too bad Nicholas Avoyelles La Cour wasn't more like Kienan. He was intelligent. He liked books, but he was more than happy with opportunities that came with ease than with hard work. Nicholas and Kienan had always acted more like brothers than best friends who'd been together since as long as she could remember.

Lacey watched as Nicholas and Quinn stopped talking as they headed over to where she stood.

Maëlle cut them off as they headed over. She said out loud. "Say Lacey, did you get your pay raise? Oh, never mind just loan me sixty dollars.

Lacey shrugged. "Sixty dollars? Why do you think I have sixty dollars to give to you?"

Maëlle gave her a wicked smile. "Because I'm your best friend, and I need the money. Besides, I went with you to the bank earlier today; I know you have the money."

Lacey couldn't help laughing. "You are so funny sometimes Maëlle, I wouldn't loan you a dime. You still haven't paid me back your last loan, remember?"

Maëlle opened her mouth but before she could respond Nicholas interrupted closing the distance between them.

"Hey Maëlle," he called.

"Oh no here we go," Lacey muttered. "See what that begging act of yours has started Maëlle?

Seconds later Nicholas loudly cleared his throat. "Oh! Ah … Maëlle," he blurted out. "What was the name of that movie we watched last Sunday after the game? That western, you remember."

Maëlle tossed back her hair trying to ignore him. "Do I look like I remember ever movie we ever watch Nicholas? She stated with a frown. "Lacey and I were talking here. Now you know Quinn is going to follow you over, here right?"

"Oh, don't be so rough on Quinn," Nicholas said sympathetically, giving Maëlle a quick tap on the shoulder. "I told Quinn earlier you said I resemble that actor. Oh, what's his name?"

Maëlle quickly studied them. She recognized the gaze between Nicholas and Quinn. She knew they were trying to draw her into something. "Have you two got any money bet on the outcome of my answer? If you do I want my usual twenty-five percent."

"Oh Maëlle? It's just a friendly…Ah debate, like always," Nicholas assured her.

Quinn quickly nodded his agreement.

Maëlle studied Nicholas. "Okay, it was the movie *The River of No Return*," she said."And what I really said was you had those rugged good looks like Robert Mitchum. Especially that little dimple in your chin."

Nicholas happily smiled. He roared with laughter, "See, I told you Quinn!"

Lacey laughed out in astonishment, "If Nicholas looks like Robert Mitchum then I look like Marilyn Monroe."

"I think you do," Kienan's voice rose out as he walked over. "Well maybe not the blonde hair. But your body," he hesitated, "It is way sexier than hers," he said lifting his brows.

Lacey was speechless.Kienan had handsome nerdish bad boy appeal in his black leather jacket and black turtle neck.

Maëlle laughed out and leaned over whispering, "Girl I told you that man is crazy about you," she smiled. "I have to use the ladies room. I'll be right back."

Kienan walked and stood in front of Lacey and said out loud. "Baby, if you were a gold mine I'd file my claim!"

Lacey shivered standing so close to him. She suddenly felt that same magical electric charge. She remembered how easy it was to fall in love with him once upon a time.

Nicholas' eyes drifted between his sister and Kienan. He considered Kienan like a brother. He knew Kienan was a true friend and he knew Kienan and his sister, Lacey, had a history together, theirs was some of special bond, that had existed since childhood. Seeing them together made he remember back.

He was alone there in his own little world of loneliness, and isolation He'd always been alone there. It was his self-exiled place. His thoughts raced.

Nicholas' eyes drifted up and caught a flash of from the huge revolving disco ball that hung high above the dance floor Blinding white light, caught his attention and blurred colors and images held him spellbound.

It was as if he was transported back in time.

He remembered the day clearly; his sister Lacey was seven years old. He remembered looking through the kitchen window to make sure Lacey had arrived back home safely, after he had left her out on the trials alone. He wasn't an uncaring brother, it was just that that day he and Quinn didn't want to get stuck babysitting his little sister and they ran off and left her on the trail instructing her to head back home.

After telling Quinn, he'd met him at Boccardo trail, Nicholas had doubled back home to make sure Lacey had arrived home safely. He hid and peaked through the kitchen window and saw his sister Lacey reach over and firmly grasped a red apple with her small hands. She heaped it out of the bowl firmly, turned and looked at the boy sitting at the table beside her father Louis.

The boy at the table watched her attentively, feeling the familiar churning of a devoted protective feeling from deep within. Eleven-year-old Kienan Egan gave Lacey one of his rare smiles as he looked back at her, oblivious to everything around him.

Lacey took a deep breath as she handed him the apple. "Here Kienan, this is for you," she said sitting down beside him.

Grand mere Catherine, thought of herself as a tough strong woman, but the tears that strung her eyes told her differently as she looked tenderly between her granddaughter and the young man Kienan. Lacey was always looking out for Kienan, just as he did for her.

Grand mere Catherine turned her attention back to the stove in front of her and hovered there with her thoughts. Her thoughts told her Kienan Egan was a well-brought up, protective man child. He was gentle, and kind in disposition. She knew he was always considerate and caring of those that he loved.

Catherine smiled softly as she filled a bowl and walked over to the table.

"Here Kienan, have another bowl of my gator gumbo. You earned it," she said with pride, as she quickly placed it down in front of him.

"Thanks, Grand mere Catherine," Kienan gratefully grinned.

Grand mere Catherine leaned over and squeezed Kienan's shoulder and looked across to where Pearl stood.

Pearl La Cour gazed nervously back at her and then walked over to the window and stared out of it.

Louis La Cour sat in silence as he studied his wife Pearl across the room. He looked back at his small tiny daughter Lacey and then looked across the room at her mother Pearl. The woman he'd fallen in love with. His daughter had the same delicate features as her mother. Everything on her was a miniature of his wife Pearl. All at once anger swelled up inside of him. "I can't believe Nicholas left his sister alone on the ridge. That son of mine is an irresponsible jack..."

"Louis!" Pearl cautioned. "Be careful. Tiny ears are listening."

Pearl La Cour glanced back over her shoulder at her husband as she struggled to get the panic out of her voice. "Don't talk like that Louis. Besides, nothing happened too Lacey and you have to admit that Nicholas has been acting more responsible lately," she said trying to sound hopeful. "Don't you worry; Nicholas always looks out for Lacey."

Louis scowled back at her. "Kienan ain't even a member of this family and I trust him better to look out for Lacey than her own brother Nicholas," his temper flared. "And you know what else I think Pearl? I think Lacey is too little to be left alone with Nicholas."

Pearl hung her head and silently turned and stared back out of the window.

"Yes, maybe you're right," she said in frustration, as she leaned her head against the cool window pane. "Those trials on Mount Hamilton can be filled with snakes of every kind, even those that might snatch a little girl like Lacey."

Lacey La Cour stared between her mother and father thunderstruck."Mommy, I'm not little. I'm a big girl," she rattled out. "Besides, Kienan brought me home. Didn't you Kienan?" she asked but didn't wait for him to answer.

Kienan nodded as he spooned in another mouthful of gumbo. "Yep."

Lacey giggled. "Kienan would never leave me alone anywhere. He's my Boaz. He's my kinsman, my protector, just like the story Grand mere Catherine read to me from the bible."

Lacey gave her father her biggest grin.

"Shhhhh...Be quiet Lacey," her grandmother said, wiping her face with a napkin.

Louis turned to the young boy sitting next to him. He admired him. He wished his son Nicholas could be more like him. "Kienan, I noticed you've finished your gumbo. Would you like some more?"

Kienan nodded, as Grand mere Catherine hurried over with another bowl.

"You're welcome in my home anytime, Kienan. Feeding you isn't a problem," Louis said looking around the room and catching Pearl's attention.

His wife Pearl nodded. "Of course, Kienan is welcome here anytime."

Louis nodded. "And my mother and my wife had better feed you anytime they even think you're hungry."

Kienan let out a snort, his mouth full of food. He swallowed hard. "Thanks, Mr. La Cour. You know I've got to say Gator Gumbo tastes just like chicken."

Louis rubbed his hand across his chin smoother out his laughter. "I agree with you Kienan, but don't let Grand mere Catherine hear you say that."

Kienan nodded in agreement.

"Kienan, from now on, you call me Louis because I'm going to look upon you like my own son. Thanks again for bringing Lacey home."

Pearl La Cour pretended not to hear her husband's kind words calling Kienan his son. The words stung. She knew Kienan was a good boy. But Louis never said kind words about their son Nicholas.

Pearl wrung her hands despairingly. Her son Nicholas could do no wrong in her eyes, but lately he was becoming more and more irresponsible. She put the blame on his new friend Quinn Rolandis.

She walked over and stroked her daughter's head. "See Lacey, now you have two strong young men to watch out for you, your new honorary designated brother Kienan, and your true brother Nicholas. You know Nicholas will always look out for you Lacey," Pearl said.

"No, he won't," Louis said in anguish. "Nicholas doesn't give a damn about anybody but Nicholas. And its time you realized that Pearl."

"Louis!" Pearl cautioned as she closed the distance between her and Louis. Please, think about what you're saying about, our son, Nicholas..."

"No, your son Pearl!"

"Louis!" Grand mere Catherine's stern voice pierced the air. "Like Pearl said, tiny ears are listening, son."

Louis eyes locked with Grand mere Catherine. He knew better than to do battle with her. He jerked his head around and stared at the boy beside him. "Well Kienan Egan if you go out on the trails with Nicholas then Lacey can go. You are more mature and responsible than either of them."

"Ahhhh! Goodie! I get to go out on the trails," Lacey yelled. "Because I know Kienan will always take me with him."

Louis turned and laid his hand on his wife's Pearl's arm. "If Kienan isn't around, you'd better keep Lacey here at home," he said softly.

Hearing his mother's voice woke Nicholas out of his eavesdropping. He'd heard enough. His mother and his grandmother had been right little ears were hearing and he'd heard what his father had said loud and clear.

Suddenly the kitchen door slammed loudly.

"Nicholas? Is that you?" Louis called out.

"Yep it's me, Dad," Nicholas called out, as he walked into the room and headed straight to the refrigerator.

Nicholas retrieved a cold soda, opened it, and drank quickly. Then he looked up and laughed. "Lacey, I guess I'm not an only child yet. I see you made it back home safe and sound. See, I told you you'd be fine."

Louis felt like a knife had just been thrust into his heart. His son was standing there telling him that he left his baby sister alone on the Mount Hamilton trails. "Nicholas," he asked puzzled. "Son, what are you saying? You told Lacey to come back home all by herself?"

Nicholas laughed. "I told Lacey to go back the way she came. She's got to learn her way back home by herself sometime. You know Quinn was right. If you keep treating her like a baby, she'll keep acting like one."

Everyone watched as Louis got up and walked over and slapped Nicholas across the face, knocking the cold soda from his hands. The can of soda flew across the kitchen floor.

Nicholas' face distorted as he cried out in fear. "Daddy don't hit me," he sobbed.

"Nicholas, don't you ever leave your sister by herself anywhere! You hear me boy? You've got one job in this family as the only son. And that is to take care of your sister, your mother and your grandmother."

Desperate with fear Pearl walked slowly across the kitchen. "Louis," her voice pleaded.

"I'm not going to hit him again Pearl," Louis' eyes beamed with tears. "Pearl I'm sorry...I'm sorry," he shook his head in disbelief. "I've never hit Nicholas before...You know that..." A deep sadness etched across his face. Louis choked out a sob and turned and walked out of the kitchen door.

A blast of cold freezing air on his face blurred the images racing through his mind, as the white light seemed to flash signaling and end to this trance. Nicholas' daydream had only made him understand the chemistry between his sister and Kienan more. Their relationship didn't bother him. But he knew someone that it did. His best friend, Quinn.He knew Quinn hated the fact that Lacey and Kienan had a special bond, relationship or not.

Suddenly, Nicholas saw the chance to get his two best buddies alone to talk, man to man. He needed to talk about business after the financial situation he'd found himself in. The Hedge Fund he had developed was having a few problems. He knew both Kienan and Quinn were great at raising funds on the stock market.

Nicholas' voice was calm. "Kienan and Quinn, could I have a word in private?"

His words registered with his two friends. They nodded in unison and followed him to a secluded corner.

Lacey found a seat right by the door leading to the roof-top patio.

She sat down and felt a nudge. She turned and glanced up at Maëlle.

"Here, I found us a couple of bottled waters."

"Thanks, Maëlle."

"If you want another one, there's a whole tub of them on the table just outside the lady's room. You would think they'd find a better place to put them."

"Or Maëlle, you could say that they were smart to put them outside the lady's room. That way they were making sure that the ladies could find them."

The two friends laughed.

"Well, it looks like the guys have got something important to talk about as usual. I don't understand it. Those guys talk more than women do," Lacey said, taking a swallow of water.

Maëlle breathed out a sigh. "What I fail to understand is how they always seem to manage to slip away and leave us alone."

Lacey nodded.

Maëlle's voice shook with surprise. "Hey Lacey, look over there walking by the appetizers table," she pointed. "There's Miss Lucy Mondragon."

"Lucy who?" Lacey asked, standing up to get a better look.

"You remember," Maëlle said, rising. "She ran for Miss San Jose several years ago, remember?" Her eyes gleamed. "She's a local celebrity and her sister is Mimi Mondragon. Lacey you've got to remember Mimi. Because Mimi and Paris London were Miss California runners up three years ago, remember?"

Lacey smiled. Maëlle Moulard had been her best friend since she could remember. When it came to people, Maëlle had a great memory. She always was good at remembering people, places and their names, Lacey thought. She was a good friend who stuck by her as close as a shadow.

Lacey looked up. "Oh yeah, now I remember."

Just then, a voice said, "I remember her well."

Suddenly Quinn came out of nowhere. "Wow man! Lucy's

pregnancy is really showing."

Lacey jumped. "Quinn you startled me!"

Maëlle turned around and stared. "Quinn, I thought you were talking to Nicholas and Kienan?" she asked but didn't wait for a response. "And how did you know Lucy was pregnant? Yours?"

Quinn chuckled out. "I don't think so," he responded with gleaming white teeth, in a deceptive mild tone. His plan was simple. Cast doubt on Maëlle. He knew Nicholas was her weakness. He knew what the effect would do to Maëlle when he said what he was thinking. "You know Maëlle I think I heard that Nicholas mentioned something about Lucy. If you're interested in her you should ask him. Maybe he knows something about the father of her baby."

Maëlle paused for a moment deep in thought. She had no idea why it bothered her to know Nicholas knew anything about who the father of Lucy's baby was. Her voice was soft when she spoke. "Excuse me a moment."

Lacey watched her friend make her exit and felt a breeze of cold air as the patio door opened and closed. A woman walked in followed by a man. The woman roared out with laughter.

Lacey felt a shiver.

Quinn seized the moment and realized the stakes of the game he was playing. His eyes were glued to her when he said, as he moved in close. "Lacey, you look as beautiful as always. I don't know what is prettier, you or a million dollars."

Lacey shivered again.

It was the perfect opportunity for Quinn. He pulled her close and gave her a hug. "You're shivering. God I've wanted to touch you all night," he whispered and blew a warm breath against her earlobe.

Pressed close against him she could smell the scent of his cologne. The effects sent Lacey's pheromones into high gear.

His deep-set eyes looked cool and deceptively conning behind his black framed glasses. "You know, I heard on the grapevine that Kienan still believes he's God's gift to women. Don't listen to him too much,"

"Oh," Lacey said, pulling out of his embrace and glancing up at him. "I can't imagine what you're talking about."

"Just look at the two of them, Lacey," he nodded his head in Kienan's direction.

Lacey watched Kienan schmoozing with the very pregnant Lucy. It was apparent he was very interested in his conversation with Lucy Mondragon. Odd sensations creep upon her as she watched the gazes on both of their faces. She didn't like the way Lucy was staring at Kienan. Was she jealous, she wondered before she turned away?

Quinn's eyes were glued to her. "All I'm saying Lacey is don't let him seduce you. Don't sleep with him," he warned. "He's not the man you think he is."

Lacey spun around but Quinn pulled her close. "Seduce me, are you insane? You can be so like my brother Nicholas at times," her jaw tightened. "Why are you telling me this Quinn?"

"I was just watching the two of you together earlier. I worry about you. I saw the way you let him take you by the hand and lead you. He's setting you up to be his victim."

Lacey glanced back at him astounded. "You…You don't have to worry about me, Quinn. I'm a grown woman."

"And don't I know it," Quinn thought, looking at the way lose strands of her hair were escaping beautifully around her face. He cleared his throat. "I noticed how you kept staring at Kienan all evening," his lips tightened into a thin smile. "I wouldn't recommend trying to set your sights on him again. I remember how he hurt you before."

He watched her. Her body tensed up from the words he told her. He knew his words had meaning for her. He reeled her in. "I'd hate for a respectable worthy woman like you to become misguided by an illusion like Kienan Egan."

Lacey pulled out of his embrace and folded her arms in front of her. "What are you talking about Quinn? You talk like Kienan is a magician or something?"

"I believe he is," he whispered nervously. "That groupie I mentioned who warmed his bed, well I heard she did every type of sexual fantasy he asked her. They say it was as if he was a magician or a drug dealer pumping her with a steady fix. And she danced for the piper," his eyes gazed over dreamily. "Can you imagine having a woman at your beck and call for every fantasy that you can imagine?"

Lacey paused for a moment. Quinn's cold words chilled her. Kienan had his bad points. That was true. But he wasn't into drugs. He never was. Lacey was beginning to realize that Quinn didn't like Kienan much.

"Look Quinn, I know you don't like Kienan very much, but a drug dealer? Come on really? If that was the case, shouldn't we be calling the police right now to have him arrested?"

Quinn quickly cleared his throat, a frown marring his brow. He didn't want to lose the hold he was having over her. "I'm sorry I didn't mean it that way. I was just repeating something I heard," he sneered. "Besides, if anyone would know if he was a drug dealer or not it would probably be that girl he's having sex with…"

Frustrated Lacey glanced across the room at Kienan. Unsettling emotions about Kienan began to surface. "Look Quinn, I don't recall telling you I was interested in hearing about Kienan's antics," her voice was sharp and brittle.

Quinn's eyes were glued to her.

Puzzled, Lacey felt him staring but couldn't control her thoughts. "I wonder who the baby's father is," she muttered, before realizing that she'd spoke.

He cleared his throat. He knew she had begun to see the truth of his words. "Oh, you didn't know that Kienan's little bed warmer is Lucy…Lucy Mondragon?"

Chapter 5

ienan Egan

The next day Kienan had just finished his interview with the reporter from the *Silicon Valley Times Newspaper*. It was the major newspaper in the South Bay and reluctantly he had agreed to the interview, after he received nomination for their Excellent Business of the Year Award and then received it.

Everything had gone well until the reporter asked him questions about his personal relationships and then noted that he had brought Naomi St. John, yet he spent the night staring at his high school sweetheart, Lacey La Cour. The reporter's revelation turned the euphoric interview into a walk down regret lane.

He'd was so happy when his secretary Gladys had interrupted and said he was urgently needed. His secretary Gladys Johnson ran interruption interference like the defensive line of the 49ers.

Gladys Johnson might have been considered by most as too plump and round to hold the position of Kienan's secretary. With her gracious disposition and down-home Southern manners, she seemed out of place in the high drama world of Silicon Valley.

But Gladys was exactly what Kienan Egan needed.She had his back. Gladys always had his back. She reminded him of his mother, Milady. Maybe that was why he trusted her. She always knew exactly what to do.

Gladys was the one who told him that he needed to get Lacey back into his life and undo the past.

His thoughts flashed back to that night at the concert. When he saw Lacey talking with Quinn from across the room, he knew Quinn was sitting his sights on moving in on his girl. Then again there was nothing he could say to her at that very moment, not when he was standing there talking with a very pregnant Lucy Mondragon just after he'd rescued her from almost falling.

Kienan Egan had been raised to be a gentleman, first by his own father before his early death and afterwards by Louis La Cour, Lacey's father who had taken him under his wing and mentored him. He was thirty-two years old. He had graduated from Stanford University, summa cum laude, with dual degrees in engineering and math. At the ripe age of twenty he obtained his business degree from Berkeley University. He was a computer expert and a financial whiz-kid with a Wall Street know-how that propelled his company EIC, *Egan Investment Company* into success. He had never married and, as far as he was concerned, the only woman who could ever live up to his expectations of what a woman should be was Lacey La Cour.

He had met Lacey when they were children. Their families had been the only neighbors for miles. He smiled with his memories.

Just then a knock sounded on his door.

"Kienan your appointment is here."

Kienan looked puzzled. He didn't have anything on his schedule for today. He gazed at his open office door.

"Hello Grand *mere'* Catherine," he said, smiling softly.

Grand *mere'* Catherine walked into his office and closed the door behind her. "Hi Kienan, how are you?" she asked but didn't wait for a response. "I need you to do me a favor."

Chapter 6

unch & The Break up

Lacey La Cour had found that lunch on a Monday afternoon was the perfect opportunity to break-up a relationship that should never have gotten started in the first place.

After eating her lunch alone for the umpteenth time that she could remember, since she'd been dating James Fairway, she knew that breaking up with him was the right thing to do. She checked her lipstick and put away her compact.

Her eyes wandered to the front entrance, longingly, one more time. No James Fairway. She sighed.

"Lacey Catherine Kadira La Cour you deserve way better than this. It's a good thing you never had sex with him"

Time had taught her that if she wanted a relationship that lasted, she'd better hold out in the bedroom exercises department. Her number one rule was no sex for ninety days. James Fairway had proven she was right.

Lacey wasn't a prude. But she heard rumors about James, sleeping with his former assistant, a blonde with big breasts.

Tired of waiting she paid her check and rose to leave.

A few minutes later she made her way down the side walk to her car. She was thinking whether it was better to call James and break up with him by telephone. Suddenly she walked smack into someone coming the other way. She reached out her arms, grabbing hold firmly, to keep from falling.

"Oh, my goodness…" she heard herself saying. "I'm so sorry!"

"No harm done gorgeous."

The voice startled her. "Kienan! What are you doing here?"

"By the way, you are forgiven for bumping into me like this and feeling me up. Now if you really want to feel how strong my muscles are, we can go to my place and you can check them out in the raw," his face broke into a charming disarming smile.

"Wishful thinking Kienan. You got any more jokes?"

"Ouch! But don't you know you shouldn't go around with your eyes on the ground like that? But still it's always a pleasure to catch a damsel in distress."

She felt good in his arms. He didn't want to let her go.

"Kienan!" She exclaimed. "You can let go of me now."

He smiled warmly at her. "No need to shout, it was you who walked into me."

Lacey raised a sardonic brow. "As always you can be counted on to take advantage of the situation at hand."

He grinned back at her, "Only where you are concerned. So why are you in such a hurry?"

Just when she thought things couldn't get any worse, James Fairway seemed to appear out of nowhere.

"Oh no!" She softly exclaimed, leaning over and trying to bury herself behind Kienan.

"Lacey, I am so glad I caught you. Please hear me out. I have a perfectly good explanation for being late," James Fairway pleaded. "My meeting ran a little over, all three of my meetings this morning ran over. Can you believe it?" James said sweating profusely. "I nearly ran all the way to try and make our lunch."

"Oh, uh James," she nervously said.

As usual James Fairway didn't notice anything unusual and kept talking. "I can't believe the morning I've been having. Can you believe it? Then on top of everything, I left my cell phone at home. Can you believe it?" he repeated.

Lacey looked back at James with little interest. It was amazing how the man came off sounding like a broken record, but didn't most politicians, she thought.

James continued his prepared speech. "Well, so then I forgot to tell my receptionist to call you and tell you I'd be late for lunch. Can you believe it?" He said checking his watch. "Come on, the noon time rush is over. I'm sure we can get a real nice table right away."

Lacey moved a little away from Kienan. She was glad James had stopped talking. She began speaking slowly. "Look James, we need to talk."

James finally noticed the man standing next to her. "Sure, we can talk Lacey. Let's talk in private, let's go in and get a table."

Lacey tilted her head and shrugged. "No, what I have to say won't take long. I can say it here," she exhaled slowly feeling frustrated.

James Fairway looked again at Lacey and the man she was standing next to.

When Lacey noticed James staring she went to again put some distance between her and Kienan. She lifted her foot moving to step away from him when her foot caught. She wobbled pitching forward almost falling.She cried out.

Kienan responded fast and reached out and caught her by the waist. He held her firmly against him. One hand firmly held her waist the other hand cupped her chin. "Are you alright *Kitten?*"

Her voice was thick with frustration, "I think I broke my shoe strap."

Kienan moved quickly and checked her foot. "Your ankle seems alright."

"Yes, but my shoe is ruined."

"I'll get you another pair *Kitten,*" he promised still holding her.

James Fairway still stood there regarding the two. He looked between Lacey to the tall man. He looked again a second time. He quickly summed up the situation. If there was one thing he knew from being in politics it was how to spot the good, the bad, and the ugly of any situation. And this situation looked ugly. He was sure of that.

"Well…Well, Miss Lacey. Who's your friend? I don't think we've been properly introduced. Sir I'm James Fairway, Lacey's Fiancé."

Kienan studied the man standing in front of him. He looked comical. "You don't say. Well I'm Kienan Egan. And I didn't know Lacey had a fiancé," he said with a devious smile as he glanced between them. "Imagine that. Lacey Kadira Catherine La Cour you've got a real live fiancé, huh? Do tell."

Mortified Lacey froze on the spot. Things weren't going as planned. *She wondered, "How could one break-up get so out of control?"*

Kienan studied the two of them. He could tell Lacey was acting real nervous about something. And James Fairway was a pompous funny looking man. He found both their antics very amusing. He decided to play up this confrontation.

All at once Kienan reached over and grabbed Lacey by the waist and pulled her close planting a big kiss right on her lips and ran his hands up and down her backside holding her tight for dramatic effect.

Lacey was too stunned to even respond.

Kienan kept a tight grip on her waist. "You feel better *Kitten?*"

"Yeah, much better," she murmured softly as if in a daze.

"Sir may I ask that you don't kiss my fiancé' like that?"

"James you can ask it, but I don't think I'm in the mood to comply," Kienan grinned, looking back at Lacey.

James Fairway gasped, "Now Lacey, look here, is this gentleman a friend of your family or something?"

"Well, it's complicated," she said.

"Big-time complicated, like you wouldn't believe," Kienan said, as he looked at James with a real big grin.

James stared between the two. The situation was annoying. "Lacey, is he telling the truth?"

"Hmmmm?" She managed to murmur softly, as Kienan kissed her again.

"His hand is on your waist," James pointed.

Finally, Lacey shook out her thoughts and found her voice, "Ahhhh hum mm you won't believe this, but this isn't how it looks," she nervously laughed.

James spoke rapidly without catching his breath. "I certainly don't think this is the sort of thing that you should be doing in public and with a stranger. I hope that is who he is to you, since you never answered me when I asked if he was family."

"I am family, sort of, my name is Kienan Egan and for the most part, Lacey's part of the family rarely likes to mention me. You know I'm on the side of the family that has the mass murder trait and that incest thing? That's why I like kissing her so much. You can read all about us *in Kissing Cousins Ain't a Sin Magazine?*"

"That's nonsense," James blurted out. "There is no such magazine."

"Look Kienan stop joking. This is serious," Lacey said.

There was a moment of awkward silence.

Lacey turned her attention to James. Then she thought about why she was there. She wanted to break things off with James. But what if he got rude. So, she figured it was better if she kept Kienan standing there. "Look James, I need to talk to you. And Kienan is just here for moral support."

Kienan boyishly grinned and pulled her closer, "Oh I believe in supporting my Lacey. Kitten you know I'm here for you," his eyes smiled with merriment and mischief. "If I place my hand on your butt it's so I can get a firm hold on the situation. I've noticed you've been working out."

Lacey looked down at Kienan's hand and stiffed at the sight she saw. She knocked his hand off her behind. 'Stop joking around Kienan."

James was a politician first and saw a chance to move things in his favor. "Cousins, I see. Well, I can take a joke. It is nice to meet you

Mr. Egan."

Lacey studied James' phony smile.

"Good Mr. Egan, just so you know, I'm pretty famous around town.

Kienan nodded. "I've heard of you. You are a local politician."

James' chest swelled. "Yes, and public manners are a must with Lacey and any family of hers," he said. "I expect Lacey to be the next Mrs. James Fairway. Therefore, I expect her and her family to conduct themselves properly in public."

It was obvious James Fairway's thoughts were only of himself. He cleared his throat. "Lacey let me be blunt. It is obvious your parents must not have understood the importance of *correct public behavior.*"

Lacey gasped. James was trying to push her too far. She vowed in her mind to be civil.

James leaned over closer. The vein running across his forehead grew bigger. He whispered. "The way you are acting here in public today is very unacceptable for a man like me," he said. "But I am willing to overlook this one mishap if you promise me you'll take that proper public manners and behavior course, I mentioned that my staff gives. Remember once we are married you must be exemplary at all times."

Lacey's anger gage rose to a level even she didn't know she had. All of a sudden, she looked hard at James Fairway and thought he looked like a rooster crowing at sunrise. She shut her eyes, trying to wipe the image out of her head. But the image and her rage refused to die.

Then Lacey did the funniest thing. She started laughing hysterically. "Damn James, you look like a pompous, overly plump rooster, in a dead man's suit!"

"Now look her Lacey, I won't have you call me names and talking to me like that in public. I am James Fairway, the better man. Show me some respect!

Lacey blinked several times. She was real angry now.

"No James," Lacey said slowly. "I'm pretty sure you are not the better man. Now take your little carrot you keep dangling in front of me, called the word fiancé, and shove it far…Far up your other wind pipe," she gestured with her hands.

James frowned. "And here I was feeling slighted because you never once introduced me to your family. Watching the way, you act now, I know your parents didn't teach you a damn thing. Parents hump! You probably were raised by a single mother; and I bet her manners are as bad as yours.Some people have no class at all, you classless hussy!"

James walked a few steps away throwing his hand in the air. "And here I was thinking I was being slighted by your family because I never got invited to your parent's home. Who eats Gator Gumbo in California anyway? You and that Gator Gumbo eating pack of swamp rats you call a family can go to hell!"

Lacey knew James had just insulted her. This was his typical behavior. James always insulted those he thought were beneath him, when they were alone together. She closed the distance between them.

"James you are a miserable, pathetic, bastard, boring-ass politician!" Lacey exclaimed rolling her eyes. "And let me tell you something. That Gator Gumbo eating family of mine has some of the best good looks, Geeky intelligence and brilliant minds you'll find any place in this whole wide world," she yelled. "But you, on the other hand, have got some of the ugliest DNA my eyes have ever seen. Therefore, that leads me to believe that not only are you ugly and unintelligent but so is your momma and your daddy too!"

"Ouch!" Kienan smirked.

James Fairway stood there staring furiously with a loss for words.

Lacey stared James down and dared him to say a word.Ferociously she yelled after him."Now, if for any reason you just don't understand what is happening right now then let me make it clear. I have officially broken up with you. It's over between us. We're through. Don't call me. Don't text me. Don't email me. Hell, don't even fax me. Do you get my meaning?"

James hissed with rage, "You…You Gator Gumbo eating trash talking hussy! You can't talk to me like that. And you're a whore if I ever saw one!"

"Ahhhh James that wasn't called for," Kienan said. "Now I'm going to have to punch you in the nose!"

Kienan went to cover the distance between him and James and Lacey grabbed him by his waist and hung on for dear life.

"Stop Kienan. Don't hit the man! I should have just shut up in the first place."

"Ah *Kitten,* this man needs to have his nose broken; I swear it'll make him look better. Just give me a second," Kienan said drawing his arm back.

"No Kienan!" She sobbed out hugging him tight. "James is just a big jerk. He's not worth our time. I should have broken things off with him a long time ago."

"Ah *Kitten*, he made you cry. You should have let me hit the guy when I had a chance. Come on, we should really be going home now, folks are starting to stare. Stop crying," Kienan said touching her arm gently.

"Shut up you jerk! I'm not crying. I'm just so mad and embarrassed and I feel so stupid for even dating that jerk," she wiped her face. "And by the way don't call me *Kitten*!"

The moment was awkward.

"But what if I did the wrong thing?" Lacey sobbed. "I dated James for almost three months. Before that, I had a dry spell that lasted over a year. What if I don't find another man? James was at least talking about marriage."

Kienan's heart went out to her. "Lacey sweetheart, James Fairway is a rotten man. He's a rotten politician, who was a rotten boyfriend, and who would have made you a rotten husband. He was just a rotten to the core. And you deserve something better."

His words sounded familiar. A light flashed in her mind. "You've got some nerve! And you got that rotten crap straight from my grandmother's mouth!"

She fumed in a rage and limped off with her broken shoe.

"You've all been plotting against me!" She ranted. "I'm such an idiot," she started whimpering.

Kienan closed the distance between them, "You know, you're being too hard on yourself. Where's all that think positive energy yoga stuff you study?"

"Just stop it!" Her voice shook. And then the flood gates opened, and Lacey couldn't stop the tears from running down her face.

Kienan gently pulled Lacey into his possessive embrace and He buried his face into her hair kissing her on top of the head. She turned her face up to him and he kissed her lips. She returned his kisses. Her tears stopped.

"Oh Kienan," she whispered. She pulled away from his embrace.

He looked adoringly at her. "I'm glad you stopped crying little one. Do you feel calmer now *Kitten?*"

She sighed and leaned in and kissed him again and then leaned her head against his shoulders. He always smelled good in an earthy woodsy way. His arms felt warm, secure, safe and strong. She could stay this way forever.

Lacey closed her eyes.

"Besides, that guy only wanted one thing, to get into your pants. But these pants are mine, aren't they *Kitten*? I can't believe you don't know that type of guy by now."

Kienan's egotistical, conceded and idiotic streak had found its way through. It jostled her back to reality.

Lacey's eyes opened fast. "I can't believe I fell for this crap. You're a miserable pile of shit. You hard-boiled crab headed, heartless snake! Don't you ever put those roaming things you call hands on me ever again!"

Chapter 7

Grand mere' Catherine

A week later, that Saturday morning, Lacey went to visit her mother and grandmother. She loved driving the road that led to her family's home. It afforded some spectacular views of the East San Jose hills known as Mount Hamilton.

The La Cour's roomy family home could be called a mansion. It sat on forty acres off of the road. Her father, Louis Antoine Nicolas Avoyelles La Cour, had purchased the land in the early 1970's.

Lacey smiled with her thoughts. She had always thought her father was a smart man. He had graduated from high school at the age of fourteen. Louis always said his greatest achievement in life wasn't graduating from the University of Santa Clara, with a PhD, before the age of twenty-four, but it was his returning home to Goldonna Louisiana to marry his childhood sweetheart, Pearl Fanay Andries.

Lacey exhaled and shook out her thoughts. Her father Louis La Cour had been dead for many years now.

At the familiar curve she slowed to make the turn onto the private road. All at once she hit the brakes and jerked the steering wheel to avoid hitting the vehicle parked on the side of the road.

A truck was parked on the side of the road. Lacey recognized the

California special plates. The plate read 4 *Horace II*. She knew the owner's real name. It was Horace Sherlock Bailey Garrison. She got out of her car and checked the truck. It was empty.

Just then a car came up the road from her parent's home. She recognized the car immediately. The sleek steel grey BMW was familiar to her.

The car drove right next to her. The window went down.

A crystal-clear pendulum hung from his rear-view mirror. It caught the light.

"Hi Lacey, I was going to call you. What are you doing checking out old man Horace's truck?" Quinn asked with a smile.

Lacey smiled softly. Her eyes noticed the pendulum and followed its movement. "You caught me. Good to see you Quinn. Where are you coming from?"

She kept her eyes glued to the pendulum as if spell bound. In a soft voice she said. "Let me guess. You've been up at the house visiting with Nicholas?"

"You know it," Quinn nodded. He glanced between her eyes and the pendulum. He smiled. Everything was working like it should. "I couldn't stay long. As you know your Grand *mere* Catherine doesn't like me too much."

"No, she doesn't," she agreed softly.

Quinn shook his head. "Yeah, but I never let that bother me. I really only came out to see if you were here. You know you are my favorite La Cour"

Lacey felt light headed like she was in a fog.She blinked hard. It helped her take her gaze off the pendulum. "Me, since when?"

He grinned. "Since the other night when you looked so good, I know you felt that chemistry thing I felt," Quinn said. "I don't want to seem pushy, but I've been feeling that way for a while. I'd really like to take you out sometime."

Her eyes focused on the pendulum.

Quinn let his finger nudge the pendulum. It flickered in the sunlight.

"Lacey, we need to do something about this chemistry. I'm betting there is something real between us. Go out with me, please."

She noticed the pendulum again. This time the light reflecting back intrigued her. She stood froze as if under a trance.

Quinn stared back at her. "You broke things off with James I heard?"

"How did you know about James?" she asked but didn't wait for him to answer. "Oh yeah I forget you are friends with my brother Nicholas."

He cleared his throat. "Just promise me you'll think about going out with me sometimes."

Lacey felt strange. She went to open her mouth.

All at once a dog's loud barking woke her from her fog. The sound came out of nowhere. She listened intently for the sound of the barking dog but heard nothing.

Quinn coughed loudly. "It looks like that's my cue to leave. You have a good day Lacey."

"Yes, I will Quinn," she said, backing away from the car.

He gunned his car engine loudly as he took off down the road.

A few minutes later Lacey pulled into the drive way of her parent's home. She climbed out of the car and spotted her grandmother waiting by the side of the driveway.

Catherine Marie Rousseau-La Cour was affectionately and fearfully known as Grand *mere* Catherine. Her seventy-year-old frame was tall and slender. Her soft gray eyes smiled lovingly back at her granddaughter.

Grand *mere Catherine,* as well as Lacey's mother Pearl, and father Louis were all born in Goldonna Louisiana. Her grandmother was the family's strong link to the old traditions of Louisiana, and she was the official record keeper of all the family's stories and traditions.

For a moment Lacey sat in her car and studied her grandmother in silence, enjoying the feelings of love that filled her heart.Some things never changed she thought. Like the way her grandmother always wore her silver hair neatly braided into a coil at the nape of her neck.

Lacey quickly got out of her car and walked over.

They embraced.

"Grand *mere* Catherine, I think I saw Mr. Horace Garrison's truck parked on the side of the road. I think he may need help or something."

Too Lacey her grandmother was her ally in the family, the one person she could trust wholeheartedly.

Still her mother Pearl Fanay La Cour was better to talk with, especially about her relationships with men.

Grand *mere* Catherine looked annoyed and agitated as she stared up the road. "That Quinn fellow left I see? Good! He's one piece of rotten apple core if I ever seen one," she said bitterly.

Lacey started to open her mouth in Quinn's defense. "Grand *mere* you forget the good things that Quinn does sometimes. Like last year when he donated 100 turkeys to feed the homeless for Thanksgiving."

"Hmmm I don't forget anything. That wasn't Quinn's idea. That has his Grandmother Ms. Ione's idea. Ms. Ione is a good-hearted woman."

Lacey looked up into the eyes of her grandmother. She was going to say more in Quinn's defense but stopped abruptly when she saw a strange look in her grandmother's eyes that chilled her. She knew her grandmother was born with a gift of sight.

Lacey stared back at her with a puzzled look. "What did you see?" She asked in a timid voice.

Grand *mere* Catherine 's eyes flashed with a deep knowing. She swallowed hard. "Nothing child…Come on into the house Lacey. I've got a pot of Gator Gumbo ready in the kitchen it will fill you up and make you feel better."

Lacey innocently looked at her. "But Grand *mere,* what about Horace's truck? He may need help."

Her grandmother eyed her quietly and suddenly chuckled lightly. "Horace doesn't need any help. He's probably just off somewhere taking a walk with somebody."

Lacey quickly grabbed her laptop off the car seat next to her and walked into the house following her grandmother.

The rich flavorful aroma of her gator gumbo wharfing into the air made her stomach growl just smelling it.

"Where's Mom?"

"Ah, your mother ain't here right now," her grandmother mumbled in her low Cajun drawl.

Grand *mere* Catherine smiled and turned away. She took lively spry steps toward the back of the house and made her way up on the porch and into the kitchen.

Lacey halted and looked after her. All at once the *fragrant aroma of the* sausage laced gator *Gumbo* soup filled the air and made her mouth water.

Her stomach growled real loud.

Grand *mere* Catherine laughed out. "From the sound of your belly growling you are a hungry child."

She followed her grandmother into the kitchen.

Lacey put her laptop down on the counter top on the other side of the kitchen next to the doorway leading to the family room. She sat down at the table and basked in the down-home warmth her childhood home exuded.

Her grandmother's kitchen overflowed with the fragrant aromas of Creole cooking. Lacey could smell her favorite. Her grandmother had made her delicious pralines again.

Grand *mere* Catherine watched her granddaughter in earnest. She loved her granddaughter and her eyes sparkled showing just how much. Lacey and Nicholas were her only grandchildren. She enjoyed cooking for her family. It was a labor of love for her.

Grand *mere* Catherine went to the stove. Several bowls sat on the counter top next to it. She quickly filled a bowl and walked over and placed it on the table in front of Lacey along with her favorite Royal Dutton tea pot. She sat down and grabbed her napkin.

"Grand *mere* don't do that. I'm a big girl. I can wipe my own face and pour my own tea."

"Don't deny an old woman a chance of reliving an old memory. I love watching your face smeared with gumbo all over it. It makes me happy to wipe your face. Besides, who knows how much longer we have to enjoy times like these together."

Lacey shrugged. "Grand *mere* stop being morbid, you ain't sick and you're not dying."

"I was talking about lose in the sense of losing something. Not in the sense of death."

"What do you mean losing something? What's on your mind Grand *mere?* Have you lost something?"

Grand *mere* Catherine shrugged. "Not yet, but I was talking about men like Kienan? Men don't wait forever."

Lacey slowly sipped her tea. "Stop playing matchmaker. You're as bad as Maëlle."

"What are you talking about?" Maëlle doesn't know a thing about matchmaking. It's us old ones who wrote the book on matchmaking."

###

Half an hour later, Nicholas walked up to the sliding patio door, turned and grinned at the man behind him and then opened the door.

"Hey look who I found outside?" Nicholas' voice sliced the air. His grin was wide. "Whew, something smells good. Where's mine?"

Lacey jumped at the sound of her brother's voice. "Who is with you?"

"Kienan!" "Grand *mere* exclaimed, smiling wide at the sight of him. "It's so good to see you."

With a sly wide smile as big as Texas, Kienan Egan's six foot four-inch frame crossed the threshold and entered the room wearing dark sun glasses. They made him look ruggedly and distinctly handsome.

Kienan took off his sunglasses and gazed around the room. His eyes beamed brightly when they found hers. The two of them stared silently before they looked away awkwardly like two teenagers.

"God Lacey looked beautiful this morning," Kienan thought. Not taking his eyes off of her.

"It's good to see you too Grand *mere*," Kienan said closing the distance between them. He warmly hugged her.

Grand *mere*'s tone was playful and kind when she murmured low so only Kienan could hear her. "I see you've still got tunnel vision when it comes to my granddaughter."

Kienan smiled back at her before he walked over and sat across from Lacey. His grin was wide reviewing perfectly straight teeth. His eyes consumed her as he lingered on her lips. "How are you doing Lacey?" He said in a whispered husky late-night voice. "I came over here today hoping to see you. I want to apologize for acting so rude the other night, when you saw me speaking to that girl, Lucy."

Lacey nervously exhaled at the sound of his voice. She felt a deep intense reaction within her. "I'm fine… Just fine! You don't owe me an explanation about the other night," she said anxiously swallowing a spoonful of gumbo.

Grand *mere* Catherine noted the reaction between Kienan and Lacey. She studied them. Suddenly her facial expression broke out into a wide grin. She had an idea.

"Ah, Nicholas you have company. Offer our guest some food. But first, please do us all a favor and wash your hands!" His grandmother commanded.

Nicholas frowned. "Yeah, like my hands aren't already clean."

Lacey just rolled her eyes and shook her head in desperation. This was just like her brother, being inconsiderate of others. "Nicky," she warned. "We have company. Wash your hands please."

Nicholas opened his mouth to respond. His sister was the only person in the world he let call him Nicky. He knew when she called him that he'd better think twice before he said something off of the top of his head. He noted the serious look in her eye and he quickly washed his hands.

A moment later, he shook his head and threw Kienan a hard look before placing a bowl of gumbo in front of him. "I expect a tip man. You won't get this kind of service at the Fairmont," he joked.

Nicholas walked back to the stove, filled his bowl and grabbed a spoon, and started eating.

Grand *mere* Catherine eyed Nicholas over the rim of her tea cup. "For goodness sake, Nicholas!"

"What? What is it now?" Nicholas asked giving her a quizzical gaze between mouthfuls of gumbo.

"Nicholas sit down! Your manners get worse every day. His grandmother drawled. "My gator gumbo will hit your stomach instead of your feet if you sit down and eat properly."

Nicholas quickly took a seat right next to his grandmother.

The silence at the table was unnerving.

Kienan and Lacey exchanged glances.

With a soft groan Grand *mere* Catherine noticed no one was talking. "Oh, for Christ's sakes somebody please say something," she griped.

"The gumbo is good," Nicholas said.

"Agreed," Kienan smiled.

Only Lacey was silent.

It was apparent that the four of them weren't having the most brilliant conversation in the word. Grand *mere* Catherine quickly poured herself more tea. Then all at once she had a thought and reached out her frail hand.

"By the way Nicholas, what have you been doing in your father's old barn all day? Anything important you think we should know about?" she asked patting his hand.

"I haven't burned it down yet," he laughed out.

Lacey grimaced and looked up at Nicholas. "You have a warped sense of humor Nicky. What have you been up to in Dad's old barn?"

Nicholas swallowed a mouth full of food. "I was just joking. Anyway, I haven't been up to a thing."

"Hmmmm," Grand *mere* smiled and shook her head. "You know Nicholas there were some strange guys out here a few weeks ago. I could have sworn that Quinn brought one guy by and then left. The guy looked like a banker, dressed in his suit and tie."

Nicholas swallowed again. "Nay, it couldn't have been Quinn. Quinn wouldn't have just left the guy here by himself. Besides, why would he be out here at the house when I'm not here?"

"You know what Nicholas, now that I recall. I didn't see Quinn's car pull up the road," Grand *mere* Catherine said shifting in her seat.

Nicholas tried to think of a lie quickly. Then a light bulb went off in his head. "Oh…Did they ever come up to the house?"

"No that's just it. The strange man never came up the road. I saw him from upstairs in my room."

Nicholas kept his eyes on his bowl, and then looked quickly up at his sister. "It couldn't have been Quinn," he said clearing his throat. "He would never come all the way out here and not try and pay a visit. At least to see if Lacey was here."

Lacey's eyes flashed back at her brother. "I heard that Nicholas."

"Grand *mere,* was Quinn disrespectful to you?" Kienan asked through almost clenched teeth.

"Oh no Kienan," she relied. "Thank you for asking. It was just annoying the way that strange fellow was looking around the property," Grand *mere* Catherine smiled.

Suddenly Grand *mere* looked up at Kienan and chuckled softly and then said. "This old bag of bones can still take care of itself when it needs to."

"An appraiser," Nicholas briskly said without thinking, getting back into the conversation. "I mean I think that was the guy who is an art appraiser. Oh yeah, now that I think about it, that must have been the day Quinn told me he brought Jeffery over. Only Jeffery Bowman, he's an art appraiser, drove himself over and got tired of waiting for me to get back. Quinn wanted to check out a painting by a Monterey artist he's been interested in buying. He'd told me that he and Jeffery stopped by looking for me."

Lacey nodded. "Ah well that makes sense. Quinn's always asking you for your opinion Nicky. You know that Quinn can't make a move without you."

Nicholas chuckled and found a way to change the subject. "Yeah, you're right," he said hesitating for a moment. "By the way Grand *mere*, how come you never talk about old man Horace coming around here?" he asked perplexed. "Isn't that his truck parked up the road?"

"Uh-huh!" Grand *mere* Catherine cleared her throat and gave him an icy stare.

Nicholas stared back at his grandmother. He knew that look. He'd better keep quiet about old man Horace's truck. He knew that she was done putting him on the spot. He could now make his exit. He turned his attention to his sister.

"Hey Lacey, could I speak to you a moment in private?" Nicholas asked before standing and walking over by the patio door.

Lacey quickly followed him over. "What is it Nicholas?"

Nicholas rubbed his chin. "I'd thought we'd give Grand *mere* Catherine a couple minutes to speak to Kienan alone. You know he's her favorite grandson."

Lacey's brows furrowed with a determined look. "Kienan's not a La Cour. He's not her grandson."

Nicholas nudged her and chuckled.

Lacey realized he'd been joking. She softly laughed. "Okay you got me their big brother," she grinned. "But I know that look in your eye

Nicky, you want something. What is it?"

"Is that your laptop over there on the counter?" He asked, crossing his arms impatiently.

"Ah, yes you know it is," she shrugged.

"Could I use your laptop to check my Gmail account?" He asked. "I huh, I left my laptop at work."

Lacey shook her head. "Can't you use your Blackberry?"

He leaned over and whispered, "I don't have the Blackberry anymore. It was work issued. They are trying to save money with the bad economy. They asked that all the employees give them back."

Lacey thought that that was odd. She walked over to retrieve her laptop.

Nicholas followed her and watched her take the laptop out of her carrying case.

"Okay Nicholas," Lacey said. "But don't be too long, I need to check my emails too."

"Thanks Sis," Nicholas leaned closer and whispered. "You remember that girl Lucy Mondragon we saw at the concert?"

Lacey nodded. "Oh yeah the one who was kind of pregnant?"

Nicholas looked embarrassed. "Yeah, well Quinn said he heard some guy has been giving Lucy three thousand dollars a month to keep her mouth closed about who the baby's father is. He said he heard it might be someone we went to high school with."

Lacey watched her brother closely. His expression was easy to read. Nicholas was in a good mood. "If he told you all of that then Quinn must know who the father is."

"Only that he thought it was Pierce Nevins," he lied and hoped his sister couldn't read his expression. "You remember that tall football jock?" He said. "He was the one that was part Samoan, part French and part African American? He looked just like Dwayne Johnson that actor. All the girls were crazy about him my senior year."

Lacey shook her head. Nicholas sounded stupid. This was just like her brother. She wondered if he'd ever heard himself talk. At least she knew Quinn hadn't mentioned their conversation. "Pierce was multiracial Nicholas," she said agitated. "That part, part, part thing? It isn't how you describe a person. Anyway, yes I remember him."

"It's the same thing," Nicholas replied smugly.

Lacey knew it wasn't worth it to try and show her brother the error of his thinking. She changed the subject "Well, as long as the baby is not yours, we don't care do we…I mean, as long as you don't have something you need to tell mother and Grand *mere*," she said darting her eyes back at their grandmother who sat at the table.

"No…No… I don't, that's for sure," he smiled. "Hey, thanks for letting me use your laptop. I'll take it into the family room. That way you and Grand *mere* won't be interrupted. Don't worry I'll treat it like it was mine," he assured her holding it carefully.

"Hey Kienan, can you join me in the family room? I've got something to show you," Nicholas called out.

She watched Kienan's back as he made his way into the family room. She wondered about what Nicholas had just said. She turned and walked back to the kitchen patio door and made sure it was locked before she returned to the table.

Grand *mere* Catherine's lips turned into a frown as she watched them go. "I'm not a crazy old woman. I may be getting old. But I know Quinn Rolandis when I see him," she shrugged and poured herself another cup of tea.

Lacey remained silent.

"An art appraiser my ass," Grand *mere* Catherine said disdainfully. "I know a banker when I see one and that fella had mortgage banker written all over him. And you know what else I know?" she asked but didn't wait for her to respond. "I saw Quinn drop that fella off and I bet, Quinn, Nicholas and that banker fella are up to something. Thick as thieves they are. A thief always looks like a thief.

Lacey looked confused. "Nicholas….

Grand *mere* Catherine interrupted her. "Yes, Lacey my grandson is a thief. So, I know firsthand what a thief looks like."

Lacey's mouth dropped open as she stared back at her grandmother. The two of them sat there in awkward silence for several minutes. Loud rapping on the kitchen patio door startled them.

"Jesus!"Grand *mere* Catherine exclaimed. "Who is it?

"I'll go and check," Lacey rose and walked to the door.

She looked through the door and saw her brothers other best friend Quinn Rolandis.

"Hey Quinn, come on in," she greeted him with a big smile. Quinn looked pumped with masculine power. Like he'd just come from working out. He always did remind her of a Mayan Clark Kent. She smiled with her thoughts remembering that was the name his grandmother had given to him.

"Hi, Lacey, you look beautiful today," he said scrutinizing her up and down. He paused and remembered where he was. "Look I just stopped by because I saw Nicholas' car parked outside. Is he home?"

"You know he is," she said, leading the way back into the kitchen.

"Grand *mere* Catherine, guess who came by for a visit. It's Quinn," Lacey said.

"So?" Grand *mere* Catherine answered. "Quinn ain't anybody special," she said rising and walking over to the stove busying herself.

Lacey looked between the two and quickly realized that she should seize the moment and excuse herself. "Excuse me, I have something I need to take care of."

The minute Lacey walked out of the room Quinn stared after her until he felt eyes staring at him. He looked back and saw Grand *mere* Catherine studying him. He dropped his head. He felt like her eyes could see right through him.

For some reason Grand *mere* Catherine just didn't trust Quinn. Then she remembered her manners. "You hungry Quinn? I've got a pot of Gator Gumbo on the Stove. You are welcome to have some if you want."

He looked up and smiled. She wasn't looking back at him. "Ah, no thanks. I've eaten already."

With her back to the stove and coolness in her voice that she reserved for careless pompous people.Grand *mere* Catherine asked. "You got a steady girlfriend yet Quinn? You know you need to quit messing around. There are a lot of disease and sick people out in the big wide world."

"Man, that old woman could be difficult," Quinn thought. Even with her back turned to him he felt she knew more than she was saying. It almost seemed like she had some sort of gift to be able to read a person's mind and know what they were thinking.

He cleared his throat. "I was just asking Lacey if Nicholas was home but…"

She stirred a pot."Nicholas and Kienan are probably out back in that old barn by now."

Quinn looked up attentively. "What did you say? Kienan is here? I didn't see his car."

She frowned looking back at him. "You heard me right Quinn. Is there something you want to say?"

As he walked toward the way he came in Quinn turned and said, "Tell Nicholas I had to go visit my grandmother. I'll give him a call when I get back."

From the shadow of the hallway Lacey watched and listened to Quinn and her Grand *mere* Catherine as they talked. There was just something about Quinn that was so sexy in a primitive animal instinct way. She thought about the fantasies she had about him.

"Lacey! I know you are standing in the hall, come here!" Grand *mere* Catherine called out.

Stubbornly Lacey entered the room and approached her grandmother.

Grand *mere* Catherine waived her over. "Come in closer, I don't want anyone else to hear this."

"Yes," Lacey asked.

"Whatever you do, don't you ever sleep with that boy Quinn, and you hear me?"

"Sleep with him? What do you mean? Like have a sleep over like when we were kids? Besides Grand *mere,* in case you haven't noticed. Quinn isn't a boy anymore he's a full-grown man. Can't you tell Quinn works out? He's built like superman."

Grand *mere* Catherine threw up her hands. "I don't care if Quinn works out or shovels shit! I don't want you screwing around with him?"

"Oh, you can be safe in knowing if Quinn shoveled shit I…"

"Lacey girl don't try my patience," Grand *mere* Catherine interrupted.

"Ah… No worries Grand *mere* Catherine," Lacey answered blankly.

Grand *mere* Catherine let out a deep breath. "People are a product of their upbringing baby girl. Things that have happened to them in the past, still affect them in the present," she cautioned. "I know you remember the good little boy that was Quinn. But the grown man Quinn, well he's got some serious issues. Promise me you'll never sleep with him."

Vigorously Lacey shook her head in agreement.

Chapter 8

*F*irebaugh California

That Saturday miles away in Firebaugh California a gray-haired old woman sitting on her front porch in the old white wicker chair with her hands neatly folded in her lap had been beautiful once, real beautiful.

"Quinn Darnell Rosolado Rolandis, where have you been?" His grandmother Ina asked with a heavy Spanish accent, "I've been keeping my good food warm for you." A deep frown creased across her soft brown face.

"I'm sorry I'm late. I just got into town, mi abuela," Quinn smiled gently leaning in to kiss her on the cheek.

His grandmother didn't smile, "You lie Quinn!" She exclaimed with a tilt of her head. "Grandma knows. My friend, she saw your car. Stay away from that woman's house!"

She gave him a blank stare.

"Everything under the sun that God made needs love grandmother," He said slowly bowing his head.

She gave him no response.

Ina Rosolado stood up straight and silent. She held her head proud, high and steady as she stared back at her grandson. Her jaw tightened.

Her eyes were determined, and she didn't utter a word.

The silence was daunting as she continued to stare.

Quinn finally sighed exasperated. He knew trying to out-stare his grandmother was hopeless. She had perfected the art of looking through him and seeing the truth.

"Fine… I will grandmother," he lied and prayed she couldn't see the truth. "Can we please eat now?" Quinn solemnly asked.

After a few seconds Ina Rosolado slowly held up her hand gracefully directing her grandson's entry into her home. "You know where the dining room is my Mayan Superman, let's eat. I made you a chocolate cake," she said gently and softly as her eyes brightened, twinkling back at him.

Quinn walked in and kept his head hung low. He softly murmured, "*Tú eres mi angel...* Grandmother you will always be my angel."

Miles away back in San Jose later that evening clouds hung overhead as Nicholas slowly walked down East Santa Clara Street. Downtown San Jose California was turning into an ugly eyesore he thought, as he strolled past another homeless person.

Nicholas whistled out slowly, as a young Asian woman with long black hair in tight jeans walked past. "Impressive, I'll make you the leading lady in my next movie," he grinned.

"What's the name of your movie," she asked provocatively as she swayed her hips exaggeratedly walking by.

Nicholas didn't need to be asked twice. "Whips, Chains and Buck-

Naked Girls," he blurted out playfully. He could see the woman playing with a whip in the role-playing sex video running through his mind. He eyed her backside approvingly as she walked away.

Instantly, he collided with someone. When Nicholas finally looked up he was gazing into the strangest looking pair of bright eyes he'd ever seen.

"Pardon me." Old bony fingers clasped tight around Nicholas' wrist. "Son, it's disrespectful to talk with women that way," the old man said.

"A bum," Nicholas quickly thought before snatching his arm away. He gently pushed the elderly man away from him.

The elderly man snorted out a quick laugh and just smiled back at him.

Frowning, Nicholas stared back at him. There was something about the old man's eyes.

The old man just stood there staring at Nicholas.

Nicholas quickly cleared his throat. His smile was condescending, "Hey, back off old man. Go beg someplace else," he said.

"Mister, you didn't ask me if I was hurt," the elderly man shrugged. "But that's okay. Can you spare some change?"

Nicholas stared hard; his eyes looked strangely familiar. He tried to recall where he'd seen that face before.

"So, are you thinking about giving me some change?" The old man asked. "Anything you have would be kindly accepted?"

Nicholas lifted his brow. "No, you will only buy alcohol with it."

The old man shrugged, "Judgmental, aren't we? Guess this wildness called life can make a man that way," The old man said.

Nicholas was taken aback. The old man's voice was mesmerizing, like God speaking. It held him spell bound.

The old man shook his head. "Sorry, I don't think I have a taste for alcohol" the old man murmured as he softly stared. "So, have you already cast me as the alcoholic bum actor in that little movie making mind of yours? You think this whole world is just a stage, a play that you call *The Cesspool*?"

Nicholas laughed. "If that's the case then I guess you're playing the part of the *poor twisted bastard."*

In an eerie voice the old man said. "Well I guess you're playing the part of the infidel. He who wears the mask, and hides his real problem, his destructive self, in case you didn't know my son, this man is truly the fool."

A knowing silence fell between them.

The old man's snarled finger pointed out judicially, "Therefore, if I'm playing a part then you are too, my son. Isn't that true my son?"

Nicholas pushed his hands deep into his pockets, shrugged and turned away. The old man was strange and weird, and he wanted to put as much distance between the two of them as possible.

The old man's voice sliced the air, "Never be foolish and judgmental too. And watch out for the rats. They run wild everywhere you know," he cautioned. "Rats can change form right under your nose."

Nicholas' ears stood alert when he heard him mumble about rats. But quickly he shook it off that the old man was crazy. He kept walking faster.

The old man stared after Nicholas, "Foolish."

Chapter 9

Spoiling my plans & Other Surprises

On the other side of town in San Jose, Lacey thought her Saturday had started out disastrously. "Grand *mere* I thought you and I were going to watch the Saturday night movie together. I wouldn't have cancelled my plans if I'd known you were going to go to bingo. You know mom's out of town."

"I'm terribly sorry Lacey. But I never promised I'd spend the whole Saturday with you," Grand *mere* Catherine's voice pleaded. "Besides, you never mentioned cancelling any plans, child."

"Hello, anybody home? It's me Gabby," Gabby Baptiste yelled as they swept into the foyer of the La Cour family home."Myrtle and I are ready to go to bingo."

Myrtle Duncan and Gabby Baptiste were two of Grand *mere* Catherine's oldest friends.

Grand *mere* Catherine walked over and swapped air kisses with them in greeting. "Ladies, it's so good to see you. Come on in and make yourself at home. I'll be ready to go in a minute," she said turning her attention. "Lacey, come here and greet Gabby and Myrtle."

Lacey quickly followed her grandmother's command and walked over and stood as both women gave her a warm hug.

Lacey, who was still standing by her grandmother's bingo friends, thought for a moment about making a scene? She stared back at her grandmother. "Grand *mere* how about I go to bingo with you and your friends?"

Simultaneously the bingo posse yelled. "No!"

Gabby and Myrtle glanced between each other.

"Oh Lacey, we didn't mean that the way it sounded," Gabby said. "But we have a system. If one us of wins the bingo jackpot we all drive up to *Cache Creek Casino* and spend the night," she grinned. "I've got a good vibe one of us is winning tonight."

Myrtle shook her head in agreement and then tried to change the subject. "Hmmm goodness, is that fresh coffee I smell?"

"Mmmm Myrtle, I think you're right." Gabby agreed taking her hint to change the subject.

"Why I almost forgot. Yes, it is fresh coffee. As a matter of fact, Gabby, why don't you and Myrtle go into the kitchen and fill up my thermos for me?"

Her grandmother waited until her friends were out of earshot. "Lacey, now you're spoiling my plans. Stop acting like a child and behave. I'm going to bingo."

###

A half hour later, Lacey sat in front of the television and pressed the remote, changing the channel again. She reached for her cell phone and pressed speed dial. The number she called belonged to her best friend, Maëlle. Instantly the number went to voice mail.

Lacey hung up the phone. She had left four messages for Maëlle already and Maëlle hadn't called her back. Even Maëlle had plans for that Saturday night.

59

Her fate was inevitable. She was going to be all alone on another Saturday night.

The doorbell rang and cured her cynicism. She shook out her thoughts. Her parent's home sat on a mountain overlooking San Jose. There was no way to get to it unless you drove.

She composed herself and headed to the front door.

"Hello beautiful," Kienan said with a smile as he strolled into the foyer. "Tell Grand *mere* Catherine I'm here to get my weekly bowl of take home Gator Gumbo."

Lacey paused a moment before she answered.

"Kienan, Grand *mere is* not home. She went to bingo."

Kienan frowned. She caught him off guard with her answer. "What, she didn't make her gator gumbo? She promised."

Lacey shook her head. Just like a man he was thinking about his stomach. "Come on into the kitchen Kienan. You know Grand *mere* Catherine made a pot of gator gumbo. It's on the stove. I'll fix you some."

At just after eleven thirty that night, Lacey couldn't believe she and Kienan had watched two movies together. It was actually nice spending time with him.Slowly she finished off the last of her well-deserved glass of wine. She leaned back against him as they sat on the sofa. It felt nice and cozy.

Unexpected emotions touched her. She knew she'd never get over how much he meant to her no matter how much she tried.

She thought back, remembering their old relationship together. Back in high school she and Kienan often spent Saturday night's enjoying a movie. If they hadn't broken up when he was in college they'd still be together, *stronger than ever,* she thought, with a smile.

He stroked her arm and then he leaned over and dropped a kiss on her neck.

She felt the heat from the feel of his touch.

Lacey's fingers reached out and touched his face. She looked into his eyes. Something flashed inside them. She tried to read the look in his eyes. She was sure he wanted her. For once she thought she was in control. She kissed him and pulled back. She was in control. She felt powerful. Never again would she be overcome by her love for Kienan.

He looked back at her eager and hungry. "Kiss me," he commanded.

"Now wait a minute. Where do you get off telling me what to?"

Kienan kissed her with determination.

Lacey's instincts told her to push him away.

He gave her another kiss and this time her lips trembled and parted willingly. The rush of pleasure at the feel of his tongue seeking hers set her body on fire.

In lightning seconds their passions brought desire and Lacey felt her arms wrap tightly around him.

His mouth tasted better than she remembered.She pulled her mouth away from his and licked her lips. "This can't be happening. You and I..."

"It is happening and what was in the past is in the past," he leaned over and captured her mouth with his and eased her back on the sofa. His fingers unbuttoned her blouse and his mouth traveled down her throat possessing her.

She moaned as her body was abased with sensations.

Just then her cell phone rang out loudly.

The phone rang again. Lacey couldn't help but wonder if she was saved by the bell. She was apprehensive about answering the phone in front of him.

"You should get that," Kienan said, with lines of impatience around his mouth.

Lacey reached for her phone. "Hello."

The phone line went dead just as Kienan pulled out of their embrace.

Lacey checked her caller ID it was blank. Then a thought occurred to her. Maybe it was Maëlle calling her back on someone else's phone.

"Oh, great someone hung up on me," she replied.

"What?" Kienan asked curiously. "You're in another relationship?"

"Ah yeah!" she laughed jokingly. "But I'm not aware of it."

Kienan didn't find her joke amusing.

The moment felt empty.

Kienan rose slowly. "Excuse me Lacey, I think I should go."

He walked to the front door and stopped with his hand on the knob. He turned with a raised brow.

"You owe me," he said, his eyes meeting hers.

"What?" She asked silently clearing her throat. Recognition hit her. The phone call earlier had ruined their evening together.

"Oh, you mean like spending time with me…Ah, like doing this again? I mean having dinner?"

He smiled. "Yes, that's exactly what I mean. You owe me dinner to make up for tonight."

"Okay, but let's make it at some place other than my parent's house and you call the shots," she shyly smiled.

"Sure, I will. But don't forget. The date and time are my choice and all you can say is yes," he said smiling again and closing the door behind him.

Chapter 10

Firebaugh, California...

Just after midnight in Firebaugh California, Quinn tiptoed out of the front door of his grandmother's home breathing a sigh of relief. If he had to watch another episode of *The Price is Right,* he'd scream. He smiled easily, remembering he'd just been saved when the old girl finally fell asleep and started snoring.

"Another wasted Saturday spent with my grandmother," Quinn thought, as he made his way to his car.

At least once every other month Quinn visited his grandmother. He glanced at his watch. It was almost midnight. He couldn't believe he'd spent almost eight hours listening to her talk and watching those TV shows she loved, with her.

Quinn smiled easily as he quickly started his car and made his way down the lane. Once he was out of view of his grandmother's house he pulled over and made the call.

A deep mysterious hoarse voice said, "Hello my friend."

"Hello, it's me Quinn. Where are you?"

In an assertive voice the woman purred into the phone. "I'm waiting for you right now lover, on the corner of North Washoe. But…" Woman voice paused. "Madame Rosa said that you could only come and pick me up if you had what she needed."

Quinn wickedly chuckled loudly as his teeth shone luminous in the moonlight. "Your friend Madame Rosa is very greedy. But yes, I'll pay her price," he asserted. "I'm on my way."

Minutes later, on the corner of North Washoe was quiet for a Saturday night. Quinn thought as he pulled over to the curb eying the woman he was looking for.

A woman walked out of the shadows and up to his car. "Hey Quinn baby," the woman purred in a low-down husky voice. "You got Madame Rosa's money?"

Quinn grinned wide. "You know I do Tabitha," he said grinning uncontrollably as he stared eye level at her breast.

Tabitha was dressed to seduce, and Quinn was a man who wanted to get laid.

"Girl, you look smoking hot and sexy in that outfit. Get in!" Quinn coolly smiled, "Where to?"

"Well, shall we head for the party? Madame Rosa gave specific instructions to only bring you back if you had her money. And since you promised you have her money I'm sure Madame Rosa will see you," Tabitha answered.

"Good," he said, gunning his engine as he took off down North Washoe heading to old highway 33.

The engine of his BMV revved up like a jet, he thought as he drove the old highway. Suddenly he smiled. He had a thought. He pulled out three one hundred-dollar bills and held them up.

The crisp bills caught the moonlight.

Tabitha's eyes widened at the sight of the money. "What do I have to do for that?"

"Blow," he ordered her, before easing the car off the Old Highway and onto a deserted dirt road.

He unzipped his pants. "Oh, and lick it good and wet," he said, smiling revealing gleaming white teeth.

"Sure, Quinn baby," Tabitha purred in her sexiest low voice, as her head moved to his lap and she took his cock in her mouth.

Minutes, later Quinn's head fell back from the mind shattering orgasm that overtook him.

###

A half hour later, he made his way to the house on little Panoche Road. He quickly turned into the driveway.

As Tabitha open his car door and went to climb out of his car, she paused and then turned and stared back at him. "You know Quinn, I never thought you believed in all that hocus pocus stuff. You do know Madame Rosa is a witch."

"I don't believe in that hocus pocus stuff," he said, his face was serious. "But I hear Madame Rosa has other gifts to offer."

Tabitha saw the skepticism in his face. "Oh, you are looking for those things, like potions," she said knowingly.

"What of it? Potions are harmless. Just fun and games."

"Be careful Quinn, you do know Madame Rosa is the real thing?"

Quinn chuckled softly. "By real thing you mean a real witch. I only believe in witches on Halloween and today isn't Halloween."

"Just be warned Quinn, her potions come with a price that must be paid," she said realizing that it was hopeless trying to tell him anything. "Pull around back Quinn," Tabitha commanded. "Madame Rosa said you'll find her out back. Oh, and have her money ready."

Quinn hurried around to the back of the old rambling Victorian House. He'd been told the grand mansion had originally been built by an English nobleman in the 1800's.

Madame Rosa was lying on a chase lounge staring up at the sky. She wasn't old or thin. She rose up as Quinn drew near.

Quinn smiled warmly at the sight of her. She was attractive with long jet-black hair and deep green catlike eyes. She had an exotic beauty that could only be described as mesmerizing.

"You have my money Quinn?"

Quinn handed her what she wanted and as he did he could have sworn the air around him changed. It smelled like sweet sin.

She smiled wickedly. "So, tell me Quinn, is your situation so drastic that you had to come to me?" She stared back at him, "You are the Wizard of love?"

"Yes, I am. Would you care to have a sample of what I have to offer?"

"Easy Quinn. Stop acting like a snake," she laughed in a deep and hoarse voice. "You do not wish to upset me before I give you what you have come for?"

Quinn grew quiet and studied her face to see how serious she was. He looked back at her and said. "Just give it to me."

She could tell that Quinn was annoyed. She quickly held out a small clear vile up to the light. "Here Quinn, what do you call it again?"

"I call it the elixir of the Wizard of Love," Quinn grinned wide. His eyes bulged as he tried to snatch it from her hand.

The woman was as fast as lightning. She pulled her hand back and the vile disappeared.

He grinned wide staring back at her.

"Have patience my friend." She wickedly smiled. She slowly lowered her hand and unzipped his pants. She placed a small drop of liquid on his penis. Gently she slowly stroked him.

Quinn breathed out slowly and closed his eyes. All the while he felt her fingers stroking his penis to an erection.

"Mmmm now it's the right size," Madame Rosa told him, as she placed a condom over his penis.

The next thing Quinn knew he felt his shirt removed as he opened his eyes and watched as she crawled back upon the pillows.

In one smooth movement he was on top of her sliding into her. It was the last thing he remembered.

###

Several hours later Quinn pulled on his jacket and strutted proudly and made his way out of the house on little Panoche Road. He felt energized. He quickly got into his car and started it and just sat there listening to his BMW purring like a tiger. He felt great as he smiled wide. He was the man.

Instantly his cell phone rang. He was glad he had left it in the car.

"Hello baby, I've been meaning to call you," he coolly said into the phone.

The familiar woman's voice brought back memories.

"Hey lover," she giggled. "I got you some chocolate cake, Quinn. I know how much you love chocolate cake."

"Sounds excellent in fact, if you're not busy, I'm dropping by real soon, say in about an hour? We can spend the day together."

Quinn hung up with a triumphant smile. His day was starting off right.

Slowly he eased his car down the old two-lane highway heading to the Interstate.

When he finally looked at the clock, it was 4 o'clock in the morning. He made his way along Interstate 5 heading to highway 152. He was just passing the Casa de Fruita Exit when he quickly wondered what Nicholas had been up to. Too bad it was late, or they could have hung out together.

The next time he looked up he spotted his exit. He sighed out heavily as he gunned his BMW, taking Highway 101 North to San Francisco

Chapter 11

An Invitation

The following Wednesday at six o'clock that evening after work, Lacey lay on the floor in the half Lotus position and thanked God for Yoga.

Soft chanting music played as she tried to focus. All at once the meditating chant ended and the music abruptly changed to the song *I want to do something freaky to you.*

The sensual sexy slow beat made her think about the feel of Kienan's hard strong rip cord muscular chest. He had the kind of body that would put an Adonis to shame. She recalled the way his shirt gashed open and revealed something powerful and feral about him that sent a shiver down her spine. He appealed to the primitive within her. He always did.

Closing her eyes and feeling the music, she slowly ran her hand down her body, imagining Kienan on top of her. It was true what she'd heard about music. It could get under your skin and cause you to want and desire human touch. The song made her think about Kienan touching her in some very wicked ways.

Lost in her thoughts, the song ended in mid-sentence and the room fell deathly silent.

Lacey looked around curiously before she remembered that she'd set the timer on her CD player for forty minutes.

Her yoga time was officially over.

Getting up from the floor, she reflected on just what had happened and walked into her closet and sat on the floor. She looked for her favorite box. She found her hiding place.

She reached for another one of her miniature hidden pleasures and opened the wrapper and took a bite. "Mmmm if I can't have sex with Kienan at least I can have chocolate."

The soft hum of her telephone ringing pulled her attention away.

She swallowed hard and awkwardly said. "Hello."

"You got a man in your room young lady?" An old woman's shaky frail voice rung out through the phone.

"Hi Maëlle. No, I'm just sitting in my closet on the floor looking at all my shoes. What's up?"

Maëlle chuckled at her friend's serious voice. "You're not looking at shoes you're eating a snicker bar aren't you? Don't you know candy bars aren't good for you little girl," she joked. "Besides, how did you know it was me?"

"How long have we been friends?" Lacey asked. "Anyway, who else knows where I hide my stash of snickers bars?"

The two laughed out together.

Lacey sighed. "Maëlle, those acting classes you took aren't working. I can still tell your voice. You need to practice more on your old lady voice and that Spanish accent thing you used on me last week, well that was just awful."

Maëlle Moulard was Lacey's best friend since kindergarten. And she loved her like a sister. There wasn't anything Lacey wouldn't do for Maëlle, and she knew Maëlle felt the same about her. Maëlle was as sweet as pie. Her personality could only be described as particular, in a special way.

"Goodness, you can be so mean and testy," Maëlle grumbled. "I don't know why I called you."

"Because I'm the only one who would listen to you do that crazy accent crap, now what do you want?"

"Wow, you are so testy. What's wrong? Didn't you find your center and that positive energy stuff when you did your Yoga?"

"I'm counting now… One, two, and three…" Lacey said between finishing her snickers. The counting was an old game she did with her best friend to let her know she was serious.

Maëlle gave in. "Okay, I was wondering if you knew where Nicholas and Quinn were this past weekend. I couldn't reach Nicholas all weekend. Did he and Quinn go to that fight in Vegas or something?"

Lacey listened to her friend. She knew she had a thing for her brother. "Sorry I don't know about any fight in Vegas," she said. Then she thought about something. "Nicholas did mention he had to find something to do, because Quinn was visiting his grandmother."

"Oh, I forgot it was visitation weekend for Quinn," Maëlle said with a hesitation in her voice.

"So, is that all you wanted, to ask me about my brother Nicholas?"

"No, I wanted to know if you wanted to go out and do something fun tonight. Like maybe see a concert."

"Not really… Okay well maybe. Who?"

Maëlle blurted. "I've got two tickets to see Leonard Cohen, but they are only good for his concert tonight?"

Lacey almost choked on her candy bar. "What! You've got tickets?"

"Yes, the concert starts at nine o'clock, so do you want to go? Unless you have something else to do," Maëlle said.

"Sure, I'll go with you! But only because I hate to see you sit through his concert alone. So what time are you picking me up?"

Maëlle coughed out, "Who says I'm driving? I got us the tickets remember?"

"Now who's testy? Okay, be over here by eight sharp."

"Okay," Maëlle exclaimed.

Lacey muttered out a soft laugh. "Oh, and thanks for getting us the tickets."

Maëlle giggled, "I'm sorry, I didn't catch that, could you say it a little louder."

Lacey felt her jaw tightening. She cleared her throat. "Why do you always have to make everything so difficult? Okay thank you."

"You're welcome."

All at once the other line of her phone rang.

"Maëlle, I'm getting another call, I have to go, bye."

Lacey clicked over quickly to her other line.

"Hello?"

Silence.

"Hello?" She repeated.

The line went dead.

Bewildered Lacey shook her head and clicked the phone off.

Chapter 12

Quinn Darnell Rosolado Rolandis

That night, Lucy Mondragon's face flushed with excitement and she felt a growing urgency as she watched Quinn's well-endowed manly body get into bed and lay beside her. Quinn softly placed a peck on her cheek before his lips moved down to her shoulders.

Lucy exhaled loudly she felt an explosion of joy when he entered her from behind.

"Lucy what did you call this position again?"

"It's called Mandarin Ducks in Japanese erotology. But you can call it spooning," Lucy purred, softly liking the things he was doing to her body.

Lucy Mondragon was stunningly beautiful and very pregnant. Quinn closed his eyes and felt the desire within liquefy as he ran his hands down her ripe naked body. He found her body to be erotic, desirable, and very pregnant. A moan escaped his lips. "Ahhhh I do like spooning with you Lucy," he murmured grinning. *"Who knew having sex with a pregnant woman could be so hot and erotic,"* he said in his mind.

"Oh, Quinn stop talking so much. I want it harder, baby. Harder!

"Damn Lucy, I've forgotten what a nymphomaniac you are," Quinn murmured

Then they both moved rhythmically moaning as each move intensified before they climaxed together.

"Oh Quinn, that was so wonderful."

Quinn lay back and tried to control his breathing.He grinned satisfied to know he could add screwing a pregnant woman to his list of conquests. "I would have to agree," he finally said. "But you were pretty incredible too, Lucy."

"Thanks Quinn, you know I love to make you happy," Lucy gushed with pride, loving the compliment he paid her. "We can go again just as soon as I finish a little snack and maybe take a nap," she said reaching for the slice of chocolate cake on the nightstand.

Quinn's predatory glance watched Lucy spoon the chocolate cake in her mouth. "Hey Lucy, don't eat all of the chocolate cake. I thought you brought that for me?"

"I brought enough cake for four people," Lucy replied, swallowing a bite of cake.

"Yeah but you're two people all by yourself," he said, whisking the plate of cake from her hand. "Besides you ate a piece earlier for that baby in your belly, and I'm not sharing another slice of my cake with that unborn crumb-snatcher."

"Don't call my baby a crumb-snatcher," she said ignoring him. "By the way, can I have the money now?"

The smile died on his face, as he swallowed a big bite of chocolate cake and licked the spoon. There was a look of impatience on Quinn's face as he leaned over to the side of the bed and retrieved the fat envelope. He knew he should never have spent so much time with Lucy. He'd been staying with Lucy for three days, ever since he returned from visiting his grandmother. Staying with a woman for three days gave her ideas that a man belonged to her.

He was getting in way too deep with Lucy. The more time he spent with her the more she was starting to think the two of them were an item. And the more she thought that the more she thought he'd just keep supplying her with money. He knew he had to keep the reason why he was there in perspective and be frank and make sure she understood.

"Lucy, I heard about your ordeal at the concert that night. I'm glad you and the baby are okay. Here's the money I promised."

She paused for a moment and then nervously said. "You heard about that? I almost fell but Kienan came to my rescue."

Quinn could sense she was coming forth with details. He was wise in his understanding of human nature and women. He knew Lucy would keep coming back to him asking for money. Money he was tired of giving her. He thought carefully as he planted the seed of an idea in her head. "Kienan Egan caught you? How lucky for you," he said in a low voice with understanding. "I grew up with Kienan, so believe me when I say he is a noble and good man," he coolly said without a trace of the jealousy he truly felt against Kienan.

Lucy shook her head in agreement. "Oh yes, Kienan is such a wonderful guy. He was like the cavalry coming to my rescue," she said briskly. "It could have been a bad situation if he hadn't been there."

Quinn's handsome face looked solemn for a moment as he studied hers. He could sense that she just needed to have that seed he planted watered thoroughly. "Kienan was heroic that night. But I must be honest with you Lucy I saw the whole thing. I saw the way Kienan looked at you. It was obvious that the man is crazy about you."

Lucy's cheeks flushed. She'd always had mixed feelings about Quinn. He could be rude, jealous and arrogant at times. The two of them had dated often but always secretly. Now with the baby coming she'd found herself clinging to him more.

Her eyes darted back at Quinn's. "Oh Quinn, you know I don't have eyes for any other man but you," she said coquettishly.

He surveyed Lucy and noticed the dark circles under her eyes.

Quinn stared back at her as if she didn't exist. Once upon a time, a long time ago, he would have loved to hear her say that he was her everything and mean it. He knew she was lying. They both were users and liars. "That was a great comeback Lucy. But I'm being honest with you. I'm a man who likes to fuck, that's all. Plain and simple," he said feeling powerful and invincible. "I don't mind taking care of a woman who's taking care of my needs. But at the end of the day, I don't have any room in my life for anything with you but sex. And I only want that every now and then."

"You know that's the same thing I want lover," she said anxiously trying to control her emotions. "We've always been great together," she said, running her fingers down his arm.

Quinn had enough problems, and having Lucy consider him as daddy material for the baby she was carrying wasn't going to be one of them. He wasn't shy with his words as he stared back at her. "You know Lucy. I'm concerned about you," he said with meanness. "You need to stay out of my bed for a while. You know and start trying to catch yourself a daddy for that baby before you start looking like you're somebody's momma."

"Damn Quinn!" she grimaced "You can say some of the meanest things sometimes!" She hissed. "Don't worry about me. I'll catch my baby's daddy."

He looked bored. "Oh really. From where I'm lying, you haven't been doing much trying. Every time I look up you're here fucking me," he blurted.

"Quinn, I don't..."

He interrupted her with a look of impatience on his face. "Look, I'm just making sure that you are not trying to stick that kid on me. So, I'm sorry to say it Lucy but there will be no more money from me. You need to get off your ass and find yourself another sugar daddy. I quit!"

Shocked and dismayed. Lucy stared back at him. "Quinn Darnell Rosolado Rolandis you're a fucking bastard!"

"No sweetness, that's what the folks in the England will call your baby once it is born."

With a parting look of hatred Lucy inched her body to the side of the bed. "Shut the hell up Quinn I'm leaving! And I hope you choke on that chocolate cake!"

He laughed. "Ah, I bet you do. But if I were you, I'd try and save some of that money I just gave you. Don't spend it all in one place! Because sister your well is died up and empty," he chuckled out. "Oh, and please lock the door as you leave sweetness!" His laughter roared out. He only hoped she wouldn't stay mad at him forever.

Chapter 13

Rats, Old man you're hallucinating

Miles away that same night, Nicholas' sleek steel gray BMW 745il quietly purred as he slowly made his way onto Embarcadero West at Jack London Square in Oakland, California.

He parked his car in the first open lot he found. The lot was nearly three blocks past the Heinold's First and Last Chance Saloon. He got out of his car and quickly zipped his jacket as a chilled wind blew softly off of the harbor.

Heinold's looked inviting. He quickly walked past. When he wasn't meeting Quinn, he often got a drink at Heinold's.

He moved quickly, pulling his collar tighter and bracing himself against the cold. The place that he was going to, was a place he'd been many times. He smiled warmly remembering. He and Quinn had first gotten in with fake ID's they made. This was their secret place, their bar. The one place they kept secret from Kienan. As far as dives go, it was where the name originated. But still it was a cool mellow place and the crowd was likeable. The drinks were cheap, and you never had to wait. Plus, it helped that Quinn got to be real good friends with Sam, the owner, many years ago.

"Hey mister can you spare some change?" A bum called to him, quickly moving into his path.

Nicholas tried to walk around the man. But he quickly implanted himself in Nicholas' path.

"Did you see that?" The old man questioned Nicholas.

"Excuse me?"

The old man's bony snarled fingers pointed, "That big fat rat that just ran past."

"No, no. I didn't see a rat. Old man you're hallucinating," Nicholas said.

"You need to be careful young man. Rats have been known to take the form of a human man."

Nicholas threw up his hand. "That's crazy old man!"

"Yes, they have," the old man insisted. "Haven't you heard of the Rat man coming to life in the Nutcracker? It's true. I've seen it." The old man shrugged. "I saw the whole play on Broadway one year. Broadway's in New York you know?"

"You ain't never been to New York in your whole life," Nicholas responded.

"Judgmental aren't you, young man? Never judge a book by its cover. One day you're the King's son, the next day you find out you ain't shit." The old man shrugged. "But never mind, you got any change you can spare mister? Please mister, spare some change for a sad old man." The old man pleaded.

Nicholas ignored the man and quickly walked over to an old store front with a brown door.

"Foolish!" The old man murmured out.

Nicholas pushed on the brown door and it quickly gave way. He walked into the darkened room and quickly adjusted his eyes to the darkness and the red lights.

He quickly walked over, "Quinn, old buddy."

"Nicholas," Quinn greeted him.

Quinn smiled and chuckled loudly, "Sam, old buddy get my best friend his usual," He said quickly pulling out a wad of cash. He laid a fifty-dollar bill on the counter. "Sam get me a bottle of Wild Turkey."

Sam just looked at Quinn.

Quinn quickly sweetened the deal and put another fifty on the counter. "Your tip my friend."

Sam took the money and handed Quinn the bottle, "Keep the bottle out of sight Quinn," he growled.

"I know the deal," Quinn smiled coolly.

Sam handed Quinn the bottle and two glasses.

"Sam, you know where to find me, at my table."

Nicholas and Quinn made their way across the room to Quinn's favorite table way in the back.

Quinn's excited voice sliced the air, "We're going to have some great fun tonight! Our agenda is full. We've got booze, women and more women," he said as he led the way.

Deep shadows filled Nicholas' face as he quietly sat down.

Quinn studied Nicholas and then opened the bottle and poured him a drink.

Nicholas took his bourbon straight. He gulped it down quickly. The warmth filled him.

Quinn eyed his friend. Pushing back his glasses, he lifted his brow. "Ah, troubles Nicholas? Is Lacey okay?"

Holding his glass to his lips, Nicholas shot back a look, "Yeah, I think my sister is okay right now. But Quinn you don't know the half of it," he said, gulping his drink down.

"What happened?" Quinn squinted through puffed fatigued eyes. "Did something happen too Lacey?"

Nicholas shrugged. "I found out she has been dating a stupid politician."

Quinn sipped his drink slowly, "Nonsense. It couldn't have been serious," he said trying to analyze how Lacey could have kept that relationship a secret.

He poured Nicholas another drink. He needed Nicholas to keep talking and confide in him.

Nicholas was silent for a moment. "I can't believe it," Nicholas said, frowning. "She's been dating him for almost two and a half months, and I didn't have a clue."

Quinn played with the drink in his hand. "A politician huh, sounds like a missed opportunity to pick up an investor."

"I'll say," Nicholas gestured with his hand. "She could have at least mentioned the guy once or twice on her outlook calendar."

Quinn saw his opportunity. He had an idea and he was sure it would get him the information he craved. "If you don't know the guy's name how did you know, he was a politician?" He finally asked but didn't wait for a response. "Nicholas, you didn't read Lacey's diary, did you?"

"Oh no, I read it on her outlook calendar. You know the one on her computer? She wrote that she was *seeing the politician* – on the days she had dates with him."

"Really, Lacey's been sleeping with a politician?"

"Now that I do know, exactly. She hasn't slept with the guy once, and she wrote that on her calendar too," he blurted. "She said she was instituting some ninety-day rule of no sex."

Quinn smiled slightly. "Nicholas, it sounds to me like you wanted to try and use that politician to get your hands on some money?"

"No? I mean maybe. I'm not sure if the guy would have been worth it," Nicholas replied.

"Well Quinn, I'm worth it and I have a proposition for you if you care to hear it."

"Certainly, I would."

###

Miles away in San Jose at almost midnight, Lacey and Maëlle were walking out of the HP Pavilion with a thousand-other people. They both had genuine smiles of happiness on their faces.

Lacey turned to her friend and blurted. "That concert was the best! I got so choked up when he sang *Suzanne*…Oh it was so great!"

She stopped abruptly and grabbed Maëlle and hugged her. "Oh, you are my best friend in the whole wide world. Thank you so much for bringing me Maëlle."

Laughing bubbly, Maëlle said. "You are very welcome; I was so happy to do it. See I told you I had a great present for you. Come on now, let's hurry and get back to the car. It's cold out here!"

The two women walked to the corner of Autumn Street and East Santa Clara Street where they had left the car.

Lacey exclaimed while unlocking the car door for her. "Goodness, it really is cold for this time of year."

Maëlle's teeth started chattering. "I'm so cold. Hurry and turn on the heat. It looks like we were some of the first people to leave the concert. We got a straight shot getting out of the parking lot."

"Yes, I agree with you." Lacey said as she edged the car onto Autumn Street and made a left at East Santa Clara Street. She caught Highway 87, heading towards home.

Maëlle's voice loudly sang out in a childlike manner."Yeah, we beat the traffic, we beat the traffic…Whew! That's what I'm talking about!"

Lacey was still a little thunderstruck that they had even gotten tickets. She knew that Leonard Cohen had been sold out months ago. She cleared her throat, "I still can't get over how great our seats were. I do thank you for getting them Maëlle, really I do from the bottom of my heart."

Maëlle continued to play with the radio. "You know; I love this XM radio. You've got so many channels to listen too."

Lacey nodded ignoring her. "But those seats must have cost you a fortune?" She checked her rear-view mirror.

Maëlle smiled back at her. "Nay, I got the concert tickets for nothing."

"Still, I'm so happy and upbeat right now that I don't care. I'm just glad that you brought me. It was a wonderful concert." She flashed a quick look at Maëlle and started to sing like she always did. "I'm just so happy…Happy…Happy…Yes that's me!"

Maëlle looked amused at her friend. "Using my line, are you? I thought you said my *happy song* was too corny and ridiculous?"

"Me? Never. You know I love that song, because you love it and made it up," Lacey smiled. And then her smile quickly faded as she suddenly thought of something.

Maëlle kept flipping through the radio channels.

"Hmm," Lacey said anxiously as her thoughts raced. She remembered what Maëlle had said. She'd gotten the tickets for nothing.

"Maëlle my BFF, I know it's not polite to ask how much a gift cost, but did you say you got the tickets for nothing? How can that be?"

Maëlle's silence felt stifling.

Lacey shrugged. "Okay Maëlle I know you can be a woman of many talents. But what did you do to get those tickets for nothing?"

"Oh, come on Lacey, please stop worrying. I didn't pay a dime," she assured her. "And no, I didn't use any of my womanly talents. Anyway, I've got other sources. Besides, I wanted to do something nice for your birthday. Whew! You are a bad gift taker," she responded sarcastically. "Happy belated birthday, by the way."

Lacey shrugged. "Maëlle I heard you when you said you didn't pay a dime for those tickets. Now I want the truth. Out with it!"

Maëlle cast Lacey a cursory glance. "Okay, but first let me tell you this. The concert tickets weren't my gift. And you've got to promise me you will use the gift certificate that I got you, on the date that is listed."

Lacey nodded. "What? No, no… I won't promise you anything!"

Maëlle teased. "Is that your final answer?" She asked. "Then I guess you really don't want to know the truth."

"Okay, what is it."

"First swear it." Maëlle flashed a smile.

"Hey look, I will, I promise. I'll do whatever you say. Heck, I'll promise you anything so that we can move on!" Lacey gripped the steering wheel tightly.

Maëlle's voice tensed. "Oh goodness, looks like someone's getting angry," she teased. "Okay here goes. Kienan wanted to get you something special to apologize for that night you saw him talking to what's her name. I told him how much you like Leonard Cohen, and well anyway a few days ago Kienan's Secretary Gladys called me and told me she had two tickets held in my name for the concert tonight."

Lacey frowned. Now she felt obligated to thank Kienan because of all the money she knew he'd spent for these tickets. Not to mention she'd promised him dinner.She decided not to mention this to Maëlle. She didn't want to start explaining how that had come about.

Then Lacey remembered Maëlle said she'd gotten her a gift certificate. She was curious to know if it was at the same salon she used before. "Okay so tell me Maëlle, where did you get my gift certificate this year? Is it for a facial and manicure?"

"Huh?"Maëlle responded.

Lacey shook her head. "You know I didn't like the salon you used the last time. They made me wait way too long and my nails were not filed the way I like them."

"Don't worry, I didn't get you a facial or a manicure this time," Maëlle replied.

Lacey looked confused. "But Maëlle you always get me a facial and a manicure."

"Not this time, and you swore to accept my gift," Maëlle answered with a slightly turned up smile. "Remember you promised."

Chapter 14

A **Mystifying Situation...**

Saturday afternoon, Lacey slowly made the drive to Fremont. Traffic on Highway 680 was light as she passed the Calaveras Road Exit heading out of Milpitas.

Her sleek Black Buick Lucerne car radio was loud as she listened to her music.

If you give it everything, trust..."

The sound of the man's voice saying trust made her think of Kienan. Unexpected emotions touched her. She knew she'd never get over how much he meant to her no matter how much she tried.

She was startled by a strange funny sound. She listened closely and realized that the chiming bell ringing sound was her cell phone. She answered it.

"Hello!"

"Hi Lacey, how are you, okay?

The last person she expected to hear from was on the line. And he was the person who'd just run through her thoughts.

Her voice was fractured with anxiety. "Hello Kienan, I'm just fine. How are you? Any particular reason for this call," she said calmly.

"No… I mean yes, I guess I just wanted to see if you… If you liked the concert, the gift, I mean."

Lacey was silent. It sounded like the line went dead.

"Lacey, are you still there?" Kienan asked softly.

"Yes," she responded and paused and said. "The concert was great! And thank you for the gift. I...I haven't forgotten about promising to cook your dinner."

Kienan's voice softened, "Uh Cool, I'm ready anytime you are," he said hoping she couldn't tell he was just about to ask her that question. "I'm just happy hearing your voice, Lacey."

Lacey knew instinctively that Kienan's offer was made with genuine concern. "I hope you're not thinking of getting together today Kienan, I'm busy all day."

"No...No... Whenever it is good for you," he paused, and realized he needed to make his preference known. "What about Sunday, two weeks from tomorrow? Are you busy then?"

Lacey decided to give in and get their dinner over with. Besides two weeks was a long time away. Anything could happen. But why have dinner when she could have a late brunch and have him out of her home before evening. Her throat was parched, "Okay, in two weeks then."

"Good, and we will make it a late afternoon brunch, say round three o'clock?"

"Wonderful! That sounds good, meet me at my house. You still know where it is, right?

"Hey! Wait a minute I thought you wanted me to cook for you," she announced.

"Ah! Well I decided to switch things up and cook for you," Kienan replied. "I know how you are always at your parents' home helping out. I thought I'd give you a rest."

"Sounds like bribery. But, okay then, I'll see you at three."

"Okay, then I'll consider that a promise," he replied.

Just as Kienan said promise, the second line on her cell phone buzzed loudly.

"Go ahead. You should take that call Lacey it could be important, goodbye, "Kienan said hanging up abruptly.

Suddenly her phone rang again.

"What was going on today, normally I never get any calls," she thought.

"Hello?"

"Hi Lacey, it's me, your buddy Quinn. How are you doing?"

Lacey took a deep breath. "Hey Quinn. What's up?"

Quinn laughed out.

"Everything is up. The stock market, my portfolio in fact I'm doing great! If you need investment advice, I'm your man. If you need a money loan, then I'm your man. In fact, I'm the best man I know."

Lacey was silent as she listened to Quinn's egotistical rave about himself. It was always the same with Quinn. He liked to call and rant and rave about how well he was doing. And today Quinn was on a *Quinn's world high.* She figured if she kept quiet, he would talk himself out of things to say.

"Lacey, are you still there?"

She tightened her lip to keep from laughing. Quinn's rant and rave routine about himself reminded her of the pitch routine used car salesmen used on television. He had the same comical stance.

"Yes Quinn, I was listening, it sounds like everything is going great for you. Your business sure is successful. Sell any cars lately?" she asked jokingly.

"What?" Quinn inquired.

"Oh, never mind. I was just thinking how sweet it must be to be your own boss, Quinn."

"Oh, it is, Lacey. I am my own boss," he gloated. "And you will never understand how running your own business and making it a success feels. It empowers you."

Quinn ranted on about his accomplishments.

Lacey checked her location. Her thoughts weren't on their conversation. She said the first words that rolled off of her tongue. "Jeez Quinn, you sound like the chairman of the board, the master of the game, you are the man."

Her compliments hit their mark.

"Yes, I am," he murmured.

Quinn's mind raced with thoughts of Lacey. He daydreamed about seeing her naked. He'd love to see her lying naked sprawled across his bed, waiting for him to do unspeakable acts to her. Was this love he wondered? The word love meant many things to many people. He thought for a moment and then he remembered it wasn't love. It was lust.

All at once he knew he had to work a different angle if he was ever going to get into Lacey's pants.

A soft note crept into his voice. "You know Lacey, I still haven't forgotten that you missed my housewarming party," he said sincerely. "And I still have your personal letter of regret, stating that you were unable to attend but promising me you could come over and plant my first rose bush with me. When are you going to come by and plant a rose bush with me, Lacey?" He demanded.

Quickly Lacey thought of a lie. "Look Quinn, I really can't talk right now, in fact I'm driving. I'm sort of going out of town."

Quinn chuckled into the phone. "What do you mean kind of going out of town? You are either going out of town or you're not."

Lacey tried to ignore the condescending tone of his voice, but it irked her in the worst way. She said the harsh words in a moment's notice. "Okay Quinn, I'm in the middle of going out of town. Big deal, it isn't any of your damn business anyway."

What had started off as an entertaining diversion for Quinn quickly changed as he felt an emotion akin to panic. No woman had ever had an effect on him like Lacey had. The minute she yelled at him her words stung him badly and instantly Quinn realized that he'd lied to himself earlier. It wasn't just lust he felt for Lacey. It was love too. She was the only woman whose words could cut his heart like a knife. He was glad she could not see the expression on his face over the phone.

He had to make amends and the opportunist in him thought of the perfect response. "If you don't want to drop by the house, that's fine. How about we go for a ride? I know how much you miss going to Copperopolis. I'll take you to see you father's old cabin."

At the mention of her father's cabin in Copperopolis Lacey grew quiet. The truth was, she'd wanted to go and see the place real bad. She had for a long time. But now wasn't the time to talk or think about visiting her father's cabin.She had an appointment. She couldn't be late.

She sighed heavily into the phone. "Let me think about it and get back to you," her voice softened. Quinn, I'm sorry for yelling at you. I've got a lot on my mind."

Nervously he laughed out, "Yeah, I understand. I'll be waiting for your call, okay?

Lacey's face twisted into a frown. "Sure, goodbye Quinn" she said before she abruptly hung up.

Instantly Lacey forgot about her conversation with Quinn. She had to focus on taking the next exit and where she was going. The Mission Blvd exit loomed in front of her. With Maëlle's help she mapped out her route before coming. She now navigated easily through the rustic old city. The road quickly turned into a scenic old highway. The area was historic and nicely preserved.

What possessed her to go through with this was beyond her. Lacey had no intentions of ever going to *Let's Get Acquainted,* until Maëlle called her a heartless shrew who took her friendship for granted and treated her even worse. Then she had to go and start crying. *Okay I'm a lot of things, yes, I am a little mean sometimes but* Maëlle *is my best friend. I love her like a sister, she thought.*

Let's Get Acquainted, Lacey thought, what a name for a matchmaking service.

Lacey looked out for the century's old grove of olive trees that Maëlle told her to look for. It signaled she was approaching the turn that would lead her straight up the hill to the Stately Mansion.

She parked her car in front of a huge old rose arbor. The rustic old-world charm of it was beautiful. She looked beyond the arch way and saw that magnolia trees stood on each side of it. Her gaze looked past them and there stood a magnificent garden.

For several minutes she just sat in her car and stared mesmerized. She wondered how beautiful everything would look at full bloom in the summer.

A few minutes later she got out of her car and took the walkway heading to the house. She had every intention of ringing the doorbell. She looked for it but couldn't find one. A strange doorknocker seemed to appear out of nowhere. A shiver ran down her spine.

Mystified, Lacey just stood there and looked at it and refused to touch it.

The door slowly crept open.

"Hello, and welcome to *Let's Get Acquainted,*" I'm your host for the night Mrs. CJ Oshun. But most people just drop the CJ."

A very petite lady waived her in and turned and started walking down the hallway. "Welcome to the Magnolia Heights Mansion."

"The lady must have been standing watch at the window," Lacey thought.

As Lacey walked behind the small frail delicate little old lady, she studied her. She was wearing a spectacular green dress that had a bold magical green effect to it. Her deep green dress was framed by an exquisitely beautiful burgundy and gold scarf that resembled the beautiful folds of a sari.

When Mrs. Oshun spoke, her voice sounded like melodious singing.

Lacey followed closely behind her, silently.

Mrs. Oshun spoke as she walked. "Your face looks like I need to tell you the absolute truth, she sung out. "My true name is Madame CJ Fortier. I have given myself the name of Mrs. CJ Oshun after my late husband. He was my second husband. He was originally from Santería Cuba. You know. In his country the name Oshun means he who reigns over love. In some cultures, it refers to a spiritual goddess." She nodded. "Anyway, that said. You may call me Mrs. Oshun," she said, as she abruptly stopped walking.

Mrs. Oshun turned and studied Lacey's face.

All at once Mrs. Oshun reached out her hands and cupped Lacey's face. "And believe it or not, I know who you are Lacey Kadira Catherine La Cour"! She exclaimed. "Oh, my…I would know your face anywhere. You look just like your mother Pearl."

Mrs. Oshun's green eyes sparkled like emeralds. "Sorry but there is no time to explain how I know you. Come, come. We must get started. She urged Lacey to follow her down the hall.

Lacey looked up in astonishment as she quickly followed behind Mrs. Oshun.

"Hurry, hurry," Mrs. Oshun's voice called softly."Right this way, it's not far. Stay close and follow me."

Soft music filled the air. Lacey could have sworn that she heard an instrumental version of the song *"Hello Young Lovers" humming softly through some hidden speakers, she thought.*

"Oh great! What kind of mind games is this old lady playing?"

They reached a strange looking door that was very old and ornate.

Mrs. Oshun abruptly stopped walking. "In here you will meet ladies just like yourself. I'm sure you'll make some new friends. Have you eaten yet?"

"No," Lacey said shaking her head.

"Good! We are serving dinner, shortly."

Lacey grew quiet as she followed her close behind.

"Just be yourself. Don't worry, everything here has a way of working itself out," Mrs. Oshun said attentively. "I have assembled just the right, shall we say, number of women for the right number of men that have been invited. There is no need to worry about finding Mr. Right in this room."

"What?"

"A penny for your thoughts Lacey but keep your questions until later. There will be no explanations until after this evening is over," Mrs. Oshun said pulling open the ornate looking door, and ushering

Lacey into a beautifully decorated room.

The room was artfully decorated with beautiful vases of fresh flowers in every size and very large pictures with abstract objects. The colors were fascinating shades of magenta, reds, yellows and tan. *"Wow, who knew the effects of color," she thought.*

"Ladies I want you to meet Lacey," Mrs. Oshun softly said while making introductions. "We are all present and accounted for now."

Three ladies stood before her.

The first one to shake Lacey's hand was a tall Blond woman named Claudia. Her perky Boston accent caught Lacey off guard.

Gina the redhead shook her hand next. Lacey almost laughed out when she heard her low country throaty drawl. Lacey was glad she had experienced plenty of relatives with worst accents from Louisiana.

The last one to shake her hand was a pretty, short girl in black glasses who had even blacker hair. Her name was Roma. Her clothes looked like they belonged to a shy, old-fashioned librarian, but her shoulder look page haircut and bangs made her look like Betty Page. Especially when you looked at the deep red lipstick and kinky black lace up ankle boots she wore with ruffled trimmed white ankle socks.

For about twenty minutes the four of them chatted easily about nothing important until Lacey said. "I wonder where Mrs. Oshun is."

Suddenly as if she heard her name. The mysterious Mrs. Oshun reappeared. "Ladies let's get back on schedule. Please have a seat, *Oui,*" Mrs. CJ Oshun said. "I will now introduce you to Glenda D'Goodwrench.Glenda will grab your attention for the next half hour or so and provide you with some expert advice."

Glenda wasn't a bad looking person in fact she looked like a former model. Positive energy poured off Glenda like the water falls at Niagara.

After her quick introduction, Lacey realized Glenda D'Goodwrench was a spell binding speaker.

All at once Glenda shot a look around the room and froze everyone to their seats. "Everyone, I won't mince my words. The secret to getting and keeping a man is simple. You need to know when to be sexy and sensual. And you need to learn how to cast your love spell," Glenda said. "I am here today to teach you how to cast a spell, a Love spell."

The redhead named Gina raised her hand. "Is this anything like voodoo? Because if it is I'd rather have the doll that looks like the man I want, that way it's easier for me to control him," she said in her soft southern drawl.

"It sounds more like some hocus pocus magical stuff to me," Roma added. "I've got to see the living proof that this works."

"Jeez! I've got my work cut out for me with you ladies," Glenda replied. "Now you've got to be open and to try new things. Otherwise you're not going to get anything out of tonight's romantic magical experience," she said, placing small bowls filled with various trinkets in front of each woman.

All at once Glenda reached out her hand and the air seemed strange and electrified. She closed her eyes and said.

"We were each born special for just one. Oh, that we might know the one that we love," Glenda's voice cackling like a low song carried by the wind. "Oh, that we might know our love to feel him, to fondle him, and to caress him until our heart grows as one."

Lacey's eyes roamed around the room quickly. For the first time she notices a strong floral scent and a sensation went through her. As if she had smelled it before, somewhere a long time ago.

Lacey shuddered at the thought and shook her head. And then she thought she heard a musical tinkling sound. She looked down at her hands. They were moving as if something or someone else was controlling the. She watched her hands as they selected and assembled small items from the various bowls.

Lacey looked up suddenly and her eyes met Glenda's. "You selected the right colors. You remind me of your mother Pearl." She said patting her shoulder. "Keep working."

Lacey turned her head and stared hard after Glenda walked away.

Her thoughts raced. *"How did she know my mother's name? And why didn't I hear her walk over?"* She thought before her logic kicked in. *"Of course, it must have been Maëlle who told them all about my family."*

All at once Glenda's voice ushered out in a soft chanting whisper.

"From our quieting minds, the truth will unfold, happiness, joy, and love to behold."

Glenda continued the strange and mesmerizingly mantra.

It seemed like time stood still.

"Ladies we are done," Glenda finally said.

Lacey looked down at her watch. Over an hour had passed.

Roma breathed out. "And what was the purpose of this…This exercise?"

Glenda just smiled and patted her shoulder. "Roma, you will see shortly."

Lacey looked up at Glenda. "But all of the little trinkets look like little pansy flowers."

"Mine have faces," Roma said.

Glenda looked down at Lacey and touched her chin. "Close your eyes Lacey and feel with your heart."

Lacey felt like she heard a soft melody play softly caressing her ear.

Suddenly Roma raised her hand. "Did we just perform a love spell?"

The room felt enchanted and timeless as Glenda slowly smiled. Her eyes looked sparkling mysterious. "Now ladies, we must keep with our agenda. It's now time for our next event of the evening. Please bring the bag sitting behind you on the back of your chair."

There was a gleeful commotion as whispers went around the room. The women all looked at each other and grabbed their bag.

Lacey reached for her bag and wondered when they put them on their chairs. They weren't there before.

The small bag reminded her of the gris-gris bag that her *Grand mere* had made her for protection when she was a small child. Things were just not making sense around this place she thought.

Lacey made her way of out the door. It led them down a massive hallway. At the end stood a huge double door that opened into the formal dining room. The room was breathtakingly beautiful. Glistening gold-plated flatware adorned the huge circular table. It was set regally. Everything was gold. The dinner charger, plates and bowls were solid gold in color. Only the crystal glassware was spared the color of gold.

Lacey noticed that every item was geometrically spaced in a geometric pattern. Even the centerpiece set exactly and were colored in gold.

Lacey and all her new friends stood silently gawking around the room. She quickly noticed that they were alone.

The room grew dim and fog slowly seeped in and to everyone's amazement.

Mrs. Oshun mysteriously appeared. She was now regally attired in a full deep green sari that matched the scarf that she wore earlier. Her presence was commandingly regal, royal and magical.

Lacey admired the beautiful Sari Mrs. Oshun was wearing.

Her soft singing voice sounded sultry and hoarse as she said. "Welcome to our dining room part of our little adventure tonight." Mrs. Oshun smiled softly. "Now Ladies please sit one seat apart and place your bows with their trinkets facing up directly on the left of you, on the seat."

Finally, each lady did as she was told. Each looking at the other wondering what to expect next. The tension was heavy in the air.

"Now, as you all know, I don't operate in the conventional methods. Your match for the night has been carefully selected not just based upon your compatibility but also based upon something that is solely unique to me."

The ladies whispered among themselves. The room felt supernaturally charged. The lights seemed to grow dimmer.

Gina leaned over and whispered. "Lacey, do you think Mrs. Oshun is using some kind of secret binding method? I hear all matchmakers use it?"

Lacey shrugged whispering. "Gina what if I told you none of it works, especially if you don't like the guy to begin with?"
"Shhhhh!" Roma said.

The room was mystically foggy and dim.

Mrs. Oshun's expression was serious. "Now ladies, prepare to meet the gentleman that has been chosen for you." She waved her hand like a magician getting ready to pull a rabbit out of a hat. And magical dust and mystical vapor floated through the air. A crimson red door appeared out of nowhere.

Heavy sighs entered the air as each woman looked toward the door.

And then Claudia, the blond-haired woman with the deep Boston accent, murmured out loudly. "I wouldn't mind going out with a guy who was as ugly as a monster or as horny as a toad. Just so long as underneath he was sweet, sensitive, gentle and kind. May my sweet soul mate walk through that door now, I command it!"

"Oh God, please don't let mine be Jeffery Dahmer's cousin." Gina said joking.

"Shhhhh!" Roma said pushing her thick glasses back on her nose. "Be quiet and let the Geek Squad enter," she smiled.

Lacey tried to suppress her giggle.

The ladies' whispers and constant body movements stopped as soon as the first Gentleman walked through the door. All eyes were on him.

The man walked slowly through the mystic fog. He wore a plain featureless domino mask over his face.

Claudia gasped and then whistled loudly. "Look at the body on that momma! Who cares what he looks like under that mask? Hmmmm talk about a Mister Good body. That one's mine!"

The man's ripped sensual muscles were clearly visible through his white shirt. He looked like he was a first-rate professional football player. He walked over and stood right next to Mrs. Oshun as if she commanded him to do so.

"He looks good and he knows it," Roma said pushing her thick glasses back upon her nose.

Lacey just looked on in amazement. She was sure her mouth was open.

The deep crimson door slowly opened a second time and the foggy mist continued. This time the gentleman walking in was more handsome then the last.

And it continued this way until the last man entered. Each man entering the dining room walked over to stand directly by Mrs. Oshun as if they had already been instructed to do so.

Each man wore the same plain featureless domino mask over their face.

Once the last man took his place next to Mrs. Oshun she commanded. "Gentleman, please take your seats."

One by one they walked around each table of ladies. It seemed they didn't even glance at the ribbon that was sitting there.The men continued to circle the tables.

The smoky foggy mist continued its flow throughout the room.

Finally, they stopped, and stood motionless.

"Whew! I've got the one I wanted!" She heard someone exclaim.

Silence filled the room.

Mrs. Oshun's voice sounded in the darkness. "Ladies I know it's a little dark in here right now, but remember I said my way is not the conventional way. Your gentleman is holding your ribbon and if you want to see if you have the correct gentleman please just look at you're charm bag." She said laughing softly.

Lacey looked at her charm bag. In the darkness it oozed with a wonderful energy. She watched as a deep soft, glowing, vaporizing colorful mist floated from it. She looked around quickly and noticed each bag was glowing and each one had a different color.

Mrs. Oshun softly laughed out low and hoarse, "Aren't the colors beautiful? They are the color of your special aura."

The smoky foggy mist continued its descent around the room.

The man sitting next to her in the mask just sat there listening. He never moved, and his gaze never met hers.

Lacey took a sip from her glass of water.

And all at once the room seemed to transform. It changed and looked enchanting and romantic with flickering lights of white candles.

Lacey looked up. The ceiling looked like a twilight star studded night, soft and romantic.

"Oh my God, look at that full moon!" Roma said. "Do you think that moon is for real, Lacey?" She asked.

Lacey turned her attention. Just where the red door once stood now stood a radiant full moon shining through an opened French doorway. And Mrs. Oshun stood in the center of it. It was like nothing Lacey had ever seen.

"Wow, this has been some night, huh Lacey?" Roma laughed out shaking her head. "It seems so all unreal."

"Totally twisted." Lacey nodded.

Mrs. Oshun cleared her throat, "Ladies please step away from your tables. Your gentleman will now join you in a dance. This is also our getting better acquainted time." She said waiving her hand. "After which you will finally get a chance to see the man under the mask, whom I have chosen for your date tonight."

"I hope you turn on some lights," Roma said. "So that we can see the men better."

"That will come later Roma, but first your next set of instructions. You must begin the dance and end the dance with your gentleman. Once the first song has concluded, your gentleman will remove his mask and then you are both welcome to roam about the mansion with your chosen companion. Or free to leave if the mood suits you," she said. "But I welcome you to please stay and enjoy Magnolia Mansion, with my compliments."She commanded. "And now let the music began."

A familiar slow song started playing. The music was easy to dance to.

A hand went around her waist and Lacey felt herself swept up into the dance. *"Good, we're almost at the end. A few more minutes and then I am so out of here," She thought.* Her feet took to the music and glided to the melody.

She tried to think of the words to the music she heard playing but couldn't seem to remember. She and the man floated over the dance floor. It was still too dark to see who he was.

The music kept playing, endlessly it seemed.

At one time she could have sworn she saw Mrs. Oshun standing right beside them. Lacey's eyes looked at hers. It was as if Mrs. Oshun was chanting Lacey thought. Lacey heard words echo throughout her mind. *"The colors of romance do shine, as a tear drop falls from her eyes, as the morning dew shines upon the rose, sooth their hearts and comfort their souls, bind them here forever more....*and then Lacey smiled up at her companion for the evening, her smile ever enchanting and inviting.

The dance seemed like forever. And then the music finally stopped.

"Gentleman, the time has come. You may all remove your masks!" Mrs. Oshun commanded."

The glee of cheers from the ladies in the room was heard cheering about the music.

Lacey felt like she'd been on a bad roller coaster ride.

She looked up.

"Lacey, I have always been in love with you," a familiar man's voice said. "And if you let me seduce you. I promise to give you the best times in bed you ever had," he said. "You will see that I am a fully equipped man."

"Why…You…You!" She stuttered

The man cleared his throat. "You know Lacey, I believe that before I was born you and I were together as man and woman on one of God's clouds and we were having a go in bed. With God's blessing of course."

Lacey looked around for her host. "Mrs. Oshun! What kind of sick game are you playing here? I'm leaving!"

Chapter 15

A week later, that Wednesday morning at nine thirty, Nicholas sat in the conference room at his office and looked over the reports. He was a study in contrasts as he sat their hiding his emotions. He'd learned over the years how to use people and today he was using the bastard Dante Channing.

Dante Channing had a nerdy arrogance that came from having been given the best education that money could buy. He was capable at doing his job, Nicholas knew, but he had weaknesses. Many of them, he thought, as he studied him suspiciously. One of them was that he loved to hear himself talk, another was thinking that he was smarter than everybody, and then there was his need to feel he was in control. But his greatest weakness, Nicholas knew, had to be Dante's lost moral values. He would do anything to make money.

Dante passed out another report. "Everyone, *Neon-Tech* is a sure winner. And we have Nicholas La Cour to thank for doing the full financial check on *Neon-Tech*, and I must say it is now starting to show a very nice, albeit tiny, profit."

Dante watched Nicholas for a moment and then walked over and nudged him whispering. "Nicholas are you paying attention? I just gave you a compliment."

He put him on the spot.

Nicholas knew that he had been thinking about something else entirely. He'd been thinking about how glad he was that he had a programming background. He knew he'd done his homework when he'd set up a dummy corporation to do his siphoning. He needed to make some extra money the old-fashioned way, quickly, silently, and secretly.

Frustrated, Nicholas looked up at the other men in the conference room. He could tell they were glad Dante's focus was on him and not on them. His smile was carefully crafted when he looked back at Dante. He shook his head. "You know I was just doing my job Dante, but thanks for the compliment," he said with a sly smile, letting him know he'd heard every word he said.

At two o'clock that afternoon, Nicholas had just sat down at his desk after returning from lunch; when a soft knock sounded on his door.

Dante walked in and quickly closed the door. "Nicholas, can I have a minute?"

Whenever Dante began a conversation with those words he wanted a favor.

Nicholas checked his watch. "Sorry Dante, I'm really busy right now. Can this wait?"

"A friend of mine has a problem," Dante began looking disoriented.

"I don't fix problems for other people's friends."

"I know," Dante said with a fraction of a pause."To be honest Nicholas, it's a personal problem that I need your help with."

Nicholas had just leaned back in his chair. "Go on, I'm listening."

Dante strolled around the room as he chose his words carefully. "It was a lucky coincidence my seeing you at that…Ah club the other night?"

Nicholas knew where this conversation was now going. He'd seen the scene. The bouncer wouldn't let Dante in. It must have been a humiliating experience he thought.

"Yeah Dante it was a coincidence," Nicholas agreed.

"I wanted to personally thank you for talking to the bouncer and getting me in, he replied quickly. "Experiences like that happen a lot to me…"

Dante stared back at Nicholas. It looked like he was truly interested in their conversation. He unloaded his soul. Finally, he felt free to talk privately with Nicholas about his circumstances. He knew how popular Nicholas and his friend Quinn Rolandis were. He'd heard about the parties the two attended. Parties where a man was treated like a king. Parties where the women serviced a man with their soft lips. Even now he felt aroused. The truth was, he wanted to be invited to one of their parties.

He circled Nicholas' desk. "I sort of heard about the parties you and your best friend Quinn attend."

"I bet you have," Nicholas chucked, under his breath. This was starting to sound interesting. He thought about what he could get out of all of it.

All at once Dante leaned on his desk with an eager gleam in his eye. "Perhaps if you are helpful to me, in say getting me into certain parties and clubs, well, I could be helpful to you. Say here at work."

"So far, it's sounding pretty good," Nicholas said shaking his head. He wanted to hear Dante tell him out loud exactly what he was willing to do to help him. "So, tell me precisely Dante, how you could help me, I mean here at work? If I help you."

Dante's smile grew slowly wide. "Oh well, there is a surplus in cash in the EFT petty fund accounts that, "he coughed out. "We could invest some in the Stock Market. The interest that we make would be totally ours to keep, as long as we don't touch the principle," he glared back at him.

"Very interesting proposition, Dante," Nicholas said sizing up the situation.

He took a moment to think it over and to watch Dante sweat waiting for his answer.

Finally, Nicholas grinned. "Okay Dante we have a deal. Now I've got work to do."

Dante walked to the door and stopped abruptly before opening it. "Well, when can I go to my first party? I hope a lot of loose woman are there."

When Nicholas looked back at Dante standing by his office door, the first thing that he took in was that he had to get Dante laid. The man was on sexual overload. He could tell he'd been working too hard watching other people's money to even take care of his own needs. He checked his calendar. Today was Thursday. There was a real big party on Saturday. He needed to show up there and introduce Dante around as being his friend, making sure he was included on the most exclusive guest list.

He contemplated for a moment more. "Okay Dante, be ready Saturday at eight," Nicholas said. "Oh, and I'm taking tomorrow off. There's some important business that I've got to attend to."

Chapter 16

He pissed me off...

Maëlle was happy when Nicholas spent time with her. That Friday he'd taken the day off from work and spent it with her taking her shopping at her favorite shopping center, Stanford in Palo Alto. He'd even treated her to a full body massage at her favorite salon *Day Spa by the Bay.*

The perfect day was now about to turn into the perfect night. She hoped as she lay in bed. She loved Nicholas. She was sure of that. But she never wanted to be vulnerable to him ever again. She knew what the price of loving him cost. She knew that sometimes with Nicholas she had to take a number and wait her turn. Nicholas saw other girls. It was what he and Quinn did. It was what made her so angry at him sometimes, enough to hate him, and sleep with his best friend Quinn.

"I'm just a little confused sometimes," Maëlle thought as she looked around the master bedroom of Nicholas condo. The room was huge and masculine-looking with an ancient headboard and a fireplace leading to the master bathroom. The room came complete with his and hers dressing rooms.

Maëlle smiled softly remembering how she'd helped him decorate. She didn't know which she loved better, the room or the sight of a naked Nicholas crossing the room to join her.

He quickly got in bed and began running his hands gently exploring her body.

Maëlle smiled. She knew exactly what Nicholas was capable of giving her sexually. When he wanted to be the exceptional lover, she thought.

All at once he took her in his arms and kissed her hard. She looked at him puzzled before she realized this was going to be a Nicholas quickie. She went to open her mouth to object and his lips silenced hers as he captured her mouth with his, as she felt him enter plunging deep as he moved faster and faster.

At last he gave one last thrust.

Maëlle lay sprawled underneath him and thought. *"Nicholas, you are a pathetic jerk sometimes."*

Nicholas chuckled as if reading her thoughts. He leaned back and looked at her. "Everything okay Maëlle?"

"Just get off of me Nicholas!" She hissed out. "I am so pissed off with you right now."

"No," he teased, his lips kissing her softly and then his mouth left hers and slid to her neck.

Maëlle melted at the soft kisses of his lips. She watched him as he slid lower down her abdomen leaving the hot wet pleasure of his tongue. She shivered as she watched his head bend toward the mound between her legs.

He began to lick. "Is this what you want, Maëlle?"

"Nicholas yes," she gasped out loud, as she spread her legs wider. She moved rhythmically feeling her need for sexual gratification.

His tongue flickered against her clit and she felt her body tremble. Nicholas stopped abruptly.

"I want more Nicholas," she begged him.

He chuckled. "I know you do. Now tell me what I want to hear."

"I love it Nicholas. I love what you do to me," she begged. "I want you inside of me."

Chapter 17

Saturday Night...

Nicholas drove his BMW at high speeds taking the curves of the winding mountainous old highway, high in the Oakland hills.

The old highway was his favorite. There was never much traffic there. He slammed on the brakes in the darkness and backed up, realizing he'd almost missed his turn. He quickly turned the car onto a dark road with no resemblance of a street marker.

The old country road opened into a driveway and a huge old mansion came into view. The old mansion had been built in the 1870's by a former sheriff who'd struck it rich in a gold mine in Auburn California.

The party was in full swing when Nicholas arrived with Dante Channing.

Nicholas drove his car down the driveway leading to the back of the house. The back yard of the house was covered with expensive cars as far as the eye could see.

"Damn I've never seen so many expensive cars parked in one place. Look, there is a Lamborghini and a Porsche...and a," Dante breathed out.

"Stop naming cars," Nicholas scolded him.

A guard was standing at the back of the house as the two men approached.

"Good evening Nicholas," the old guard greeted him.

"Good evening Harold. This is a good friend of mine, Dante Channing. You might want to memorize his face. He'll be a regular soon I'm sure."

Harold nodded as he studied Dante's face.

"Come on Dante, let's go in. Uh, by the way Harold has a photographic memory. He never forgets a face. Harold will always let you in so long as you obey the rules," Nicholas said.

"Rules? What rules?"

"There is only one. Don't abuse the ladies, or Harold will have Big Bobby the Bouncer escort you out. And the word *escort* means thrown out on your ass that is after Big Bobby gives you a thorough ass whooping."

"I understand," Dante nodded following close behind Nicholas.

All at once a woman walked up dressed in hardly anything with the nipples of her dress busting out of her bodice. "Mimosas?" she asked.

Dante grabbed a glass off her tray and quickly gulped it down. The girl just stood there.

"What do you prefer Dante, white meat or dark meat?"

Dante chuckled. "Both. I'm ashamed to say it but I prefer to call it having my chocolate ice cream with a little white milk drizzled on top," he giggled. "But that might be too much to ask on the first night."

"Let me tell you something Dante," Nicholas said taking his empty glass and placing it back on the girl's tray.

"I'll take him up to room seven," Nicholas told the girl. She nodded, and she quickly walked away.

"Dante, everyone in life has a dream or a fantasy and you just told me yours.There's nothing to be ashamed about. You do know this is a whore house? Whatever you desire is yours for the asking and the price," he paused. "You do get my meaning?"

Dante swallowed hard and thought he'd finally found heaven.

Nicholas took him up a flight of stairs and down a hallway.

"Well here is your room," Nicholas said opening the door for him.

Just as Dante and Nicholas walked into the room, two women came in through another door. One was African America with large firm breasts that you knew were real. The other girl was boney with blond hair and deep blue eyes. They were both topless.

Dante stood there giggling with his mouth open. "Wow you are both naked."

Nicholas took charge of the situation. "Ladies I want you to meet a good friend of mine, his name is Dante. I know I'm leaving Dante in capable hands," he walked to the door and paused. "Oh, and if he passes out before the morning, will one of you make sure he gets home safely?"

The blue-eyed woman said in a heavy Russian accent. "Don't worry, we will take care of our new friend."

"Nicholas, "Dante called, "If I'm not back at work in a few days, cover for me."

"Sure," Nicholas said closing the door behind him.

Both women began unbuttoning Dante's shirt and then removed his pants.

The Russian ceased his stiff erection and licked it.

The women's hands were everywhere as they stroked his body, kissing and licking him.

Dante closed his eyes. "Oh…Oh baby, this is good," he groaned out. "Oh, please I've got to ram me some dark chocolate now!"

Chapter 18

*Y*ou instigator...

A week later, that Sunday morning, Lacey slept late. The instant ringing of her telephone woke her.

She groped for the phone. "Hello."

"Lacey are you still asleep?"

It took a moment before she recognized the voice. "Maëlle is that you?"

"Yep it's me," Maëlle said.

"Maëlle girl I've been calling you for days. Where have you been?" Lacey questioned her but didn't wait for an answer. "Oh, let me guess. You are mad at Nicholas for something."

"Yeah, you are so right. Anyway, once you gave me the details about the fairy tale dinner at *let's get acquainted,* I figured I'd better stay out of your way until you got over being mad."

"How true," Lacey said sitting up on the side of her bed, reaching for her robe.

"So out with it," Maëlle stated. "What are you wearing today?"

Lacey responded. "My usual pair of jeans and a sweater," she reminder her. "Oh, are you inviting yourself over today? You know

I'm visiting Mom and *Grand mere*."

"No, you're not. Have you forgotten?" Maëlle answered. "Today is the Sunday you said you'd drop by Kienan's."

Lacey sat motionless holding the telephone away from her wishing she'd never told Maëlle that she'd promised Kienan. Not to mention she had forgotten what day it was.

"Don't you even think about not showing up," Maëlle hissed out.

Lacey whispered. "Lucky me!" She cleared her throat."Okay Maëlle, I need to get up and get dressed."

In her most stern voice Maëlle declared. "Think about it Lacey," she said. "Don't you know this is your opportunity to get back your highness of geekiness for all the stupid things he's done to you? For instance, have you forgotten the way he dumped you when he was in college?"

Lacey smiled she hadn't thought about it that way. Maëlle was making a lot of sense. "Okay, you, instigator. So, what do you suggest I wear?"

"Oh, and I know you'll probably wear a pair of jeans so dump the ugly oversized sweater that you always wear. In fact, wear something dangerously seductive like that champagne beaded sweater that clings in all the right places."

"I'm hearing you sister," Lacey wryly smiled.

"Okay, then it sounds like my work is done. I'll talk with you later, bye," Maëlle softly said, feeling she had planted the seed.

Maëlle was glad Lacey couldn't see her smile as she hung up the phone. At least she knew Lacey would be busy for the rest of the day.

Chapter 19

Lacey & Kienan

That after noon at just past three, Lacey and Kienan dined on huge steaks, creamed salmon, roasted potatoes, sautéed green beans, chocolate cake, and it was served up with hot coffee in a sterling silver pot and a white table cloth centered with a vase filled with perfect cut red roses.

They ate, drank, and talked for what seemed like hours.

Lacey studied Kienan. She knew he had a kind, giving heart. When they were children, he'd always been protective of her. But now the child was gone, replaced by the man who was sitting in front of her, the man who had once hurt her deeply.

Kienan Egan's soft gray eyes stared back at the woman he'd loved since childhood. He knew she no longer carried childhood illusions about living happily ever after with him. During his college years' success had gone to his head. His fondness for women grew. He'd run amok. His disloyalty had taught her to be cautious. He knew she'd vowed never to trust him again.

"Mmmm, I am so stuffed. Everything was so good," Lacey said savoring one last bite. "I can't believe you did all of this Kienan," she said admirably.

Kienan laughed out. "Cooking for you was a pleasure. You have my mother to thank for teaching me how to cook. But thank you. I'm vain, I love the compliment."

She sipped wine and gazed back at him. She was amazed that that old sense of rage at being dumped by him surfaced. She remembered it like it was yesterday. Kienan was twenty-one and working on his master's degree. She was sixteen at the time when they slept together. She'd lost her virginity to him. It was right after that that he broke off things with her. The matter had left her disillusioned, heart-broken and crushed.

She shuddered with her memories. "I guess I should say thank you. But I'm sure your true motive will come out in the end and I will probably regret saying so," she said coldly.

Her cold words startled Kienan out of his daydream.His fingers tightened around the stem of the glass he held. He knew he'd hurt her badly when he'd dumped her in college. His eyes held hers mesmerized. "You know this is my way of apologizing for all those years long ago when I…" he hesitated. "You don't like me very much anymore, do you Lacey?"

"Come off it you Geek King, I'm here," she replied, praying for strength. His mesmerizing piercing gray eyes were her short coming. They always had been. She looked away.

He smiled and reached out and touched her hand."You haven't called me the Geek King in years. Maybe I am making progress on getting you to forgive me."

Abruptly Lacey pulled her hand back. As her thoughts preyed upon her she told herself she was in complete control. She was all grown up now. This time I won't be any man's fool. She cleared her throat. "Don't misunderstand my intentions. I'm just here acting as a friend, helping you eat some of this good food. Yep, that's my story. I'm having brunch with a lonely geeky friend, that's all."

Their eyes held fast.

"Well that's a start Lacey and this lonely Geek King will take what he can get at this moment. Cheers!" he said raising his glass in a toast.

At that moment, Lacey's rage subsided as she looked back at the man who was always her childhood hero. She could never stay made at him. She knew she still loved him, probably always would. "I'm confused," she thought and then laughed out.

"Okay cheers!" she said clanking glasses.

The two of them laughed together like old times.

She rose gathering the dishes. "Come on I'll help you clear the table and stack the dishes in the dishwasher."

"You don't have to clear the table," he said, reaching for a plate.

"Oh yes I do. You have a nice home and I want to get a chance to see the rest of it."

Kienan smiled. "I was hoping you'd say that. I've been anxious to show you around. You know, I was lucky to buy this house. It came on the market and the price was just right. I just brought it. Besides, I was set to graduate from college and I needed a place to live,'" he said as they stacked the dishes and cleared the table.

They finished cleaning and clearing away what had been a beautiful brunch.

Kienan poured the two of them a cup of coffee and the two walked out of the patio door and admired the waterfall flowing into the pool.

Opening the patio door. Lacey walked toward the caressing sound of cascading water flowing from a natural rock waterfall into Kienan's large oversized pool. The turquoise blue water was mesmerizing Lacey thought as she got closer.

Lacey took a step back and looked between the house and the pool. "You know, I hate to say it, and maybe I'm talking a wild guess here, but this house is so like everything I ever dreamt of having in my own home," she said somewhat perplexed.

Kienan's gray eyes gazed at hers and clasped her hand. "Is that what you think?"

Sparks of something electrifying shot between them, as they exchanged glances.

Lacey shivered, and sighed. "Can we go back into the house Kienan? I'm cold."

He led her back inside, past a wide foyer and straight up the winding stairs to a huge bedroom with a stone fireplace. The bed towered in the center of the room sitting on a pedestal.

Lacey's heart was beating fast she tossed aside logic staring around the room. *"Was this really going to happen,"* she thought as she threw caution to the wind. *"I will be in complete control, this will just be having sex,"* she told herself.

Hardly aware she was moving she turned and stared back at Kienan. She could have sworn she saw his undying love for her. He pulled her against him. "Lacey, you are all I ever think about. If I could undo the past I swear to God I would! I… I'm so sorry for hurting you," his words were drowned out by his hungry kisses.

She didn't want his gentle words of forgiveness right then and there. The only thing she wanted was his sexy lips on her. She pressed her body closer and kissed him hard, hungry for more. Shudders of excitement raced through her body as she moaned, wrapping her arms around him.

Hurriedly Kienan pulled the champagne beaded sweater that clung to her body in all the right places over her head and instantly snapped off her bra. His hands worked feverishly tugging and pulling off her jeans.

Within minutes he removed his shirt and jeans and the two of them stood their naked and enthralled with each other.

Suddenly Lacey gasped out when he shoved her back on the bed.

He slid on top of her and held her close. She smelled so good. She was everything he'd ever wanted. "You are so beautiful," he said, running his hands down her firm breasts.

Greedily they kissed.

Lacey felt her body ignite and erupt with pleasure at the feel of his touch on her naked body. *"Oh God,"* she thought. *"I'm so twisted. I love being pawed and used by this man."*

"I need you Lacey," he said, before his mouth claimed hers again, as he drove himself into hard and deep.

Instantly Lacey felt a rush of pure pleasure. She cried out falling into ecstasy.

Chapter 20

etting Even...

That evening, Maëlle sat on the floor in her living room flipping through a stack of old magazines. She was just going to reach for the TV remote when her telephone rang.

"Hello Maëlle?" Quinn said into the phone.

Maëlle sighed. "What took you so long to call me Quinn? I was horny over a week ago."

"Well, you don't sound glad to hear from me," Quinn said, getting all defensive. "It's not like you need an invitation to come to my house. Why didn't you just drop by when you didn't hear from me?"

"This isn't a relationship Quinn."

"Yeah, I suppose you're right," he admitted. "But know how it is between us. We're just two old friends," he said, and then thought. *"That love to sleep together."*

"What's the matter Quinn, lonely? What, you can't find your side-kick Nicholas?"

"Huh, you know how it is between me and Nicholas. I stay out of his business and he stay out of mine.

"Yeah, I do," she replied. "Besides, you know I don't want to be seen in public with you."

"Then come by my home, in an hour," he replied. "In fact, I'll leave the garage door open just like before."

Within the hour Maëlle was sitting in her car, in Quinn's garage, waiting as the garage door closed.

She got out of her car strode into the house and went to the bedroom.

Quinn grabbed her as soon as she walked across the threshold. He kissed her warmly.

"Maëlle, you know you're my best friend," Quinn said. "I want you my best friend. I want you," he said dramatically. "And you know you want me. He leaned in to nuzzle her neck. Puzzled, he pulled away. "You're not wearing our perfume?"

Maëlle studied him. He was so easy to read. "No Quinn, you, melodrama Shakespeare crazed lunatic. Your screw buddy is not wearing our perfume. You're twisted," she blurted.

"I know," he assured her. The desire drained from his eyes.

"Can't get into your fantasy without it, huh Quinn? The perfume I mean," Maëlle said.

Quinn just nodded. "I have some… Some perfume, you know."

"Oh, go ahead and get the perfume and spray me Quinn. I'm just as twisted as you are," she murmured. "Besides, I have to be out of here before the sun comes up. I've got to go to church in the morning."

"Church?" Quinn looked back at her in surprise.

"Yes, it's my Cousin Anael Paschar's first sermon tomorrow," Maëlle said. "He'll need me there for support. If I'm not there he'll be too nervous to speak."

"Then I'll get the perfume," he said getting out of the bed and retrieving it quickly.

Watching Quinn walk over to retrieve the perfume Maëlle started having second thoughts. Why was she playing this game with Quinn? "Quinn, don't you think this has gone on long enough? I mean, don't you ever think about the people we are hurting by sleeping together?"

Quinn turned and grinned at her wickedly. There wasn't one shred of understanding in his cold dark eyes. He instinctively knew that to pursue the subject that she was trying to bring up would be fatal. He had miscalculated her anger at Nicholas' cheating on her and her best friend being the object of desire of the only man that he was sure she had ever loved. "They don't think about us so why should we care about them? If you don't want to play the perfume game, that's fine," he said putting the bottle down.

His mind was focused. He was not about to lose control over the situation.He was greedy when it came to possessions he owned and the people he thought he owned. And Maëlle was one of those people. He was not willing to relinquish his control over her so easily. He turned and studied her.

He saw a way to make sure she stayed angry at Nicholas. "So, tell me Maëlle, when did you learn that Nicholas only took off from work Friday, because he knew he was taking a friend from work to the best little whore house in Oakland?"

Disbelief flooded her face. "What?"

Quinn kept his thoughts to himself as he watched her face. The emotions traveling across Maëlle's face reminded him of a spell binding performance at an opera he once saw. Jealousy, grief and revenge turned over in her eyes as he studied her digesting what he just said. He knew she knew he'd spoken the truth.

Pulling herself together Maëlle thought for a moment. Her eyes landed on the open bar sitting on a side table. She rarely drank anything harder than wine and maybe a strawberry Margarita occasionally, and she never did drugs.

"Quinn I'll have a shot of that tequila."

He crossed the room and grabbed the bottle of tequila. Seconds later he handed her the shot and watched her throw it back. He quickly poured her another one.

Maëlle barely squinted at the hard burn of the liquid going down her throat. It numbed her pain.

He watched her down the second shot and put the bottle down. "Come here Maëlle," he said tenderly holding out his arms. "I worry about you. You are too beautiful to be letting Nicholas drive you to drink," he said, brushing her hair back from her face, as he kissed her.

He pressed a kiss to her brow and said, "We've been through all of this before. You know I'm here for you always. We're just two old friends who get together from time to time and sleep together."

He kissed her again. He put his hands under her sweater and helped her pull it over her head. He released her bra and played with her nipples.

Maëlle's instincts told her to push him away, but the warmth in her groin wasn't hearing a thought she had. Her judgment was clouded. She knew she should hate him. What is wrong with me she thought? For some reason she liked being pawed by Quinn. She moaned, fumbling with his belt buckle.

Quinn retrieved a condom before yanking off his pants and tossing them to the floor. He lifted Maëlle and carried her to the bed. Throwing himself on top of her, he spread her legs with an urgency to be inside of her.

Maëlle let out a throaty moan.

The sound aroused Quinn like a wild animal. Next, he was ramming her hard until they both shuddered and climaxed together.

A few hours later Maëlle grabbed her purse and keys. She made her way to the door and looked back at Quinn.

"Oh Quinn, do me a favor and don't call me again. Even I have standards," she said. "Besides, I'm not paying my cell phone bill anymore. You won't be able to reach me."

"Don't worry! Just send me your cell phone bill. I'll take care of it. In fact, I'll take care of whatever bills you need," he paused. "I mean it Maëlle, whatever it is you need, just let me know. Besides, we're not through, we'll never be through. I haven't finished telling you all my bad habits yet," he said jokingly.

Maëlle stood at the door and stared back at him. "Do you really mean that?"

Quinn leaned back against the pillow. "Of course, I mean that I said it didn't I?"

"Thanks, so much Quinn, I'll take you up on that offer," she said gratefully before closing the door behind her.

Chapter 21

Horace, Sherlock, & Bullet

It was before eight in the morning the next day, when Lacey turned onto the private road leading to her parent's home. She spotted the late model truck with personal license plates that read *4 Horace II* and instantly slowed. She had seen the truck parked there before and pondered why. She slowed her car to a stop as a man slowly approached.

It was Horace. He had been Lacey's father Louis' best friend.

Lacey always thought that Horace Sherlock Bailey Garrison was a very handsome man. She figured it had to do with his mixed-race ancestry that he could trace back to the legacy of his Irish Jamaican roots. His middle name Bailey was a result of his White Irish Great-Great Grandmother.She was also the reason for his deep vivid green eyes. He was witty and had a natural good spirit.

"Hey there little darling," Horace smiled. "I swear you and your mother could be twins. But you did steal all the height from her," he joked. His smile was contagious as he walked over to her car.

"Yeah, I guess I did." Lacey laughed as she got out of the car. She thought she caught a glimpse of someone in the distance walking through the bush on one of the trails. She couldn't make out the figure.She heard the bushes moving.

The rustling sound startled her.

"How are things Horace?" she asked but didn't wait for a response. "Say, why are you parked so far up the road from the house? You know you are welcome to park in the driveway up at the house anytime."

Horace shrugged. "I've been walking these trails and looking at the hills. They are beautiful this time of year." He smiled heartily.

Lacey laughed out. "As I recall, you did love to bird watch this time of year?"

"Bird watching, yeah now that's a right proper name for it," he spoke with passion and a flicker of humor in his eyes. "I do love getting in my share of bird watching. Yes, I do. And in fact, I believe I've discovered a new species of bird to watch," he laughed out playfully.

"Mr. Horace, why don't you come up to the house with me? I'm on my way for a visit and I bet mom and Grand *mere* would love to see you," she said tossing back her hair.

He lifted a brow and cleared his throat. "Oh well now, I don't think I should. You see my bird, the one that I got my eye on might get away, you see?"

All at once a bark sounded.

Lacey was startled by a wet nose nudging her hand. "Bullet, where'd you come from?" She said playfully as she rubbed the back of a deep golden yellow Labrador retriever.

Bullet walked abruptly to Lacey's side to be patted and then walked over and sat beside Horace.

Lacey looked between Horace and Bullet.

All at once Horace cleared his throat. "You never know what to make of who an animal will go to. Look Lacey, I really think I need to get going. You have a nice visit with you grandmother," he paused. "And oh, mother too."

Horace headed for one of the famous Alum Rock trails. A second later Bullet barked loudly frolicking cheerfully behind him.

"Oh, Bullet come back. Horace doesn't want to be bothered with you. You'll scare his birds away,"

Horace stopped and turned around. "Don't worry Lacey. I'll make sure Bullet gets back home once I'm done with my walk."

Instantly Horace and Bullet disappeared down a trail thick with trees and bushes.

###

A few minutes later she sat on the huge back deck her grandmother called a porch and watched an eagle soaring high above.

Lacey's laptop sat gently in her lap. She finished checking her emails. She could feel her grandmother's prying eyes on the back of her head anywhere. She closed her laptop and put it aside.

"What is it Grand *mere* Catherine?"

"You've got company out front," her grandmother said in her low Cajun drawl, smiling like she just won the lottery.

###

Minutes later, Lacey walked to her driveway and stared at Kienan as he stood in front of a slick Black BMW M6.

"Damn, the girl looks like a supermodel with those long legs and the sexy sway of her hips," he thought as she walked toward him.

"Wow Lacey you've never looked lovelier," Kienan gushed.

"Thanks, is this car new?" She asked. "Is it yours?"

"Yes, and yes." He answered smiling back at her.

"Impressive!" She softly murmured inspecting the car. And then pointed. "What's this thing right here? It looks like a miniature ruler, and look here this is a Cadillac, a miniature Caddy! This is chrome."

"The first one is a slide rule," he said. "I'm an engineer and that is an engineering tool. It's a memento for my college major. The miniature car is a replica of my mother's Cadillac. It's just a little something to remind me of her, or rather my way of honoring her," He smiled holding the car door for her.

"Oh yeah, I remember your mother, Mrs. Milady Egan. She loved her Cadillac Sedan. I always wanted a personal license plate on my car just like hers. I even fell in love with her Cadillac. She looked so stylishly cool," she gushed out. "Oh and that personalized license plate of hers was so romantic. It read *4 Milady.*"

Kienan snorted out a laugh. "Okay if you say so, it was romantic. Now are you going to take a drive with me? Or are we just going to stand in the driveway talking?

Lacey held her head regally and proud and said in her best British lady-like accent, "Of course my King Geek, but might you open a lady's door?"

Kienan's lips quivered into a smile. "Madam you're Geek King is at your service," he said in his best British accent. "I am so glad to hear you do those old impressions. It's just like old times."

Kienan closed her car door and got in and started the engine. The car ran smooth and quiet.

There was an awkward silence and then Lacey resumed the conversation about his mother. "Everything about your mother was romantic. From the sound of her musical voice that I loved to her and that accent. Where was she from again?"

Kienan tenderly looked at her and smiled. "I didn't know you remembered so much about my mother," he said as his lips curled into a soft smile. "That was the musical voice of her island home, Barbados."

Lacey smiled, "Oh I remember a lot about her. I remember hearing she moved away from Barbados when she was very young?"

"Yes, she did. She was maybe six or seven years old when her family moved to California," he said. "But she could never lose that slight accent, no matter how much she tried."

Lacey sighed. "Whatever happened to her old car?"

He cleared his throat. "I still have it. The car, I mean. It's in storage. It's a classic you know? Refurbished and everything."

"Wow, you must have a lot of cars?" She said, toying with the flap holding the makeup mirror.

"Yes, I mean no. I only have the three cars. The Escalade, Milady's caddy, and now this one," he said. "I'm not a car hog."

Lacey smiled and turned away. "Don't worry I wouldn't judge you about a thing like that. I had a father who loved to collect cars especially old Buicks."

She adjusted her seat belt and her hands relaxed at her side. "I bet you didn't know I went to your mom for tutoring in math some Saturdays. Your mom was an excellent teacher and I know she had her PhD."

His face beamed with pride. "Heck, she was the reason I loved going to school. Most people didn't know it but my mother had her masters in Science and a PhD in Math," he said proudly.

You're right, she was a great teacher and a wonderful mother."

Lacey turned and looked at him. "Now I see why having the chrome logos on your car are so important. One is a symbol of your mother's love and the other a symbol for the love of education that she gave to you."

Kienan cleared his throat, "Yes, it wasn't easy getting that chrome logo piece made with both a slide rule and a caddy. But it was worth it."

She listened attentively, "I bet it was. You must be proud of it? But aren't you afraid some teenager may pull it off and steal it"

He shrugged. "Nope, you know it's embedded into the body of the car? That means that baby isn't going anywhere. I dare a teenager to try and pry it out. They'll need a magic saw that can cut through a product made from tungsten." He assured her, shaking his head and laughed out proudly.

The enthusiasm in his voice caught Lacey's attention. She could tell Kienan was happy.

Lacey smiled at his happiness. "I'm impressed," She said. "Does Nicholas know about this car?" She asked. "I'm sure he doesn't, or he would have said something to me by now."

He shook his head, "Just so you know, you're the only one who does know." He softly smiled. His voice was low and tender, "And you're the first person to ever ride in my new car and the only person I really, really wanted to, very much."

Lacey hadn't anticipated this. Her pulse flirted like the wings of a dove. She tried to conceal her smile by looking out of the window. She murmured low, "Is that so? I'm amazed and flattered."

Kienan exhaled deeply and then grinned big with happiness. He reached into the back seat and handed her a clear box. "This is for you. It's for your hair. I remember how you like to put a flower in your hair."

Lacey opened the box. "A purple and pink orchid, it's beautiful!" She exclaimed softly.

"It has a hair clip wired to it," he smiled.

"I can take the hint. You want me to wear it." She quickly pinned it in her hair. "How do I look?"

Kienan whistled out. "You're gorgeous...Whew let's get going before I get other ideas."

Lacey leaned over and kissed his cheek. She felt alive with happiness being with him. This is how it always was when they were together, she remembered. She smiled wide and leaned back and enjoyed the ride. The car was soft and quiet except for the soft roar of the engine.

She cleared her throat. "This car looks different than your average BMW. Do you have an upgraded?"

He smiled and checked his rear-view mirror, "No, it's just a standard BMW M6 engine, pretty soft huh? I did have the dealer make a few custom changes to the body. Something they called the pimped 6-Series," he said, flushed and embarrassed using the word pimped.

Lacey's face registered surprise. "The Pimped 6-Series huh?" She said repeating his words. "What is it with guys and the word pimp? Every movie you see on television now-a-day has got some young guys that want to be a pimp. I guess somebody in Hollywood got the idea that old Pam Grier Blaxploitation films using the words pimp and pimp mobile was now a hip up to date thing to say."

"For the record, just so you know, we are establishing that I'm not a pimp," Kienan said, cocking his head to the side.

Lacey laughed out, "That is a firm Yes!" She exclaimed, laughing at him.

"You sir are definitely not a pimp, and this is not a pimp car. But it is a beautiful car. But why did you buy it, ego? What?"

He silently said a prayer and decided to talk to her and tell her how he was truly feeling. "I had three purposes when I bought this car. One was as a healing gift, to get over the death of my mother. He sighed as his thoughts raced. He heard the words inside his head. "The next reason I call a renewed hope in believing all things. And well, finally, I thought of you when I bought it."

"Well, has it worked?" She asked. "I mean getting over your mother. As a wound healing present?"

Kienan paused and checked his rear-view mirror. "Yes, I think it did, because it renewed my hope about many things." He said.

Lacey watched him. "Renewed hope in what things?"

Kienan seemed to concentrate. Finally, he said, "Well, you for one thing... He paused. "Boy, you ask a lot of questions."

The moment was silent.

He simply glanced quickly back at her, as his thoughts raced. *"You haven't got a clue what I been through after losing you Lacey, he said in his thoughts. "Mainly I want you in my life for keeps Lacey."*

Finally, he spoke. "Life can be complicated," he said softly.

The silence in the car grew.

Lacey swallowed hard. "By the way, I'll probably be sorry for asking, since I know you always give your cars names. So, what do you call this machine?" She asked

Kienan tapped his fingers lightly on the steering wheel. "I call her *Kitten II.*"

She turned to look at him "Please promise me you won't call it that in front of Nicholas and Quinn?"

"No, I won't say a word to them. And just so you know, I'd like to keep both of them from knowing I have been going out with you. At least until I'm ready to tell them."

"Agreed," he smiled.

Kienan drove the sleek German car with ease. The car's quick response and lighting speed jetted easily down highway 680 heading north towards Sacramento.

"This car is so awesome!" Lacey blurted out smiling, enjoying the ride.

Chapter 22

❧

***N**icholas's little problem...*

"Time, banks, and women can be cruel," Nicholas said to himself as he sat alone at work. All three of them could cause you heartache, pain, and misery. He thought of Dante Channing and laughed.

Dante Channing was rarely at work. Dante had fallen victim to becoming a regular *John* at the house of ill-repute he'd introduced him to in Oakland.

Nicholas' fingers caressed his chin as he thought of something he read once by Mark Anthony. *"O Marcus! O colossal child... able to conquer the world but unable to resist temptation!"*

He keyed another command into the computer. He'd just pulled up a financial summary report when his telephone rang.

He stared at the caller ID. It was Jeff Weinberg from the bank.

Reluctantly he picked up the phone. "Hello Jeff."

Breathless Jeff blurted. "Nicholas I've been trying to reach you for days. There's not enough cash holding in the old mansion to make your refinance request. You need to look somewhere else to raise the rest of the half million."

"Look Jeff, this project benefits you too. Where am I going to get that kind of money?"

Jeff's tone was cool. "Come on Nicholas, you knew what costs were involved when you got involved in this real estate development deal. You'd better come up with the money and quick. Remember, your family's home is on the line."

"What are you trying to say Jeff?" Nicholas replied.

"I'm saying your family home could be foreclosed on if you don't get the money, and quick."

Awkward silence hung between them.

Finally, Jeff said. "Look Nicholas, you've got a couple of well-off friends. Hit them up for the money. Hell! Think of something like making one of them a silent partner, getting him to marry your sister, for Christ's sake, I don't care what scheme you come up with just get the money."

Chapter 23

A Trick of the Eye

Two weeks passed. Early that Sunday morning Lacey walked down the hall leading from her bedroom. She caught a glimpse of herself in the full-length mirror just off of the living room. Was that the face of the same girl that Kienan remembered? She wondered, as she stared back at her reflection. She caught sight of several old pictures hanging in a frame on the hallway wall. One was of her and Kienan when they were young. That day he had been trying to help her learn how to hit a baseball. She looked at herself smiling happily. She was always drawn to him like a moth to a flame. That old emotion stirred.

Her thoughts raced. *"What if I'm setting myself up for failure falling back in love with Kienan? He broke my heart once.*

She weighted her options as she watered her plants. She should date other people until she knew for sure that Kienan was serious. A thought came flooding back into her mind. She remembered back to her junior high school days. She and Maëlle had gone to a slumber party. One of the girls with them told them a story about her older sister sleeping with Quinn and saying it was the best sex she'd ever had. Then there was that time when she saw Quinn swimming in the lake naked and they had exchanged glances that had sent shivers up her spine. Her body quivered remembering how sexy and attractive he looked.

Lacey shook out her thoughts and went back to her chores.

A few minutes later she turned to walk back into the house. Her house phone rang just as she walked past the table in the hallway. She quickly picked it up.

"Hello."

"Hey Lacey, it's me Maëlle. Are you watering plants? She asked. "Say did you ever decide what to put on that back patio of yours?" She curiously asked. "Now that place could stand some improvement."

Lacey quietly listened to her best friend."No, you know I still haven't decided what to do with the back patio?"

She quickly walked to look out of the front window and enjoyed the peaceful hillside views.

"Look Maëlle, you always seem to know what I'm doing and when. Maybe you can check that crystal ball of yours and tell me when my patio will get some plants and a makeover?" She joked. "Anyway, where have you been? I didn't hear from you all week?"

"Missed me huh? I haven't been doing much, going to work and sleeping late on Saturday. I had to run a couple of errands for my Auntie Joan," Maëlle said.

"At that Hoodoo head shop your family owns?" Lacey inquired.

"We like to refer to it as that Magickal, one stop shop."

"Maëlle, you know I still don't understand that sign hanging over the front door of the store right before you walk in."

"Oh that… It's the symbol known as the *Girdle of Isis* or The Buckle of Isis. Some call it *the blood of Isis.* It's supposed to have the magical powers of Isis, the magic power of the Eye. It protects you from any wrong being done to you.

"When I see that symbol, it makes me think of some Cleopatra Pharaoh divinity, you know godlike."

"Yes"," Maëlle said. "My Aunt Joan says it lets you know you are protected by the Great One."

Lacey sighed heavily. "Where does your aunt get all those crazy ideas from and all those customers from anyway? There's no name on the place, just the freaky old symbol, and yet the place is always crowded."

Maëlle laughed out. "Don't you know anything? My Aunt Joan's place has been located on Murphy Street in Sunnyvale for years. Besides, all that information that she knows can be found in the Egyptian Book of the Dead," she said. "And I guess you never listened to me all these years when I told you my aunt's shop is really called *Aunt Joan's Magickal Enchanted Gift's and Things.*"

Lacey sighed heavily. "Yeah, you're right. I haven't been listening all of these years."

"So, tell me Lacey when are you and Kienan going to see each other again?"

Lacey cleared throat. "Kill the thought. You're just a wishful matchmaker. Who says I'm seeing Kienan again? A girl got to keep her options open."

"Hmmmm...Options," Maëlle softly murmured. "Well, we both know Kienan should be option number one and only. Kienan's a good man. Lacey, you amaze me how obtuse you can be sometimes."

The phone line grew quiet.

Lacey's voice grew solemn as she continued. "Come on Maëlle, you know Kienan's still a womanizer."

Maëlle cleared her throat. "Maybe he's changed. At least give him a chance.

"I'm just confused right now. I've got a lot of things going on."

"Like what? Keeping you options open?"

The line went quiet again.

"Lacey, are you still there?" Maëlle asked.

"Yeah I'm still here. But you are wrong about Kienan.Now change the subject or this conversation is over, okay?"

Maëlle sighed heavily into the telephone, "Okay fine then, we will change the subject. How's your mother Pearl and Grand *mere* Catherine?"

"They are both fine. But I think mom might be seeing someone? My grandmother keeps dropping hints."

"She is a grown lady, Lacey!"

Lacey's voice grew tight, "Yeah, well it ain't your mother, now is it?"

"Okay, Miss Grouchy. Hmmmm...Changing the subject again. What is really bothering you Lacey?"

Lacey sighed heavily. "I don't know but Quinn..."

Maëlle chuckled softly. "Hold on Lacey, if you're thinking of setting your sailboat on Quinn, may I remind you that boat's name is *You are a Fool*?" She said. "Really Lacey, I can't believe you sometimes."

"I am not a fool, Miss Maëlle Annie Moulard!" Lacey said curtly, "And I am shocked and offended at you..."

Maëlle cut Lacey off in mid-sentence. "Oh! Got to go! That's my other line ringing." Her words tumbled out quickly.

"But Maëlle!" Lacey said.

"Isn't today your day to visit with your mother and grandmother?"

"Yes," Lacey said.

"Good, I'll catch up with you there later, Lacey bye!"

Click!

Lacey heard the line go dead. She slowly clicked off the phone.

###

A couple of hours later Lacey sighed out heavily. "MMMMMM I'm too full to move."

"I just love Gator Gumbo." Maëlle said lounging lazing in Lacey father's old chair.

Maëlle and Lacey sat in the family room just off the kitchen.

Lacey stood looking out of the huge bay window looking at the beautiful rolling foothills and country side, slowly sipping her hot tea. She hadn't been able to take her mind off what her grandmother said earlier. Her eyes constantly traveled back and forth from the green rolling hills to her fathers' old barn. She'd hoped she would see Nicholas. She wanted to study him to see if he looked like anything was wrong, like he was up to something. Her thoughts raced. She didn't want to confront him because Maëlle was visiting today.

She heavily sighed, walking back to the kitchen and had just stood in front of the kitchen patio door when she felt the chill before she saw the figure instantly appear before her eyes. It was like vapor materializing out of thin air, as it took form standing in front of the kitchen patio door.

Lacey stood there frozen to the spot and openly stared and thought it was just a trick of the eye.

The figure standing before her resembled an aluminous shining bright being of light, like nothing on earth she'd ever seen. She thought for a moment and decided it reminded her of something she'd seen standing at the foot of her Grand *mere* Catherine's bed. One night long ago, when she was a child, she had crawled into her grandmother's bed because the old house had been cold and scary.

Then the figure slowly faded away.

Lacey breathed out slowly and smiled with her thoughts, her grandmother had always told her the dead watches the living.

"What are you staring at Lacey?" Maëlle asked.

Lacey swallowed hard and rubbed her arms. The chill was going away. "Oh! I'm just gazing at the magnificence of the Mount Hamilton hillside being lush and green this time of year."

"Yes, it is," Maëlle said leaning into the sofa.

Lacey waived her hand. "Say Maëlle," she said softly. "Come over here. I want to talk."

Maëlle quickly closed the distance between them. "What is it?"

"There's something I realized I never told you," Lacey moved in closer. "Remember when you said I should not set my sights on Quinn? Well, there is something you don't know," she hesitated. "Do you remember that summer you couldn't go with us to the cabin, remember?"

Maëlle grinned. "Yeah, I do. We were fourteen that year, right? Wait a minute as I recall Kienan couldn't make it either, his family had their family reunion that week."

Lacey stopped abruptly and shook her head. "That's right. I had forgotten about that."

"Go ahead, what were you saying Lacey?"

"Well, what I never told you. On one of the mornings I got up real early to walk by the lake and guess who I saw stark naked taking a swim?"

"Quinn no doubt," Maëlle said impatiently. "He never did like to pass up an opportunity to strut his stuff in the nude."

Lacey looked puzzled. "Oh really?"

"Yeah Lacey, I saw Quinn naked a year before you.His body was beautiful, right?"

Lacey hesitated. "Yes, and in all the right places."

"I know what you mean," Maëlle giggled. "It made you weak in the knees, huh?"

"Yes…I felt strange sensations all over. I stood there stuck to the spot as we both gazed at each other. It seemed like he wanted to do things to me. Sexy things, nasty things and dirty things"

Maëlle shrugged. "Hmmmm, that sounds like Quinn. He's always trying to fill a girl's head with dirty empty-headed thoughts."

Lacey cleared her throat. "Maëlle, haven't you ever wondered what it would be like to be with a well-endowed man, like Quinn?"

"Shhhhh Lacey…Be quiet there's Nicholas." Maëlle whispered. "I hope he didn't hear us."

Both friends grew silent.

"Hey Nicholas," Maëlle called.

"Hey Maëlle, you sure do look nice and sweet today," Nicholas grinned.

He looked up at his sister. "Hey Lacey, have you got a minute?"

"Lacey, I'll wait for you out front," Maëlle rose, grateful for the chance to walk away.

Nicholas put his hands in his pockets and watched as Maëlle walked away. "Oh yeah Lacey, can I use your laptop while you're gone? I need to check my emails."

Lacey looked hesitative. "Sure, just be sure to put it back on the table where I left it. I don't want to be looking all over the place for it."

Nicholas cleared his throat. "You know; this old house constantly needs repairs."

Lacey lifted a brow in puzzlement and then nodded agreement.

"We agree, right?" He asked.

"Hmmmm… Maybe," Lacey shrugged, "So what are you saying Nicholas?"

"It's just that repairs aren't cheap. I just want you to know that," he said." As you can see from looking around the place, I have already had a few things done."

"Oh really?"

Nicholas wiped his brow. "And I'm just trying to make you aware of the cost, that's all."

Lacey's thoughts raced as she studied Nicholas. He seemed agitated. She cleared her throat. "Well Nicholas, I need to see any receipts for supplies, materials, or parts, which you have. You do have receipts don't you Nicholas?"

Nicholas seemed nervous. "No, no. That's not what I meant. I just wanted you to be aware about…The ah repairs." He pushed his hands in his pockets looking nervously around. "Nobody's called you? I mean to get approval for any repairs."

Lacey folded her arms and stared at him. "No, why should they?"

Flustered Nicholas' eyebrow rose. "No reason, I was just checking," he hesitated. "That's good. It's a good thing. Sometimes those construction types get so antsy for their money." He looked around awkwardly. "Its' just that I 'err was out of town for a minute. And well I kind of let something slip my mind. But it's all taken care of now. No worries."

A long silence as Lacey fixed her eyes on her brother. She went to open her mouth.

"Hey Lacey, don't forget, I'm waiting" Maëlle voice suddenly sliced the air.

"Looks like you need to get going Lacey, "Nicholas' voice was cool. "Maëlle sure sounds lonely without her best friend."

"I'll talk to you later Nicholas," she said turning away.

Nicholas nervously rubbed his brow as he watched his sister walk away. He needed to get started on his next plan of action.

<h1 style="text-align:center">Chapter 24</h1>

F ootball, Family, Players & Underachievers...

A week later, that following Sunday Lacey glanced up from the tray of bowls of gator gumbo she was carrying just in time to see Nicholas jump out of his seat yelling.

"Run with the ball...Run!" Nicholas screamed out at the wall mounted sixty-inch television.

She shuddered, startled by Nicholas' outburst and turned back to stare at him.

She glanced up at Kienan.

"You're okay?" He softly asked.

She smiled back at him and nodded.

Lacey smiled, watching Kienan sit back down in her father's old chair. The memory she remembered the most was of her father sitting in his chair watching the game before he passed away. She turned her head to stare back out of the window.

"He's got the ball! Touch down!" Kienan yelled. "That's the play of the century the game is over..."

"Wow what a play! What a play!" Nicholas yelled. "Did you see that play Lacey? Lacey, did you see that? The game is over, San Francisco wins."

Lacey just nodded her head and placed the bowls of gumbo on the table.

"That was an awesome play." Kienan shouted. "The whole game was. For that matter it was a totally awesome game. I can't wait to see what the Raiders do in their game."

Her brother Nicolas shared in the excitement of the game. "Man was that a great game or what? Ain't nothing can stop them 49ers! They BAD…I said they BBBAD!" Nicolas laughed with glee.

Immediately Kienan got up and walked over where Lacey sat. He sat down next to her.

His expression was happy, "Great game huh?"

"Yeah, the little I saw, but I heard most of it." She said softly. But you know it was a great Sunday spent with *Football, Family, Players and Underachievers.*"

Kienan laughed. "I'm hoping you didn't lump me in the under-achiever's category," he joked.

Playfully she blurted. "Never!"

Seconds later, her mother Pearl's exuberant voice called. "Oh, Lacey Kitten, come give momma a hand."

Obediently Lacey answered. "Okay mom."

She glanced back at Kienan. "Excuse me for a moment."

From across the room Nicholas saw his chance and closed the distance between them.

"Kienan, you got a moment, I'd like to ask you something?"

"Ah, well your sister will be back any minute Nicholas."

"No Kienan, I don't think so," he shook his head. "My mother has taken Lacey out back to retrieve all those empty gumbo bowls I've left out there. And besides, I think my Mother wants to talk too Lacey about something. And if you add Grand *mere* to their conversation, I don't think she'll be back this way anytime soon."

"Okay, start talking."

"How about we do this again next Sunday?" Nicholas asked. You know the Raiders are playing Dallas. What do you say Kienan?"

Suddenly Grand *mere* walked up from the side of the house. She walked over. "Kienan, are you leaving us so soon?"

Kienan laughed and shrugged. "Yes Mam, I've got work tomorrow. Thanks again for dinner. You and Mrs. Pearl cooked a great meal."

Grand *mere* gave him a keen look. "Lacey cooked that meal. Anyway, you will come back and see us soon?"

"I was just asking him the same thing Grand *mere* Catherine. Kienan and I were just talking in private,"

Grand *mere* Catherine twisted her head and locked gazes with Nicholas. Her gray eyes probed him sternly.

"Oh, I didn't mean any disrespect." Nicholas quickly said clearing his throat. "In fact, you didn't let me finish. I was trying to say can we please talk in private?"

Grand *mere* Catherine studied Nicholas and let him squirm before she turned away from him. She tilted her chin and let her gaze fall on Kienan. Her eyes grew admiringly attentive to Kienan. "You are always welcome in our home Kienan." She softly and tenderly smiled. "Too bad I can't say the same thing about some of my own flesh and blood." She nodded stiffly at Nicholas before turning to walk away.

Nicholas rubbed his hand through his hair. He quickly checked to make sure they were alone. He quickly closed the distance between them, "What about next Sunday's game? Can you make it, my best friend?"

Kienan grew quiet thinking.

Before he could respond Nicholas', voice halted him in his tracks. He blurted out, "Hey man what about that loan you promised me?"

"What?" Kienan turned and moved in closer to Nicholas. He eyed him sternly.

Nicholas' eyes burned with rage. He hated to beg any man. "You know Kienan, that loan we talked about, the one you promised to lend me?"

Kienan glanced back at him. Nicholas was getting tense. He wondered about what trouble Nicholas had gotten himself into this time.He had enough problems of his own lately and he attempted to lighten things up. "Hold up my old friend. Let's talk about this rationally. Money doesn't grow on trees."

"Kienan, I need money!" he blurted with a disdain tone in his voice.

His hands balled into a fist by his side as he moved closer in to Kienan.

Kienan watched him out of the corner of his eye.

"You're a cheap bastard who just wants to hear me beg," Nicholas muttered viciously beneath his breath. "Man, we had a deal, where's that money you promised to lend me?"

The moment seemed to stretch out endlessly.

Kienan's stance braced. His eyes narrowed like a panther ready to strike. His gazed locked with Nicholas. His glance was ferociously cold and unflinching. "Nicholas my old friend, what is wrong with you? Are you on drugs or something?"

All at once recognition seized him. Nicholas was out of his element if he got into a fight with Kienan. Kienan looked like a tall giant staring back at him. He knew Kienan wasn't a violent man or even a fighter for the fun of it. But if Kienan was provoked, and you were in the wrong you didn't want to be on the receiving end of one of his fists.

Nicholas quickly dropped his grip. "I'm so sorry man. I've just been under a lot of stress lately."

Quickly, Nicholas backed up a foot away from him, a flare of desperation showed in his eyes.

The awkward silence grew between the two friends.

Nicholas finally spoke. "Look man, I didn't mean to yell. I'm just sort of in a bind."

Kienan's voice was calm as he shook his head. Nicholas was like a little kid at times. Like the kid brother he never had. He slowly breathed out, "Look Nicholas you were supposed to fax me the specifics, a business plan, showing me, you had a way to paying back the money. You never did."

Nicholas swallowed hard. His voice was apologetic. "But I was going to, I…just forgot to finish it, man. Besides, we had a deal!"

With a caring tone Kienan smiled, "Come on Nicholas it's time to grow up. You can't just expect someone to hand you half million dollars."

Nicholas studied Kienan; his presence alone could make him feel disconcerted. He didn't really want to have this conversation. He swallowed hard and shook his head. "Come on Kienan. You're loaded," his voice grew intense. He clenched his teeth, "What about my investments? Can't you help me? I've got to cover my investments."

"You mean your call options or whatever get rich quick scheme you've come up with this time," Kienan sternly corrected him.

"Yeah, well…It's the same thing," Nicholas snorted out derisively.

"Look Nicholas, first of all we had no agreements! I helped you before, this isn't the first time, remember? And I let you off on paying me back some of that money." Kienan's movements were strained as he stared back at Nicholas' hand. He slowly let his gaze return up to stare straight into his eyes. His calm was wavering.

"Sorry man, I just don't know what to say. I know you've helped me out before and I thank you," Nicholas said, taking a step back. He didn't want to anger Kienan. He owed him much. He knew their conversation was over.

Slowly the two friends exchanged nods of understanding. They'd been friends too long to let it end this way.

Kienan was silent for a while. When he finally spoke again he smiled softly, "The Raiders aren't playing next Sunday Nicholas old friend. But the Sunday after and if you want to catch that game, then yes I'll be here." He shrugged breathing out slowly, "And Nicholas, just hang in there."

Nicholas nodded and watched as his best friend walked away. His anger had not subsided. His thoughts raged. Slowly he looked out over the hillside. He needed to stay calm. *"Yes, old friend, come back for the game next Sunday. Who knows, maybe I'll have a specific plan on how to get you to loan me the money,"* he thought. *"Or maybe I will get it from somebody else.*

###

Grand *mere* Catherine twisted her hands as she stood beside of side of the house well out of view watching Kienan and Nicholas. She was too far away to know what the two of them had been talking about. But she had learned a lot in life just watching people's behavior to know when something wasn't right. Catherine Marie Rousseau-La Cour was nobody's fool.Her slender tall seventy-year-old frame came out of its hiding place and silently she strolled over.

"Kienan, you're not leaving yet are you, son?" Her gray eyes probed him sternly.

"Grand *mere* Catherine, where did you come from?" Kienan asked, startled, by her sudden appearance.

"You looked lonely standing there. I thought I might keep you company for a moment," she said, as she laid her hand on his arm. "Come walk little ways with me."

Kienan nodded and they slowly took a stroll.

<h1 style="text-align:center">Chapter 25</h1>

❧

Today is the beginning of the rest of your life...

Pearl felt bad watching her daughter Lacey walking down the stone path leading back from the old barn. She felt bad making her help her retrieve all the empty bowls and dishes Nicholas had left there. She vowed to be more diligent about making Nicholas clean up behind himself.

Lacey looked tormented and sad. Pearl knew that she hadn't been at home lately. Her secret admirer had been keeping her busy.She still didn't feel comfortable telling her son and daughter about her new-found friend.

Pearl Fanay Andries-La Cour was beautiful, with a gentle spirit, with a delicate and a curvaceous build. She was an exact build as her daughter Lacey except she was a lot shorter, petite as some would say. She stood on the back deck and watched as Lacey slowly approached. She looked so much like her when she was young, except she was tall like her father Louis.

"Come inside Lacey, I want to talk with you," Pearl said beckoning the way. "Sit down at the table. I want to talk. I made some tea; I'll pour you a cup."

Lacey did as she was told.

Pearl went to the stove and retrieved the tea pot and grabbed two cups before walking back to the table.

She poured them both a cup of tea and sat down.

The fragrant aroma of Jasmine tea filled the air.

Lacey cupped her tea cup in her hand. She breathed in deeply the rich aroma. "This is so good mom. I like it a lot."

"I'm glad you like it. You know a long time ago Jasmine tea was your favorite," Pearl said.

"Was it? I don't remember."

Pearl thought that maybe the Jasmine tea could help her make her point. "Yes, it was. In fact, you stopped loving to drink Jasmine tea…" She paused and chose her words carefully. "You stopped drinking it when you let others decide what you were supposed to drink and to like."

Lacey winced, thinking back, she'd always gone out of her way to make others happy. She sipped her tea.

Pearl nodded squeezing her hand. "What do you want Lacey? What makes you happy?"

Lacey gazed out the patio door into the Mountain View beyond. The sky was a cloudless blue.

"You are so much like your father sometimes. I wonder if I'm getting through to you. "

Lacey shrugged shyly and bowed her head. "Just what a girl wants to hear, she looks just like her dad. No wonder I can't get a guy to marry me."

Pearl shook her head and smiled. "You know; you've got my curvaceous body. I can recall seeing many men admire that body of yours."

Lacey stared for a moment into her mother's eyes. Her eyes held her. They seemed to hold secrets she wanted to share. She looked embarrassed and looked down at her fingers holding her cup of tea.

The silence lingered between mother and daughter.

"You're so much like Louis, whenever he didn't know what to say, he'd get quiet and look away to keep from facing the person too."

Lacey held her tea cup tighter.

"I don't say that to upset you Lacey. In fact I'm so proud of how you handle yourself, how you handle life, your brother Nicholas, and when Kienan broke up with you… I'm real proud of you Lacey." Pearl smiled. "I can see why Kienan loves you so much," she said as her eyes misted over. "Don't live your life doing what Nicholas wants or anybody else. Even for me or for Grand *mere*."

Lacey stared back at her mother puzzled.

Pearl reached out and touched her daughter's hand. "Do you love him Lacey? Kienan I mean?"

Lacey's mouth dropped open wide.

Pearl shrugged. "Don't answer that, just listen. After your father died Lacey my heart was broken, and I was very lonely."

Pearl closed her eyes tight. "I want you to know I loved Louis. I loved your father, you understand?"

Lacey nodded.

Pearl took a sip of her tea. "Well I've lived a long life my daughter and over time I've learned a few things and I've come to understand many things," she said. "Most importantly I've learned that if you live long enough you learn not to judge people. You even learn to have faith in people who have let you down," she paused. "Whatever you do in life Lacey, don't let pride stand in the way of you being happy. Follow your heart and love the person you've got tucked away there. Yourself, you've got to love yourself before you can love others. We all make mistakes, even with the ones we truly love. But what we do to make ourselves happy is what is truly important."

The moment was quiet.

Pearl placed her teacup down gently and turned to stare at her daughter. "Lacey, whatever you do in life, do what makes you happy, okay?"

Lacey was quiet and then she slowly nodded.

Pearl reached out and touched her arm. "Life is lived best when you see yourself loved through the eyes of the one who truly loves you. Without the one you love your heart is broken into like someone has sliced it with a sword."

For the first time Lacey's eyes really studied her mother.

Pearl rose and leaned over and hugged her daughter.

"Be happy Lacey."

Lacey felt a sob catch in her throat.

###

Lacey walked outside and followed the stone path to the front of the house at the precise moment her Grand *mere* Catherine and Kienan where returning from their walk.

Grand *mere* Catherine patted Lacey's arm as she walked past her.

As soon as Grand *mere* Catherine was out of sight Kienan said. "Lacey, walk with me to my car. I want to talk to you about something."

Surprise registered in her eyes and the corners of her lips turned up into a soft smile, "Sure."

Kienan reached out and took her hand in his.

Her heart skipped a beat at the warmth of his touch. She smiled gently back at him.

He met her gaze and kept holding her hand as they walked to his car.

Kienan clutched her hand tighter, as they strolled over and stood in front of his SUV. He turned and stared at her.

There was a long moment of silence.

"First of all, I want to tell you how badly I wanted to talk to you alone. I really came here today for that purpose," He said gently. He looked at her attentively and then blurted out. "But you have the most incredibly beautiful gray eyes that I've ever seen, and then I get distracted and forget what I was going to say." he said, his voice guff with deep emotion.

Lacey drew in a deep breath as emotions surged in her eyes.

She looked up at him and her gaze locked with his. She could smell the deep woodsy oriental amber and citrus orange blossom of his after shave.

Suddenly it was all as right as rain, Kienan reached out and pulled her close. He kissed her, long and hard. And Lacey melted into his embrace.

Nothing prepared her for his kiss. She was crushed against his hard-lean body as heat flooded her.

Finally, he stopped abruptly and pulled away. He couldn't tell her the truth. Because at that moment he didn't know what the truth was.

All he knew was that sometimes a man did stupid things like let a woman ask them to make them a wild promise. He'd been such a man, but for some reason he didn't want Lacey to ever know that about him.

Kienan took a step away from her. "I'm sorry for kissing you like that. I guess I was just happy about the game and got carried away. You know Lacey; I need to tell you the truth. We should not see each other for a while. Things are starting to get hectic and chaotic in my life. Having a steady girlfriend doesn't fit into my plans."

Waves of shock and anger shivered over her. Kienan was dumping her just like before. It was the same stupid tired speech he told her before, back when she was sixteen and he was in college. Lacey shivered and just stood there looking up at him. Was she that dumb that she hadn't seen this coming.

He smiled gently. His gray eyes probed her, "Well, thanks for inviting me to dinner." He murmured.

"Wait a minute!" She yelled. "Is that all you've got to say? Is this some kind of joke? I mean you just tell me your life is hectic and chaotic. What is that supposed to mean?" She held his eyes unflinchingly.

"Calm down, Lacey," he said in a low voice. Feeling the tension rising, he hesitated. He had already gotten into confrontation with one La Cour that day. He didn't want to add getting into confrontation with another one. "I've got a few business issues in my life that I need to give my full attention to for a little while. As soon as everything gets under control. I'll give you a call and maybe we can start going out, maybe date or something."

Furious she breathed out slowly. She felt her heart breaking all over again. She knew she should have never trusted him again. "What kind of game are you playing Kienan?" She threw up her hands. "No… No don't even ask that Kienan. I don't want to waste your valuable time. Just don't bothering to call me. In fact, I'll make this easy for you. I'll call you when I feel like…Oh I don't know, feel like screwing you again."

"Now Lacey you don't have to become hysterical…"

"Hysterical," she snapped. "Over you? Kienan you are one dumb ass Geek King Jerk! Just go home now!"

Abruptly she turned and marched toward the house.

Kienan watched as she left.

The next day, dawn slowly broke as the sky changed from a dazzlingly midnight blue over the horizon and slowly faded into the golden early morning sun.

Nicholas was pulled into consciousness as the morning sun slowly seeped through the barn's window. He'd slept in his father's old chair.

Quickly he reached for the desk lamp and turned it on, trying to focus his eyes. He smiled brightly when his eyes settled on old Bullet sleeping nearby.

The old barn brought back old memories.He wished that his father was still alive. Maybe he would have never made a mess of things if he was.

Nicholas shook his head and quickly looked around. His father Louis' old barn was equipped with a small kitchen.

The chair squeaked nosily as he pushed himself up and made his way to the small kitchen nearby.

He started the coffee maker. As he waited, he walked over and glanced out of one of the windows and rubbed his brow.

He needed answers and he needed them quick. He heard the coffee maker finish and hurriedly walked back and poured a cup.

Except for the uncomfortable feel of sleeping in the chair, Nicholas had slept soundly. It had been the longest he'd slept in weeks.

Slowly he balanced his streaming cup of coffee as he walked back over to sit back down at his father's old desk.

He smiled as he sipped his coffee, "Hmmmm," He thought. "Coffee, you are the elixir of the Gods."

A short time later Nicholas finished his coffee and intensely watched his hands slowly line up pencil after pencil. He'd just managed to spell out the word Y-E-S when the bottom part of his Y slowly rolled off the desk.

Nicholas quickly reached down to retrieve it. His fingers trailed along the smooth side of the desk. As he slowly brought the pencil up his fingertips touched the smooth surface lightly and gently.All at once the smooth surface hissed loudly.

"Clang, Clang, Click!"

Nicholas' eyes grew wide as a drawer snapped open. He looked on in amazement as he pulled the drawer out.He looked closely at the smooth surface of the side of the desk. It was apparent no drawer indication had ever been there.He pushed his hands deep into the drawer.

"Oh my God!" He loudly exclaimed.

Instantly, a huge triumphant smile creased his face.

Chapter 26

Anael Paschar

Over a month later, that Friday Lacey regretted how rude she'd been to Kienan the last time she'd seen him. She'd been rude and mean and wanted to apologize. Finally, she'd gotten her courage up and broke her own rules about calling men first.

She quickly shut the door to her office and called Kienan.

She was startled when all three of his telephone numbers went straight to the answering machine. She thought it was a fluke.

There was a knock on her office door.

"Who is it?"

"Lacey it's me Maëlle. Did you forget we have a lunch date today?"

"Come in Maëlle."

Lacey sat silently staring at her best friend for a moment.

Maëlle looked at Lacey strangely. "Well, have you forgotten we have reservations? Come on, let's go to lunch I'm starving."

"Oh yeah," Lacey muttered, giving her a quizzical glance. "And where are we going?"

"We are having lunch at *The Rock* of course, your favorite restaurant."

An hour and a half later, Lacey remember how much she loved having lunch at the crowded casual eatery. She took another bite of her prawn salad. The prawns were so huge she thought and as succulent as a lobster tail. She looked at her empty glass of Jamaican Ginger beer and motioned for the waiter. "I'll have another ginger beer please."

"Make it two," Maëlle said.

The waiter brought over the two ginger beers.

Lacey took a sip. "Mmmm the Jamaican ginger beer here is always excellent. I don't know which my favorite, the food or the ginger beer is. They both take my mind off venting about Kienan."

"Lacey, you just need to get over Kienan. You said you weren't interested in him."

"I'm not."

"Okay then just forget about him and for Christ sake leave him alone," Maëlle said, as she took a big bite of her crab stuffed mushroom. "Hump, this is so good," she said swallowing.

"You're mistaken Maëlle. I am over him," her voice said coldly. "Didn't I tell you I was going out to nightclubs, parties and seeing other people?"

Maëlle laughed. "Oh yeah, I forgot you are a swinger," she said looking up just at the precise moment a man entered through the door of the restaurant.

The waiter interrupted them and brought over a streaming plate of grilled salmon.

Lacey shrugged. "We didn't order this."

"Ah I did," Maëlle interrupted, wiping the corners of her mouth with her napkin.

At that moment a man's voice sliced the air. "There you are cousin!"

Maëlle grinned. "Anael cousin, how are you? Lacey, you remember my cousin Anael?"

Lacey's eyes followed Maëlle's silently. She knew her cousin Anael. Anael Paschar was in seminary. "Hello Anael, it's so good to see you again."

Anael nodded as he sat beside her. "My beautiful Lacey, it's wonderful to see you again," Anael said making it a point to caress her hand, before taking the seat right next to her.

Suddenly he grabbed his fork. "This salmon smells so delicious I'd better eat it before it gets cold."

Maëlle shrugged. "I had the cook prepare it just the way you like, Anael."

"Oh, how caring of you Maëlle," he smiled and turned his attention too Lacey and smiled at her as he ate his salmon.

Lacey took a sip of ginger beer and kept her expression blank. It was going to be a long lunch.

Anael smiled at her. "Lacey, my cousin Maëlle tells me you're not dating anyone," he stated but didn't wait for her response. "Maybe the two of us could go out sometimes?"

Lacey exclaimed. "Oh, Anael I'm so busy…"

Anael frowned. "Oh really,"

Maëlle coughed loudly.

"Ouch!" Lacey blurted.

"Oh, I'm so sorry Lacey was that your foot?" Maëlle muttered with a weak smile, giving her a hard stare.

Lacey glanced up at Anael with a swift change in her mood. "Listen, Anael I just remembered I'm available to go out with you. I had a sort of cancelation."

###

Lacey's first date with Anael wasn't the disaster she thought it would be. He'd impressed her with his knowledge of the Technology Museum. Now she waited for him sitting on a bench at Cesar Chavez Park. She studied him as he bought popcorn from a nearby vendor.

He grinned and waved back at her.

She waved back as her thoughts raced. *"Why did she always seem to attract geeky guys,"* she wondered.

Anael returned with the bag of popcorn and frowned as he walked over. "Here's your popcorn. I hope you enjoyed the Tech Museum, Lacey?"

"Yes, I did."

"I was just afraid I might have been boring you. You look like you were thinking of someone else when I waved to you."

"No, I was just a little tired from all the walking we did," she said.

"Good, then I'm happy to hear that I am not boring you. For a minute I thought that you were ready to end our date."

They chitchatted for over an hour sitting in the park.

Finally, Anael said. "Lacey if you don't mind can I make a stop before I drop you home? You see I promised Father Perez I would stop by."

"Father Perez of the Church of the Good Shepherd," Lacey inquired.

"Yes, it is. He's been so kind to help me write my first sermon."

Nervously she shrugged. "Sure, I can wait in the car for you, no problem."

He shook his head. "Oh no, I wouldn't hear of it."

Chapter 27

Kienan Egan

That evening, Kienan pulled his Escalade into the garage alongside his BMW. The last time he'd drove the car Lacey had been with him. He could still see her sitting there smiling. He walked over and opened the car door and sat down where she had sat and breathed in deeply remembering. He'd vowed no woman, but Lacey could ever drive it or ever ride in the M6. This was Lacey's car. She was the only reason he'd ever bought it.

That night as Kienan dreamt he went to a party. It was held during the rainy season. He knew this because he saw a storm blowing and lightning swirling outside the huge mansion's floor to ceiling windows.

Lacey was dancing, wearing a beautiful royal blue gown. She was dancing with a man, and without saying a word, she was promising the man she was consenting to do whatever it took to make him happy.

When Kienan looked up the scene had changed. No longer were Lacey and the man dancing on a ballroom floor. But now Lacey was lying on her back in the center of a bed and the man was walking forward to the bed.

"I want you! I want you!" Lacey softly kept repeating at the man walking toward her.

Kienan then realized he was standing in the room watching. Who was the man? He had to get closer and find out.

All at once, lightning flashed, and a warm golden light flooded his bedroom brightly.

Kienan thought it was the sun. The moments seemed to spin out of time. He opened his eyes and looked up. It was Louis La Cour. Lacey's father standing before him. But it couldn't be. Louis was dead.

Around Louis' head a ring hung like a halo.

Kienan quickly realized he wasn't dreaming.

"Who is the man with Lacey, Kienan?" Louis asked, but no sound came from his peaceful face. "The storm is coming Kienan. Be ready! Be ready..."

A bright light emerged from Louis whole being. It grew and grew until it seemed to fill the room, and then it was gone.

Suddenly a loud piercing noise rang slicing the air. It was the high-pitched warning sign of Kienan's monster cable line connected to his computer. It gave off a signal that a power outage had occurred.

Kienan woke with a start and sat on the side of his bed.

Chapter 28

Solutions & Problems...

"Hi Maëlle, it's good to see you again."

Maëlle rushed past giving her an air kiss. "Hi Grand *mere*, sorry, I'm in a hurry this dish is so hot!"

Lacey took up the rear and nodded as she tried to rush past her grandmother. "Remember, I told you we were going to watch movies here today?"

"Hold it right there, Lacey! Don't you dare cross my threshold?" Grand *mere* Catherine muttered pulling her aside.

"What?" Lacey stopped at the door riveted to the spot where she stood.

She leaned in close and hissed. "Miss Lacey, now I know, beyond a doubt, you are going straight to hell!"

"Ouch! Grand *mere* you pinched me! What did I do now?" Lacey asked.

"A priest Lacey, you've been dating a priest!"

Lacey rubbed her arm. "No...I mean. You mean Anael? Well I've only been out with him a few times and for that matter, he's not going to school to be that kind of priest."

Grand mere Catherine rolled her eyes. "I'm going for a walk."

"Oh yeah, Myrtle Duncan and Gabby Baptiste car were pulling into the driveway as soon as we arrived. You wouldn't by any chance be on your way to bingo?"

"Don't worry about where I'm going *Miss Smarty Pants*, just clean up that mess you started with that priest and his crazy cousin. Get yourself some better friends. You ain't getting me in trouble with Jesus," she commanded.

Lacey watched her grandmother storm away.

"There you are, Lacey the food is ready," Maëlle's cool voice sliced the air.

Maëlle and Lacey chatted easily as they watched their favorite movie, "*Falling for a Dancer.*"

Lacey pulled the comforter closer around her chin as her eyes glistened over with tears. "Good I just love this movie. The heroine, after getting pregnant by a jerk, is forced into an arranged marriage by her parents. She finds love and happiness with a handsome romantic loveable hero at the end."

Maëlle saw her chance. "Speaking of finding your handsome romantic hero at the end, do you remember you had dinner at *Mrs. Oshun's let's get acquainted*? I know you didn't want to talk about it. You never said a word, but I know you made a connection with my cousin."

Lacey shook her head. "Maëlle, I never said a word about that because your Cousin Anael Paschar is a priest, for God's sake!"

"Okay, I mean, sure he is" she shrugged. "But first of all he's not going to be that kind of priest and well, second of all he is willing to give it all up for you. He loves you. And my Uncle Jesus Paschar is willing to give Anael back his trust fund if he marries you. That means you'll be rich. You can then learn to love Anael. Money will do that you know."

"Maëlle, you are insane," Lacey said, rolling her eyes.

"Oh no my friend I'm not," Maëlle said, as she stood up and paced the floor. She said in her thoughts, *"But there are just some things I can't tell you about."*

Maëlle sat back down. "Think of it this way Lacey. What if one day you find yourself with a problem that's money related, not just a little money problem but something huge that required a million of dollars. You don't have that kind of cash money in the bank. But my cousin Anael's trust fund is loaded with that and much… Much more."

Lacey stared back at her coldly. "Maëlle, my grandmother was just saying something to me about not getting her in trouble with Jesus and that I needed to get myself some better friends."

"Hump!" Maëlle scowled. "You're lucky Lacey. I never give up on a friend. I'm ignoring your remarks and I'm taking what's left of my homemade *Chicken Marsala* to my cousin."

###

Later that evening, after Lacey got home, she headed for the kitchen refrigerator and retrieved an icy cold Jamaican Ginger Beer. She quickly poured it into a wine glass and watched the bubbles.

The silent moment made her focus on the quietness of her home. She walked into her family room and turned on the TV and then clicked on the DVD player. The last movie left in the DVD player flashed on, the movie was *Happy Go Lovely*. It was an old classic movie with David Niven, and Vera Ellen. The story line made her think of Cinderella finding her millionaire boyfriend who saves the day at the last moment. She just lay on the couch and enjoyed the movie.

All at once watching the movie, she pictured Anael Paschar. He was Maëlle's cousin and they shared a strong family resemblance. He had inherited his father, Drake Paschar, strong facial features. But he wasn't an ugly man. In fact, he reminded her of the actor Jeremy Irons, but with a brown complexion. She shook her head wondering if, like the actor, Anael could change himself to fit the part he was playing.

She remembered the time when she and Maëlle were playing with Maëlle's cat, *Mrs. Pickles,* and a neighbor's dog ran *Mrs. Pickles* up a tree. Anael rescued *Mrs. Pickles,* and Lacey remembered calling him the bravest boy she knew.

He rewarded her with one of his rare smiles. He followed her around like a love-sick puppy for the rest of the summer. Still, she remembered how strange, possessive and bossy Anael started acting around her after that incident. Anael didn't stop until Kienan noticed and told Anael his behavior was becoming annoying and a little strange. He told him to stay away from Lacey or else. Anael did exactly as Kienan had asked him to and never showed any interest in Lacey again until now.

She shivered, thinking back on that incident, and then shook out her thoughts and resumed watching her movie.

Loudly her telephone rung-out, on the second ring she picked it up. Instantly the line clicked off.

"Damn! Who keeps calling me and hanging up," she mumbled under her breath?

Chapter 29

*Z*odiac Club…

Days later, that Friday night, Maëlle paid her and Lacey's way into The Zodiac Club. It was Lacey's favorite night club in San Jose. She hoped it would smooth things over with the two of them.

"I just love this club, Lacey said, adjusting the clingy red dress she wore. "I can't believe I let you talk me into wearing this dress."

Maëlle nudged her. "Stop fidgeting girlfriend. You look marvelous,' she commented with a grin. "Bingo! I found us a table, right by the dance floor," she said, grabbing her friend by the hand.

Lacey breathed out. "Now this is a nice spot."

A waitress, with a short dress and long fingernails, took their drink order.

A high drum roll filled the air. "Maëlle, what's that noise?" Lacey inquired.

"Oh, hold on, that's the new ring-tone of my cell phone," Maëlle shrugged.

"Hello, oh hi cousin Anael," Maëlle said.

Lacey cringed at the sound of Anael's name. She felt trapped.

"Oh, hang on Anael, Lacey's right here," Maëlle said handing her the cell phone. "Lacey it's for you."

"Hi Anael, how are you?"

Anael's voice filled the phone. "I'm fine Lacey. Say you know, I forgot to ask if you'd like to go to breakfast with me Sunday?"

Lacey felt trapped. At that moment she would have agreed to anything to get him off the phone. "Oh yeah sure."

"Okay good, then let's say I'll pick you up at eight o'clock? Is that too early?" Anael asked excitedly as his words tumbled out.

Lacey noticed the music's volume grew loud. "On no it's not too early. But not this Sunday, the next one," she stammered out. She could have sworn she heard him agree over to her changing it to next Sunday.

The music was intense.

"Good then we have an early breakfast date," Anael whispered. "I'll be there early."

She didn't catch the last thing he said. His voice was barely a whisper. "No problem, okay then I'll see you then," she said abruptly hanging up.

A half hour later Lacey was ready to go.

"Miss Maëlle Annie Moulard!" Lacey said curtly, leaning across the table and tapping her hand. "I can't believe you talked me into coming out to this club and you think I'm going to sit here all night."

No sooner than the words were out of her mouth a voice rang out.

"Excuse me! Maëlle is that you, a buff guy that looked like a football player stopped at their table.

"Oh my God! Look Lacey it's the football player, Xavier Newhouse," she grinned. "Damn Xavier you are still fine!"

"Lacey, it's so good to see you!" Xavier smiled.

Lacey frowned back at him. "Xavier, I see the Zodiac club does not have a no dogs allowed policy," she said wryly.

Xavier chuckled. "You're still kind of mean aren't you Lacey?"

Lacey rose. "That's my cue to leave. I'm going to the dance floor, if you're looking for me Maëlle."

Xavier shook his head and took her seat. "In case you didn't notice Lacey you don't have far to go. The dance floor is right in front of you," he replied.

Lacey ignored him, moving onto the dance floor in clear view of them. She let the music take her as she moved her body. Her moves were fluid and sensual. It helped her to think. When she danced it was impossible not to see clearly? She had protected her heart this time just as she'd promised herself, she would do the last time Kienan had broken things off with her. It was all clear now that she was in control of her own happiness, just like her mother had told her she had to be. She would be happy now. She promised herself.

Nicholas and Quinn were sitting at the back bar in The Zodiac Club.

Nicholas thought about his father Louis and wished he'd been more like his father. The thought made him throw back the low-ball glass of bourbon he held in his hand. It was his third glass. Next time when he ordered again, he would make sure he just said the word double.

He knew Quinn was in love with his sister Lacey. He had been since they were kids. Quinn was rich, and he had an excellent credit rating with any bank. All he needed was for Quinn to sign the loan and his investment would be secured in seconds. But Quinn wasn't about to do this favor for him without something in return.

Nicholas caught the eye of the bartender.

"Say Bob, set me up with a double this time," Nicholas said waiving his hand.

Quinn nodded. "Make mine a low ball again, Bob."

The bartender sat their drinks in front of them.

The only thing that stood in the way of Nicholas having the success he wanted was measly half a million dollars, Nicholas thought to himself as he took a sip from his drink. He was sure his sister would overlook his slight absence of judgment in using her to help his cause.

The lie rolled easily off his tongue. "So, there's my plan Quinn. I'm telling you I heard it myself. My sister is hot for you. A few compliments from you and a few well-planned dates where the two of you are thrown together and sparks just have to fly. Before you know it, she's yours," he wryly smiled. "You just sign my loan with the bank in the morning and make it happen and I'll make sure you know my sister's whereabouts at every second."

The corners of Quinn's lips turned up into a smile. He always knew Nicholas had a knack for being a pimp. He cleared his throat. "Oh, I'll sign the loan first thing tomorrow. Are you sure she doesn't know anything about your coming to see me?"

Nicholas threw him a look. "You know I wouldn't lie about a thing like that. What do you say Quinn? Have we got us a deal?

Chuckling Quinn shook his hand. "Yes, you know we do."

And then suddenly Quinn thought for a moment and cracked a slight smile. "I don't know Nicholas. Now that I have thought about it maybe I was too quick to agree to this plan of yours. I don't even know when I'll see Lacey again."

"Oh, I don't know, she might be closer than you think," Nicholas said moving so that Quinn could get a better view of the dance floor.

Quinn spotted a woman in a red dress dancing all alone on the dance floor. "Damn that girl dances wicked."

"Where?" Nicholas feigned innocence. He knew who Quinn was looking at.

"That woman there, on the dance floor," Quinn pointed.

Nicholas followed his glance and kept up his charade. He'd known when his sister had entered the place and he'd seen her out of the corner of his eye when she'd headed for the dance floor. "Oh, for Christ's sake Quinn, I told you about wearing contacts! Put your good glasses back on."

"Why?"

"That's no woman! That's my sister Lacey!"

Quinn grabbed his glasses and put them back on.Lacey quickly came into focus. He noticed something else too. Maëlle was sitting at a table talking to Xavier Newhouse.With Maëlle around he couldn't get closer too Lacey. He thought for a moment.

He chuckled lightly and said, "Nicholas maybe you need glasses too!"

"What are you talking about Quinn?"

"Look at the table, your girl Maëlle is hugged up talking to Xavier Newhouse. You know the football player?"

Nicholas looked across the room and then threw back his drink and swallowed hard. Maëlle being with Xavier hadn't been part of his plan. "That heifer is just trying to make me jealous. Let me go and get my woman and take her home and show her what she's been missing."

Quinn, still holding his drink, watched Nicholas and Maëlle leaving and then eased on the dance floor right next too Lacey and admired her sensual movements for a second too long. *Damn, I feel the beginning of an erection,"* he thought.

Quickly he threw back the glass of bourbon. It burned going down. The burn in his throat quieted the nature of his body.

"Hey Lacey, you're looking hot in that dress. By the way, I think you might need a ride home, "he said dancing beside her.

She threw him a withering look. "Why would you say that?"

"Cause Maëlle just left with Nicholas and I saw her car when we drove in. So, I'm guessing she gave you a ride."

"Damn, you're right."

Quinn's eyes were glued to Lacey's. Instantly the music changed to a slow song and Quinn pulled her close.

Dancing close to Quinn, Lacey could smell his aftershave and found herself feeling aroused. She wondered if it was because she was so angry at Kienan.

"Damn dancing close with you is like having sex and eating a luscious slice of chocolate cake all at the same time."

Lacey cocked her head and stared back at him.At that moment her tongue felt so dry from all her dancing that she really wanted to get a drink. "Quinn, I'm not drunk enough to have sex with you tonight," she said, pulling out of his embrace. "And right now, I need a drink."

"Come on then I'm buying," Quinn replied, as they headed to the bar.

Hours later, they were chitchatting about nothing through a few drinks.

When Lacey looked at her watch, it was close to midnight.

"God, I've forgotten what it was like to sit at a bar and talk about absolutely, completely nothing for over three hours," Lacey stated.

"Sorry I wasn't better company," Quinn replied.

Lacey's brain was scrambling to remember who the voice belonged to. Then she remembered. "Oh, I'm sorry Quinn, I didn't mean to hurt your feelings, it must be all of those drinks that you bought me making me talk too much," she giggled. "Say, what was in that Femme Fatale drink you bought me."

"Oh, that was just a mixture of cognac and champagne."

"Well, all I know is cognac is some rough stuff. Maybe I should not have mixed it with all the strawberry margaritas and daiquiris I had to drink," she snorted out with laughter.

Quinn shook his head and chuckled. "Nonsense, none of that sound like potent stuff to me."

For some reason Lacey could not avoid yawning.

"I guess I'm boring you right now Lacey?"

"No, I think I just need to go home and get my beauty sleep."

All at once Lacey dozed off feeling herself relaxing in total bliss.

Quinn nudged her. "Okay, then I'll take you home."

"That won't be necessary," a male voice said slicing the air.

It was Father Perez of the Church of the Good Shepherd. An attractive priest in his mid-forties who walked the streets of San Jose at night looking in and out of night clubs for wayward people that needed him to minister to.

Quinn sucked in his breath. "Damn…I mean how are you tonight, Father Perez?"

"I am fine Quinn. How is your grandmother, Senora Ina Rosolado?" Father Perez asked.

"Oh, I'm sure she is just fine," Quinn murmured, feeling like his luck couldn't have been worst if he broke a mirror into a million pieces.

The priest's eyes bore through him. "So, tell me Quinn, is this kind of place your grandmother would want to know you hung at? Is this the place where you go to spend time purging yourself of old habits, worldly inclinations and sensual struggles?"

Quinn shrugged. "I get your point Father; as a matter of fact, I was just leaving."

Father Perez nodded. "And then I will see to it that Lacey gets home safely."

For a moment neither one of them said anything.

"Yes, Father Perez, you do that," Quinn said, rising and taking his leave.

###

When Quinn walked out of The Zodiac Club that night heading to his car he reflected on the wasted night. He could not understand why his elixir had not worked on Lacey he knew he had placed enough drops in her drinks when she wasn't looking. He needed to take her someplace where they could be alone.

Feeling horny, he spotted a drop-dead gorgeous bleached blond he remembered from high school named Goddess Martell. Goddess was legendary in high school for doing anything a guy asked. She'd fuck a guy or suck a guy real good as he recalled with a smile. Right now, he needed a blow job real bad.

He gave a low chuckle, as he boldly said in a sexy husky voice. "Hey Goddess, you gorgeous Diva, you're looking hot and sexy in that dress."

They exchanged looks.

"Hey Quinn, you still a nasty old devil just like you were in high school?" Goddess asked as she walked over. "I thought I recognized you back in The Zodiac Club. You aren't leaving already?"

"Yeah I was going to turn in."

"Hmmm I'm taking a wild guess here," Goddess said. "And I'm guessing you got tired of buying *Miss stuck up Lacey La Cour* drinks?"

"Sadly, yes," he mumbled.

Goddess purred and closed the distance between them. "Hump, you should have been setting those drinks in front of a sure thing like me, Quinn."

Quinn's predatory eyes lingered on her breasts as he licked his lips. "How right you are Goddess. I wonder if it's too late to make amends."

She leaned over and whispered. "It's never too late to make amends Quinn especially if you are a well-behaved, appreciative, and very generous bad-boy," she said, flicking her tongue against his ear.

The tickle of warm tongue in his ear made him chuckle gleefully. "Oh yes Goddess, I am a bad-boy and I will give you whatever you deserve.

She licked his ear

'He chuckled. "Oh, damn I like that.

Goddess grabbed his arm. "Isn't this your car Quinn?"

"Yes."

"Let's get in."

###

That night Lacey slept hard and she dreamed she was at her father's cabin at Lake Copperopolis. The mountain peaks of the Sierra Mountain glowed luminously bright as they loomed in the distance. The sky was clear, blue and cloudless. The trail leading to the cabin glistened with drops of rain that were mesmerizing like miniature diamonds.

Lacey made her way slowly towards the cabin, stepping lightly. She looked down and saw that her feet were bare and that her feet felt like they were walking on a cushion of the finest silkiest sand.

The smell of pine was thick in the air. As she neared the cabin she looked up and saw her father waiting, standing on the front porch of the cabin, smiling.

She ran to greet him. He smiled tenderly to her. He held out his hand inviting her to come inside the cabin with him.

Lacey ran to the porch and stood in front of her father for just a moment.

In her dream she was just so glad to see her father. His eyes glowed brightly. They seemed so unreal.

"Come inside," he said, his lips never moving, as he beckoned her to come inside the cabin.

She followed him.

"You have strength in your secret place inside of you," her father smiled softly.

He reached out to her and held out his hand.

She quickly reached out to put her arms around him.

"No, I am not of a physical body," his eyes cautioned her. He held out his hand, "Here take this. You will need it to get you through the storm."

"The weatherman didn't say a storm was coming."

"There are many storms in life Lacey. Some storms are within. They are our very emotions. They come to teach us many things and to make us masters of our own fate. Look to the childhood friend you loved most."

Her father's hand never touched hers but when Lacey looked at her hand, she held the most beautiful brilliant pendant she'd ever seem. She looked closely, and it was filled with a fine shimmering mist. She focused her eyes and she could have sworn she saw words written inside of it.

"You will know what to do with it when the time comes." Her father said.

And then all at once her dream faded and Lacey woke up.

When Lacey got out of bed the first thing that hit her was that she needed to get control over her personal life.

Chapter 30

All in the Family...

Grand *mere* Catherine picked up the phone and then put it down. She muttered something in Creole under her breath and then checked the clock. It was just ten minutes past five o'clock. She picked up the phone again and quickly dialed the number.

"Hello! What is wrong? Who's in the hospital?" Lacey screamed into the phone.

"Hello Lacey, it's just me Grand *mere*. Are you still sleeping?"

"No, I'm up," she said sitting up in bed.

"I want to invite you over for an early supper today." Her grandmother said. "Oh, say three o'clock."

Lacey shook her head. "And I bet I better not say no, right?"

Grand *mere* Catherine laughed. "Bingo, you've got it right. Now guess what else I'm thinking."

Lacey sat up on her pillows. She knew this answer required even less thought. "Let me take a guess, you don't want Maëlle invited."

"This is for family important," Grand *mere* Catherine said. "This Queen Grand lady is calling a family night and I don't want to see any unofficially invited guests. And that means your little friend. You understand me Lacey?"

Her point was taken. Yes, your royal subject humbly understands oh Grand and Great Queen," she mumbled under her breath, too low for anyone to hear.

"Hmmm did you say something Lacey?" Grand *mere* inquired but didn't wait for her to answer. "Oh, never mind. Be here at three o'clock sharp."

"Will do.

"Goodbye Lacey," Grand *mere* Catherine said before hanging up the phone.

That Saturday evening Lacey tried to concentrate hard as they played *contract rummy*. She sat at the table across from her mother and stared back at her and the man sitting next to her.

Seeing Horace Garrison sitting easily next to her mother felt strange. She studied them and watched her mother's face soften and light up with a deep expression of happiness whenever she gazed back at Horace.

Lacey thought it was unusual seeing Horace take her father's place. But seeing Horace sitting there beside her mother didn't seem wrong at all, in fact it felt right.

Lacey's mind drifted, trying to remember a story from the bible that she'd once read about a brother who took his dead brother's wife to be his own. This must be how it would feel to a child born from the first brother of that union watching their mother with the uncle. Lacey had always seen Horace more like her uncle.

All at once Lacey watched as her mother Pearl turned to stare back at Horace. She seemed to be looking past his eyes deep into his soul. She smiled softly and all at once Lacey felt a stab of jealousy watching them. They were in love. They loved each other deeply and it showed.

"Grand *mere* Catherine, it's your turn." Nicholas called out.

"Let me see now," she said as she concentrated on the cards in her hand.

Lacey turned her attention back to the game. Her grandmother sat on the right of her and she quickly tried to sneak a peek at the cards in her hand.

She clasped her cards close.

"You're still too slow Lacey. You're never learned how to be a professional card sneak," Nicholas laughed.

"Oh! I almost forgot to say May I." Grand *mere* Catherine laughed easily. "May I…" She grinned victoriously before piling down her cards. This game is loads of fun, huh Lacey?"

"Yes, if you're winning, which you are," Lacey said pushing away from the table and getting up to stretch.

Grand *mere*'s hand reached out. "Oh, Lacey can you come over tomorrow about eight o'clock in the morning? I need you to take me to the flea market. You know I like to get there early to get the best produce?"

Lacey smiled. "Sure, Grand *mere*."

"It's getting late. Isn't family night over yet?" Nicholas shrugged.

"Hold on now, it's only eight thirty in the evening," Pearl said. "What? My son doesn't want to spend a few hours with his mother?"

"I didn't say that mom," Nicholas said.

Pearl smiled back at him. "Good, can I get my son to make us all a *Cocktail à la Louisiane*?"

Nicholas rose. "Mom, you know I'll make your favorite cocktail anytime. In fact, I'll make us a whole pitcher. You're trying to mellow me out before you tell us anything, smart, very smart."

"Nicholas I'll have tea," Lacey said. "If Grand *mere* Catherine wants to go to the flea market in the morning, I don't want to have a hangover."

Pearl turned and looked at Grand *mere* Catherine. "Mother

Catherine you want tea also, don't you?"

Grand *mere* went to raise her hand to protest. "Why should I? I won't be the one driving, Lacey will. I'll have a *Cocktail à la Louisiane!* Just like everyone else."

Twenty minutes later, Nicholas strolled back into the family room carrying a tray loaded with a pitcher of *Cocktail à la Louisiane*, several glasses and a small pot of tea, with a cup and saucer.

He placed the tray on the table and then served everyone their drinks.

Grand *mere* Catherine eyed Nicholas suspiciously. "Took you long enough Nicholas. How many of those *Cocktail à la Louisiane* did you drink?"

Nicholas roared with laughter.

Pearl's voice was excited. "Oh, let's all stay on a happy note. Tonight, has been fun. Come Nicholas sit down next to me. Everyone, I have something important to say."

"Good news laden with we've just won the lottery is the best news I could hear," Nicholas said placing the pitcher of *Cocktail à la Louisiane* in front of him.

"Shut up boy and let your mother talk." Grand *mere* Catherine said.

Pearl's voice was steady as she continued. "The real reason we called you both over for family night, is because I wanted you both to be told together that Horace and I have been seeing each other for a while now. And it looks like we are starting to get serious. We are even thinking of getting married," Pearl said her eyes admiring Horace."We just wanted you to hear it from us."

Lacey's mouth dropped open in surprise and then she grinned big.

Nicholas didn't look happy. He took a big gulp of his drink before lapsing into a tense frown and leaned back in his chair. "Why? What do you want to do that for?"

"Because they're in love and that's what people in love do. Get married," Lacey said. "Besides, Momma's a grown woman it ain't none of your business."

Nicholas downed his drink and poured him another one.

"Oh mom, I'm so happy for you," Lacey said. "Now I remember all those times I saw Horace's truck down on the road and I didn't even guess that the two of you were together. No wonder Bullet came up to Horace that day. It all makes sense, now."

Pearl laughed. "Oh yes, I remember that day. I was hiding in the bushes that day. What I can't understand is that you never became suspicious or anything."

They laughed easily together.

Nicholas watched the whole happy family scene and kept drinking.

Lacey walked over and put her hands on her brother's shoulder. "Well, it's we all know now, and we are happy for the two of you, aren't we Nicky?"

Nicholas pulled away from his sister and got up. "Speak for yourself Lacey. But since I guess old people need to have a little fun every once in a while. I'll overlook it."

He sternly looked back at his mother. "Since I'm the man in the house and I say our mother is too old to be getting married!"

"Nicholas Avoyelles La Cour don't you dare take a tone like that tone with your Mother," Grand *mere* Catherine bellowed. "Boy you don't want to get me started on defining what a man really is! Now sit down!"

Nicholas threw up his hands. "Whatever," he said before taking a seat.

Horace's gaze settled on Nicholas. Nicholas wasn't bad at heart; he just always had a tough time trying to fill his father Louis's, shoes. "Nicholas, as the man of the house, I asked you before I started dating your mother if it was alright with you," his voice was kind. "Just like now I come to you with the hopes you are okay with it if we decide to get married."

Nicholas braced himself at the sound of Horace's voice. He quickly downed his drink in one gulp. He rubbed his mouth and then he spoke slowly. "I wasn't alright with it when you asked me before. Why would I be alright with it now?"

Astonished, Lacey gasped. "Nicholas you knew about Horace and Mom dating?"

"Yeah, I guess I did," he shook his head. "Horace came and talked to me a few months ago. I didn't think it was going to be a big deal. I didn't think they would get serious," he said taking another gulp. "I just thought he just wanted to fool around with her a minute or two. If mom wants to sleep around who was I to stop her having some fun?"

Grand *mere* Catherine's mouth thinned into a frown. She held her head erect, and her voice was stern. "Nicholas you're turning into a drunk and I despise drunks. Your mother is a good woman…A good woman! And Horace is a good man. And he was a good friend to your father," She shouted. "Pearl has always been faithful to your father and devoted to him, me, you and your sister." Her gray eyes steadied their gaze. "I will not have my grandson saying such vile and contemptible things in front of me!"

Nicholas laughed out. "Well then you better cover your ears, because I'm going to say something even worse."He turned his gaze to his mother. "Ah, so tell me mother, when did you seduce Horace? Before or after dad was dead?"

"What?" Pearl gasped, shocked and embarrassed.

Nicholas stared blindly and savagely between Horace and Pearl. "Don't pretend mother that you didn't hear me," he chuckled. "When did you and Horace really start sleeping together? Was it while my father was alive?"

Horace's deep hoarse voice was calm. "Look Nicholas son, you are way out of line. Your mother and I respected your father in life and death. Your father has been dead for several years," he said.

Frustrated and angry Nicholas rubbed his brow his voice rose, "First of all Horace I ain't your son. And secondly tell me this; do you want everything that was my father's or just his wife?"

"Stop acting like a jerk Nicholas." Lacey shouted. "And stop drinking so much."

"Mind your own business Lacey and shut up," Nicholas yelled.

"No, you shut up Nicholas!" Grand *mere* Catherine scolded. "And I'm going to be minding this family's business for the rest of this night. I'm the CEO and you will listen to me. My experience is telling me that you're acting like a drunken fool. You'd better apologize to your mother and Horace right now before I get on the phone and call our cousin Rufus and tell him to find his way to San Jose and whoop your ass!" Grand *mere* Catherine bellowed.

Hysterically Nicholas laughed out. "Rufus and that family of yours in Goldonna can kiss my...!"

"Nicholas!" Grand *mere* Catherine yelled

With an effort to try and control her anger Pearl rose to her feet and in an exhausted voice said."Nicholas you have embarrassed me enough for one night. Get your drunken ass out of my house and go and sleep it off in the barn! Damn I need some fresh air. Horace I'll be sitting out on the front porch if you need me," she said, tossing up her hands.

Nicholas sucked in a deep breath and lowered his head.

"Okay mother, I'm sorry...I'm sorry," Nicholas apologized with sadness in his eyes. "Yes, I'll go and sleep it off in the barn," he said watching as his mother left the room.

Nicholas swallowed hard watching his mother leave. He wasn't stupid. He was getting his mother angry something she rarely did. He didn't want to get on her bad side. Life could be unbearable for him if he had his mother, grandmother and his sister pissed off at him. Besides he thought. Horace wasn't a bad man. In fact, he'd always been good to Nicholas.

The muscles in Nicholas face and neck twitched. He knew he'd had too much to drink. His brain felt heavy and he tried to logically make a thought, but it wouldn't come. He couldn't believe it was his own voice when the worlds rolled off his tongue. His voice was slurred, and he swayed. He walked over to Horace, stood in front of him and steadied himself.

"Horace my man can I ask you something?"

Horace nodded.

"Can you be my father's best friend when he lived? And now that my father is dead feel so easy taking his wife?"

Grand *mere* Catherine was complete taken aback she took a step toward her grandson. "Nicholas, how dare you speak to Horace that way?"

His gazed settled savagely on Horace. And he stammered out. "You're one lucky happy man, ain't you Horace, you're getting everything you wanted, my mother is even stepping in to fight your battle," he gulped down his drink.

Grand *mere* Catherine leaned in close and studied her grandson. "You disappoint me Nicholas."

Just as Nicholas threw back his drink he lost his balance. Horace caught him just in time.

"Damn I think I'm drunk."

Grand *mere* Catherine's icy voice sliced through the air. "Horace you should have just let Nicholas' drunken ass hit the floor. That would have knocked some sense into his brains."

Lacey felt sorry for her brother. She put her hand on his shoulder. "Come on Nicholas, I'll help you to the barn."

"No thanks," Nicholas snapped, shrugging her had off of his shoulder. He turned and then staggered out of the room.

###

Hours later that same evening Lacey waited until after Horace had left. She made her way to the back of the house and out to the barn as Bullet followed close behind. She opened the barn door and glanced up. "There he sits, Bullet, our big brother in all his misery. Do you think we can cheer him up?" She asked Bullet scratching his ears just the way he liked it. Bullet seemed to understand and backed away from her and darted into the yard barking as he left.

"Bullet I never knew you were a coward," she called pushing open the door.

She quietly walked over to her father's old desk and looked back at her brother. "I knew you weren't that drunk Nicholas; I've seen you drink harder stuff than a pitcher of *Cocktail à la Louisiane*. You deserve an Oscar for that big fake performance."

Nicholas looked up at her as she neared. "I wasn't acting childish, Lacey. Okay, maybe a little. But I remembered things and besides, I was kind of hurt, knowing that Mom wants to get married again."

"I'm not judging you Nicholas," she said, as she walked over and took a seat.

Nicholas rubbed his brow and took a seat beside her. "I'm just stressed with everything that's been happening."

"Do you want to talk about it?" Lacey asked.

Nicholas' face was set in a sulky line. "For starters you know Quinn is still mad at us for inviting Kienan and any of my other male friends to our family gatherings."

Lacey's eyes flashed. "Yes, I've been pretty much aware of that."

"Mainly he's just jealous, the guy has a thing for you," he said. "But that's not the real reason I'm stressed."

Nicholas stared off blankly and spoke without giving her his attention. "I have this memory that won't go away Lacey."

"What are you talking about Nicholas?"

He shrugged. "I don't even know how old I was, I just remember that I know something strange happened," he said rubbing his face. "I remember that day like it was yesterday. I walked into the kitchen that morning and Grand *mere* was holding you sitting there crying. Dad," he paused. "He was…I don't know; he was just gone somewhere. It seemed like back then dad was gone all the time. I think he was working," He said quietly. "Then I asked Grand *mere* where mom was, and she looked at me with this funny look like she was going to start crying again. She was so sad Lacey, real sad."

Lacey's heart went out to her brother watching him tell his story.

Nicholas took a deep breath and continued. "The next thing I knew Grand *mere* put you in your highchair and told me to watch you while she made a call. She walked in the kitchen and picked up the phone."

Lacey listed attentively.

Nicholas' expression was sad as he went back in his thoughts. "At first I didn't know who she was calling. Then I heard her say."

"Hello this is Catherine Marie Rousseau-Andries. Is Horace there?" Nicholas' voice said in a whisper.

He turned and looked back at his sister. "And then her voice grew really faint, almost as if she knew I might be listening. But I paid attention and listened, but I couldn't hear her. The next thing I knew Horace came over. He was driving this big fancy black car," he paused. "Then Grand *mere* Catherine bundled us both up and we got into that car.We went looking for mom, I'm sure of it, because mom had left us."

Lacey glanced sharply at Nicholas. He looked like he hadn't been sleeping well. His eyes had dark circles under them. "Mom would never leave us."

His voice shook. "Yes, she did, and I know because all four of us, Grand *mere,* Horace you and me, we drove for what seemed like days to find her. We went to Goldonna Louisiana, I know that. Because I remember all the trees, and I asked what kind of forest we were in and Grand *mere* Catherine said that was the Kisatchie Forest. I'll never forget that name."

Lacey took a breath. She knew he was telling the truth. "Uncle Rufus' house is on the outskirts of Kisatchie Forest. I've heard Grand *mere* Catherine say that."

She remembered Uncle Rufus was a health fanatic. He'd been on the U.S. Olympic wrestling team when he was a youth. He still kept his figure. No one in the family knew how old he was. "Continue telling me your story Nicky."

"Anyway, cousin Rufus sat in the back seat with you and me and then we drove to this house sitting on the bayou somewhere; only it wasn't a house but a nightclub. Rufus went with Horace inside and when they came out momma was with them," he said. "All I know is that they say nobody messes with uncle Rufus."

"But…Why was momma in a night club?" Lacey probed.

"Don't know why," Nicholas sighed out heavily and looked back at his sister. His voice shook with a sob. "I don't know why but she left us," he choked back a sob. "Then Horace drove us back to Goldonna. I know because it was the same Kisatchie Forest, and I said the name and Grand *mere* Catherine said. "*You said the name right my child. We were going back up in our woods now, where our kin live, and we can get some rest for the night. Ain't anybody going to mess with us with our kinfolk around.*"

Lacey gasped "But maybe someone was bothering momma. Or maybe somebody was sick in the family, or somebody died. Yes, that's got to be the reason why mom went back there. That's why we all went back to Louisiana, I'm sure of it."

Nicholas leaned on the desk and cupped his head in his hands. "I wish you were right but Lacey, Horace took us to Aunt Delta's house, we all stayed there" he added. "I remember Aunt Delta was real nice. She let me eat anything I wanted, cake, ice cream, candy. I was in a kid's paradise and I ate so much I could hardly keep my eyes open. She put both of us together to sleep in a bedroom that was located on the side of the house above the garage and she must have left the window open. I heard a car engine and it woke me up in the middle of the night," he paused. "I walked over to the window and looked out. And then I heard them…Then I saw them outside the window," he said, with quiet watchful eyes. "It was mom and Horace and they were arguing."

The way he said it she knew Nicholas had seen it all.

Lacey perched on the end of her chair. "Where were Grand *mere* Catherine and her sister Delta when all this was happening?"

"I don't know. They were sleep or something. Do you want me to finish telling the story or not?"

"Go on," she said.

He shrugged. "Mom and Horace sat in the car. Then she got out and she told him she wasn't ever going back to California. And he told her that her place was with our father, Louis and us kids. I remember Horace yelling at her that she had to grow up and be an adult and let go of childish things. He told her what kind of woman didn't love her own babies enough to stay with their father and raise them up right," Nicholas took a deep breath.

A tear rolled down his face.

"Nicky, are you alright?" Lacey tenderly asked.

"Yeah, I just remembered something. That night when mom started crying Horace wiped her face with his hands so gentle like and talked to her so softly. He told her everything was going to be alright as he held her just like she was a child and let her cry. And then he hugged her tight and then he told her to go into the house. He'd be ready to take us home in the morning. Mom walked back inside, and Horace just stood there and watched her. The next thing I remember is mom came upstairs and got into bed with you and me. In the morning we all ate breakfast together like nothing had happened. We got into Horace's car and drove back to California. I don't ever recall Grand *mere*, Mother, or Horace ever saying a word about that time. But I remember it...I remember it like it was yesterday. I remember because our mother didn't even want us, she wanted to go back home to be with her kin folks in Louisiana. She left us Lacey, she left us..." his voice was a whisper bitter sob.

Lacey got up and walked over and took Nicholas in her arms. Her voice trembled. "Nicky you missed the whole point of your story. Momma never left us, Horace wouldn't let her. It was Horace that kept our family together. It was Horace who made mother stay and keep us all a family."

Nicholas' whimpering stopped and looked at her and managed a nod. "You're right. I guess I never thought of it that way.

Chapter 31

❧

*C*laiming mine...

The next day, When Grand *mere* Catherine had called her and canceled their trip to the flea market, Lacey was happy she had decided to spend the morning cleaning out her closet. She'd even made herself a small pitcher of *Cocktail* **à la Louisiane**, since she'd missed out on having a drink the day before.

With all of tasks completed. She finished her glass of *Cocktail* **à la Louisiane** and was now lying sprawled out on her bed.

She found the shoebox she'd placed the velvet bag that she got at the *Let's Get Acquainted Dinner.* The beautiful soft bag held good and bad memories for her. She thought as she laid sprawled on her bed staring at the ceiling. The feel of the soft velvet bag made her think of Mrs. Oshun and the woman who'd taught that class. She could hear Mrs. Oshun say. *"I will now introduce you to Glenda D'Goodwrench."*

Closing her eyes, Lacey felt like she was drifting off to sleep. She felt like she was on a string and Kienan was the puppet master. She imagined Kienan was on top of her. All at once her eyes flew open. She wanted him. She didn't care about her pride. She didn't care if it made her look desperate.She shook out her thoughts and reached for the telephone beside her bed. "Besides, old friends help each other

187

out all the time, even when they have an itch they can't scratch. She dialed the number.

The phone picked up on the first ring.

"Hello," Kienan said.

"Uh hi old friend," Lacey nervously said. "How are you? I hope you don't mind my calling."

"No, I don't mind at all Lacey. Is everything okay?"

"Yes," she muttered. "I was just missing you and I haven't seen you in a long time, and I was going to invite you over," her words tumbled out. "This is so embarrassing."

"I'd love to come over, you mean right now, right?"

"Yes!"

By the time Kienan rang her doorbell twenty minutes later, Lacey wasn't thinking about her manners, when she leaned over and kiss him hard on the lips. "Oh, maybe I should invite you in first."

"Maybe you're right," he said, as he quickly closed the door behind him.

Hardly realizing she was standing there staring, Lacey tossed logic to the wind. "Would you like to see my bedroom? It's upstairs"

"Ah uh," Kienan's head nodded.

They both grinned wide knowing they wanted the same thing.

"Just in case we can't make it to the bedroom the sofa is right in there," she pointed.

"Let's take the sofa," he said, as he pulled her against him, lifted her and carried her to the sofa.

They tumbled back against the sofa as hungry mouths, and urgent hands removed clothing.

Lacey moaned, fumbling for his belt and Kienan helped her keep his lips glued to hers.

The instant he was free, in one swift movement, he entered her.

Lacey gasped with pleasure. This was how sex was supposed to be. It was passionate and rhythmic and touched something she couldn't name deep within. Like two soul mates connected it was heavenly, wonderful Lacey thought as they both climaxed.

###

When Lacey woke up the next morning, she had a splitting headache. She thought for a moment. *The Cocktail à la Louisiane was a good idea last night, but a bad one this morning, she said in her thoughts.* She turned her head and there was Kienan and the old memories came flooding back as she watched him sleep. Having sex with him was a good idea yesterday but she had forgotten the strong connection between them and how dangerous he was to her heart.She'd been foolish trying to play his game.

All at once Kienan stirred and opened his eyes wide and smiled.

Kienan experienced a rush of feeling for Lacey when he woke up and saw her. This was the only woman he'd ever loved. Too bad he couldn't express his wish for the two of them to have a life together. His life was complicated now. When she telephoned him and invited him over, it was the last thing he'd ever expected her to do. But he was weak for her, he'd missed her.

Finally, he said the first thing that came to mind. "Hey beautiful, you were wonderful last night," Kienan breathed out enthusiastically. "Damn, I get hard just looking at you. So what are you going to fix us to eat? I'm starving."

Lacey stared back at him. She slanted her eyes feeling the effects of her hang-over. Why couldn't men just keep their mouths shut sometimes?

"Yeah that was a freaking fantastic time we had last night," she muttered. Her thoughts raced. *"But the screw-fest is over you Geek King Asshole and I've claimed what I wanted, now you can get the hell out."*

Brushing her hair from her eyes she peered back at him and softly said. "Kienan, baby could you please go home, I have a splitting headache," she hesitated, when she realized he was still grinning at her. "Now, please."

Kienan sorted out with mirth. "What no shower?"

"Of course, if you need a shower. Oh, hell just take one at your own home," she muttered getting out of bed.

"What?"

She got out of bed and pulled the sheet with her. "Yes, I meant it. Leave now!"

"Wait a minute..."

"No, I'm not crazy Kienan," she interrupted him, grabbing his pants and tossing them to him. "Here put your pants on."

Kienan put on his pants. "Wait a minute Lacey I'm a little confused right now. You've got to tell me something here. What is this all about? I've never seen you act like this before."

Lacey searched for her house shoes. "Very well Kienan listen up! I decided to change my life. From now on I'm thinking like a man," she said putting her shoes on. "So, if I'm horny and I want to get laid then I'm going to pick up the phone and call you. Then when I'm fully satisfied and done with you, I'm going to tell you to go home."

He laughed out a tad sarcastic. "Oh really?"

"Yes really, Kienan and if you are finished laughing at me you can go home."

"Holy shit, you're serious!" he exclaimed.

"Yes I am."

He finished dressing. "Okay, I get this part. Right now, you're trying to prove something by calling me over here sleeping with me and then kicking me out," he paused. "You are mad at me and you're getting me back for all the stupid stuff I ever did. Everything, including when I dumped you back in college and probably for now when I've been ignoring you… I don't blame you for doing any of this," his voice trailed off. "Am I right?"

Silently she hung her head, she knew that her sexual frustration at his having been the first man she'd ever slept with had clouded her judgment. Not to mention that since they'd been apart, she hadn't bothered to sleep with anyone else. Beyond a doubt, she knew that phoning him and inviting him over had been a bad idea.

"Talk to me Lacey, please!"

"Damn Kienan, I don't know, maybe. All I know is right now I have the worst headache and I want you to leave."

Then a thought struck him. Maybe she just didn't know how sorry he was at how everything had gone down between them. "Lacey for what it's worth, I just…" he stared, and then rubbed his chin. "I just want you to know that I'm sorry for all of the stupid things that I did to you in the past," he stuttered.

She felt her chest tighten as she made her way to the front door and held it open. "Please just go…"

Kienan walked to the door she held open for him and abruptly stopped. He took her chin in his hand. "I know my life is complicated…But know this, I never stop loving you. I want to do something to show you how much you mean to me. When you feel like it, call me and we can take a drive up to Copperopolis. I'm sure it would give us both a chance to enjoy some fresh clean air."

Lacey managed a weak smile. He was working overtime trying to be nice. "I'd like that; it sounds like a plan."

"You'll call me when you are ready to go?" Kienan asked.

"Yes," she said

He let his fingers trace the bottom of her lips, hesitated and then released his hand. He then turned and walked out of the door.

Lacey watched Kienan drive away.

Loudly her telephone rung-out, on the second ring she picked it up. Instantly the line clicked off.

"Damn! Who keeps calling me and hanging up, she mumbled under her breath?

Chapter 32

*C*opperopolis *CA*

A week later, it was a beautiful Saturday morning when Lacey and Kienan made the drive to Copperopolis.

Kienan's sleek shiny black BMW M6 roared down highway four easily.

Kienan's driving was calm, steady and normal. He kept the speed within limits. Every once in a while, he'd look over at her and give her his charming boyish smile. It allowed them to chit chat easily together throughout their drive.

They approached the turn off at O'Bymes Ferry Road exit. It would take them straight into Copperopolis. The rustic area had never experienced commercial development at any level, so the place was like stepping back in time.

Copperopolis was known as a hidden gem in the Sierra Foothills in Calaveras County. The picturesque, historic town was known not for gold mining but cooper. The second largest copper ore vein was found here in 1860.

The old road was beautiful, peaceful and quiet. The familiar surroundings were comforting too Lacey as she took them in.

All at once she said in a whispered low voice, "thank you for bringing me here."

"My pleasure," he assured her.

Lacey was amazed when Kienan made the familiar right turn. He knew exactly where the old country road begun.

"Kienan you remember how to get to the cabin. I'm amazed."

"Your father's cabin was like my second home. Remember your father Louis brought Nicholas, Quinn and me up here every free chance he had."

Lacey laughed. "I remember that it was mainly you and Nicholas. Quinn usually came up with some excuse to get out of it."

"Yes, you're right. I completely forgot about that.

They made the way down the paved country road. Their car crept slowly up as the road began climbing into the hills. Picturesque breathtaking views of the Sierra Nevada mountain range met their eyes. All around were scenic hills covered with wildflowers and tall tree groves stood strong and erect guarding the hills forming the most beautiful and breathtaking view the eye had ever seen.

"Kienan look!"

Her father's cabin loomed in front of them. The cabin was really an old rustic ranch house fashioned in the old Mexican hacienda style.

Kienan kept his eyes on the road. "I'm glad you let me bring you to the cabin. I know how much this place means to you and to me."

They sat there in the car a few minutes staring at the cabin.

Finally, Kienan said. "Oh, by the way, press the glove compartment for me."

Lacey did as she was told. She pressed the latch and the glove compartment snapped open easily. "There's a box," She looked at Kienan.

"Take that box out for me," his voice grew soft and gentle.

Lacey reached her hand in and pulled out a plain brown wrapped box and went to hand it to him.

"No open it for me," he said.

Pausing she looked inquiringly at Kienan. She looked again at the eight-inch-long box.It was too long and wide to be jewelry she thought, breathing a sigh of relief. She pulled off the brown wrapping paper and beneath was a blue box marked Tiffany.

Sitting in the center of the box was an exquisite huge Pearl. It was flanked by two large rubies set in a prong setting and surrounded by a legion of small round rubies set in a Pave'.

Lacey gasped, "Kienan you didn't have to do this! Is this a *Mikimoto Akoya Pearl?*"

"Do you like it?" He asked.

"Yes, you know I do." *Akoya Pearl* is my favorite. "But you shouldn't have, I don't know…I couldn't…"

She smiled and closed her eyes griping her finger tight feeling the ring on her finger. This looked like the ring she'd asked him to buy all those years ago when she had first thought they would always be together. She couldn't believe he had remembered. And then she thought of their break-up and shook out her thoughts. Today was a very happy day, she didn't want to ruin it by remembering things that had made her sad.

He watched her and knew she remembered that was the ring she pointed out to him many years ago. But this one was not the same. This one wasn't the small inexpensive ring the teenager Lacey had picked out. This one was the one , the man knew a queen like Lacey deserved.

Finally, he spoke. "Now don't sit there trying to think up reasons for not keeping it. You're keeping that ring. I insist. It's a little something I wanted you to have. To say I was sorry." He said. "Now I don't want to hear you won't accept my gift, I won't hear it," he said throwing his hands up. "Besides I'm trying to make the *Best Apology Ever Hall of Fame.*" He said. "You don't want me to feel like I didn't make the hall of fame now do you?"

Lacey laughed. "Okay in that case then grab the groceries that

I brought," she blurted. "I hope I still remember the code for the alarm. Do you still like London broil?" She asked but didn't wait for an answer. "The grocery story was out of porterhouse steaks and I remembered you liked London broil and seafood, so I grabbed some scallops and prawns too."

Hours later, after they dined and cleared away the dishes in the kitchen Lacey couldn't remember having a more enjoyable evening as she watched Kienan remove the storage tarps from the deck lounge furniture. He dusted off a lounge chair and settled into it in content.

Lacey carried over a tray of coffee, cups, and brandy and placed it on the table.

"Here Kienan your coffee and brandy," she said, before she walked over and leaned on the railing and looked out on the beauty of Lake Tulloch. Her eyes held a deep sadness as they scanned the surrounding Mountain View. She felt a peace within her soul.

She sighed softly while taking in the wonderful views of the valley canyon below and whispered out a cry "Daddy I miss you, and we have to thank Kienan for bringing me home today."

"You're welcome," Kienan said standing right behind her. "I had forgotten how much this place means to you Lacey."

Lacey turned her head in his direction. "I'm sorry; I didn't see you standing there," she said wiping a tear that escaped down her face.

She turned and looked back at him with a grateful expression. "I do thank you for bringing me here."

Kienan smiled back at her. "Like I said, I was so happy to do it."

And then he leaned in and kissed her.

The next thing Lacey knew he swept her up into his arms and the kiss got out of control and instantly she moaned.

All at once the patio door flung open wide as a loud piercing noise startled them.

"What's going on here?"

"Nicholas, what are you doing here?" Lacey said aghast.

And then Quinn walked up behind Nicholas into view.

"See Nicholas, it's a good thing we got here in time. Looks like there were trespassers on the place," he chuckled.

Defiantly Lacey turned her gaze. "Shut up Quinn, the only people who are trespassing are Nicholas and you."

Nicholas loudly cleared his throat. "You know Lacey, unscrupulous and criminal stuff happens all the time and the alarm was triggered, I guess by you and Kienan showing up today. The alarm company called, and I took a ride down to check things out. Of course, Quinn, being the good friend that he is, joined me to come and check things out."

She leveled her gaze at her brother. Maybe he'd been right about the alarm code. She did wonder if she had entered it right in the first place. But the alarm company normally called the family home first and not Nicholas directly. Something was a little suspicious about his story.

Nicholas walked over and greeted Kienan. He shook his hand. "Hey Kienan man, how have you been?" he asked but didn't wait for a response. "I just thought I'd check out the old cabin and see if everything is okay. If I'd known, you were here…"

Kienan leveled his gaze on Nicholas. He leaned in close, so no one could hear. "I didn't know you were so interested in your father's old cabin," his voice was stern. "Or keeping tabs on where your sister is at all times."

Nervously Nicholas shrugged embarrassed. Kienan could always make him feel like he was the younger brother getting into mis-chief.He looked up into his eyes and then turned away. He wondered sometimes if Kienan could read his mind.

Lacey looked up and saw Quinn. For some reason tonight, his rich dude attitude held an overdose of sleaze, along with a sinister quality Lacey hadn't notice before. Maybe she thought, it was because he was dressed too over the top, with his expensive suit and a starched collar. He looked out of place with everyone else wearing jeans.

Her eyes searched for Kienan, he was staring directly at her as if they both understood that they weren't the trespassers there.

Finally, Lacey blew out a breath and spoke, "Well Nicky you can see that all is well here. Perhaps it is time you and Quinn left."

Nicholas laughed. "Quinn and I were hoping to stick around and maybe play a game of cards or two. I do smell your famous London broil. You got any left baby sister?"

It was close to eleven that night and the four of them had been drinking and playing poker for hours when Lacey finally folded in her hand.

"That's it. I'm out, okay guys I'll make a pot of coffee," she said rising and heading for the kitchen.

Lacey busied herself cleaning the glasses they used. The dinner dishes had been washed earlier and put away. Next, she tackled the coffee.

A few moments later, she almost jumped out of her skin, as a man's hand slipped around her waist.

"Mmmm that coffee doesn't smell as good as you do Lacey," Quinn whispered against her ear.

"Why aren't you still playing cards with Kienan and Nicholas

Quinn?"

Quinn's lips curled into a grin. "They are so involved in the game they didn't miss my leaving," his voice took on a false note of concern. "I just thought I'd check on you and see if that Geek King Kienan tried to make a move on you earlier, before we got here," he inquired.

Lacey laughed surprised.

"I take that as a yes," Quinn stated angrily.

"You can take that as it's none of your damn business Quinn."

A red flare seemed to flash behind Quinn's eyes.

Quinn moved in towards Lacey determined to kiss her and cause some major problems between her and Kienan. Suddenly he took Lacey's face in his hands and drew her toward him.

All at once a bright twinkling light flashed. It was followed by a rapid flow of icy cold breeze that whipped in out of nowhere.

A shrill loud eerie high-pitched moan shrieked out around the room. The haunting sound's cackling whisper broke the tension in the room.

Tinged with fear Quinn abruptly stopped and stared at her.

"Lacey, what the hell was that noise? And that strange eerie light earlier, how did you do that?"

Lacey looked around her. The room felt weird. A gust of wind blew softly and ruffled her hair.

Nothing seemed normal. "I don't know what's going on here Quinn, but I didn't do anything. This is like one of those times Grand *mere* Catherine would say that the dead be watching the living and don't like what they do."

"Oh, Lacey the world is full of surprises. That was just some strange occurrence. Come on let's get back to what we were doing. Give me a kiss."

"Get away from me Quinn," she said, reaching to grab the hot pot of coffee.

"I thought you liked me," Quinn said.

Lacey's breath surged in and out as she held the pot of coffee tight. She was ready to do battle if she needed to. "Well you thought wrong."

They both stopped and looked at each other.

Then Nicholas rushed into the kitchen. "Hey Lacey and Quinn, did you hear that wild animal screaming earlier? You guys missed it. Kienan and I rushed out on the deck and we saw a mountain lion on a kill," he said taking in the situation.

Kienan in came behind Nicholas. "Lacey are you okay?"

"Yeah…Yeah that wild animal scream just caught me by surprise," she lied.

Kienan closed the distance between them.

Instantly Nicholas walked over to his sister. "Here Lacey, let me get that hot pot of coffee for you, he said. "Thanks for making it for me."

He walked over and leveled his gaze at Quinn. "Come on Quinn and help me find my Dad's old thermos. It's got to be in one of these cabinets. We need to get on the road. It's getting late."

A half hour later, Quinn slammed his car door. He was furious with Nicholas as he got into his car.

Quinn blew out a breath. "So, Nicholas, did you have a nice time playing big brother? I hope you know we didn't obtain our goal."

Nicholas shook his head. "And neither did Kienan. Don't you see? He and Lacey are driving right in front of us?"

Quinn gripped the steering wheel. "Yeah, I can see that man, but it doesn't help the fact that right now I'm one horny ass man."

"Yeah, the Hacienda is right on the way back to San Jose," Nicholas said.

"Ah what?"

Nicholas laughed out. "Quinn don't tell me you have forgotten Angel's Hacienda located just outside French Camp California? We are almost there."

Quinn shook his head. "Oh yeah how could I ever forget the delicious and ram-me-hard Miss Brandy," he laughed out. "Okay Nicholas you're off my shit list now."

Quinn gunned his BMW. It roared like a tiger as he covered the miles to French Camp in under forty minutes.

Chapter 33

I saw what you did...

The next day Lacey slept most of the day. That evening she woke up, took a shower, and fixed herself something to eat. She had just finished clearing away her dishes when her telephone rang.

"Hi Lacey, is everything okay? I hadn't heard from you in a while," Maëlle's cheery voice said.

"Hi Maëlle, I'm fine. What's been up with you," Lacey nervously inquired. She wondered if Kienan had told Maëlle the two of them had slept together or visited Copperopolis. News among old friends sometimes traveled fast.

Maëlle sighed loudly. "Nothing much, listen, I'm glad I got a chance to talk with you. You know Nicholas told me about what happened that day at the big family gathering you guys had," she laughed out. Your mother laid some serious head trips on you guys what with her dating Horace and all."

Lacey let out a sigh of relief. "Yeah that she did. But you haven't talked with Nicholas since?"

"No, and to be honest, I haven't really seen your brother in a while. You know how Nicholas and I are? Our relationship is…Well I know that he sees other people and sometimes I see other people."

"Oh, my goodness, why didn't I think of it before," Lacey's voice was soft. "When we were at the Zodiac club and you saw Xavier Newhouse…"

Maëlle interrupted her. "Yeah…Yeah we both know Xavier Newhouse always had a thing for me. So, what I've been seeing him?" she said. "Besides, I'm not a fool Lacey. I don't sit around waiting for your brother Nicholas to figure out that I'm the best thing that ever happened to him. Plus, Xavier Newhouse gives some of the best parties in Oakland. The last one had that Singer Pearl Grey singing her latest hit song."

"Okay now you are making me jealous. You don't have to tell me about Xavier's fabulous parties. I've been to three and I know they are legendary."

Maëlle's voice held a mean edge. "Oh yeah Lacey, I know I can trust you but keep the info about Xavier between us."

The edge in Maëlle's voice caught Lacey off guard. She grew quiet. She felt hurt. She had never given away any of Maëlle's secrets before.

As if Maëlle could read her mind through the telephone, all at once she said. "Lacey, I'm sorry for sounding so shrewd. It's just that…" she paused. "Look, we've been best friends for a long time and well I've always been a little jealous that you have more than one man in love with you and willing to do anything for you. While I have a guy, who sleeps around with every female walking and doesn't give me a thought."

"Look Maëlle I understand. Don't worry. You and Xavier are safe with me. But right now, I'm kind of feeling under the weather," she said, telling herself she really wasn't lying. She was recuperating from all the drama of last week.

"Oh my God what's the matter, something serious?"

"No, of course not," Lacey replied. "I just got a little tummy ache from something I ate. That's all."

Maëlle breathed out a sigh of relief. "Oh, that's good. I don't mean that you don't feel well but because it's nothing serious. You know we have London and Art's wedding to go to?"

"That's right, thanks for reminding me. I almost forgot."

"Maëlle I really should go. My tea is getting cold."

"Okay, Lacey, but remember Nicholas and I are picking you up for the wedding. So, don't worry about driving."

"See you then, bye," Lacey said hanging up.

No sooner than she hung up the phone her front doorbell rang.

"Anael, what are you doing here?"

Anael Paschar stood in her doorway.

"May I come in Lacey?"

"Of course, Anael, do come in," she said once the shock wore off. "The family room is the warmest place in the house. I'm afraid I don't turn on the heat in the living room."

"You have a lovely home," Anael said following her into the spacious family room and taking a seat on the couch.

"Can I get you something to drink? I'm having tea, but I've got coffee, water, wine, brandy, and oh there's a bottle of Johnnie Walker."

"What's the label color?"

"Black."

His eyes beamed. "I'll have a glass."

Lacey grabbed the bottle and a glass and brought them over to the coffee table and poured.

"Thank you," he said, his face expressionless as he picked up the glass. He tasted his drink. And then took a big swallow.

Lacey took a seat right next to him. "Well what brings you over, something you want to talk about?"

"Don't you know you are a very special woman, Lacey? My cousin Maëlle always bragged about her great friend Lacey La Cour. I'd heard about you so much that when I finally got to see you for the first time when I visited my cousin, I knew it the first moment I saw you I was in love with you."

She breathed out with a great sigh. "Oh Anael, kids think they can fall in love but it's just a crush that really is a mirage. It's never real."

He played with the glass in his hand. "You should take me seriously Lacey and listen attentively. Your family situation may depend upon it." His thoughts raced as he looked at her. *"I know something that you don't know," he said to himself.*

Puzzled she looked at him. "What are you talking about?"

Anael's steady gaze held her. "You know Lacey, I'm not as dull as I seem. I once dated an actress. She said my tongue's ability to find a woman's hot spot was legendary," he said, as he slowly took a sip of his drink, as his eyes studied her. "I do seem to have a knack for pleasing a woman in all area below the navel."

Lacey felt his eyes were trying to possess her. *"Oh Christ, this priest is making me feel hot. Grand mere was right. I need to quit messing with a priest,"* she thought staring back at him.

She cleared her throat loudly. "Yeah, well who knew you were a sex machine. Scratch that I said that," nervously she sipped her tea.

Anael was enjoying watching Lacey squirm. "Did you know I took her to the Carnival in Rio de Janeiro?"

"Oh really, did you date her while you were in Seminary?"

He chuckled. "No, I was just an ordinary undergrad attending Pepperdine University. That's where I met the actress on the beach at Malibu. That actress was a lot like you Lacey, very intelligent and wise."

Her eyes studied his. "So, was she beautiful?"

"Yes," he looked away.

"Seems like you liked her. Why didn't you use your trust fund to keep the actress?"

He frowned and sighed resignedly. "That actress wasn't worth me playing God in her life for. Why change a person's life if that person doesn't respect other people's feelings? If I'd offered to give that actress a huge sum of money it would have just sent her down a darker path in life. She was a user like so many people are in this world."

"So Anael, you believe in playing God and you are judgmental too.

What a combination," Lacey stated patiently.

He shrugged. "Every man and woman on this earth plays God at one time or another," Anael told her. "You are an intelligent, kind-hearted and loving woman; a man would be proud and honored to do anything to make you his wife. You would make me happy." His thoughts raced, *"Including giving you money, to buy your love and affection,"* he said to himself.

Lacey was silent for a moment as she studied the calm aura about him. "So, are you playing God right now Anael? I mean with your offer to help my family?"

He took another drink from his glass and savored it for a moment. "If that's playing God in your book, so be it. That actress would have cheated on me the second we said our vows. But Lacey, you would understand that marriage as a wise investment and a sacred oath. You and I both know that you can grow to love the person you are with," he hesitated. "For my part, I'm willing to overlook your little, shall we say, untruthfulness and sign any agreement you would like for me to. And in return, I will give you two million dollars' cash up front."

Lacey shook her head with laughter. She wasn't taking his comments seriously. She decided to play along with his gag. "Really, so tell me how much are you offering if your wife says, has a child? So, tell me what you're going rate is for child?"

Anael didn't blink. "Once you marry me, I'll give you three million dollars for each child we have, and of course all your daily living expenses will be taken care of," his lips curved up into a smile. "I'm hoping for two children, a boy and a girl. But if you wish to increase your baby allowance, and have more than two children, that would be fine with me. Just think of it if you produce five children that fifteen million dollars, the limit is all yours."

Lacey's laughter died on her face. The man was serious. "You can't be serious."

Angrily he stared at her. "I'm serious, and you come from a long line of intelligent women who never let a man make a fool of them."

"Okay now I'm not so sure I'm following you."

"Your mother and Grand *mere* are both honorable women who know and understand arranging marriages as an investment for their future. Your untrustworthiness earlier I can overlook."

Bewildered, she stared back at him. "Why do you keep saying this word *untrustworthy?*"

His eyes flashed coldly. "I saw what you did. I came by here that day you had Kienan over. And I saw when he left. Kienan offered to take you to Copperopolis and I'm guessing that he did yesterday. Because you weren't home when I came by then either," he said. "Anyway, I think you think you are in love with Kienan but he's just using you. Don't be his fool."

"Why were you spying on me?"

He shook his head. "No, I wasn't spying on you, that Sunday when I came over and saw the two of you, it was the Sunday that you'd promised to have breakfast with me."

Lacey looked puzzled. "I'm terribly sorry but I don't remember…"

"I believe when I asked you. You and my cousin Maëlle was at some club. When I called and asked you."

The moment was tense.

"This is so awkward," Lacey breathed out, "You are so right, I did say that. Look Anael, I am so sorry. I had forgotten all about my phone call with you that night," she said as she silently leaned back on the couch and stared trying to collect her thoughts.

They both sat there in silence.

The phone rang and broke the ice.

Anael leaned over and kissed Lacey on the cheek, as he got up off of the couch. "You should take that. I'll show myself out."

"Anael, I'm sorry, really I am," she got up and followed him to the front door. "We need to talk about this."

"Don't worry Lacey I'll give you a call," he said closing the front door behind him.

The phone rang again, and Lacey picked up the one on the table in the foyer. "Hello."

"Hi Lacey, it's me Nicholas. You do know we've got that wedding to go to?"

"Yes, I remember," she said. "But Nicholas can I ask you something?"

"Yeah sure," he said.

"I've been visiting with Anael Paschar, you know Maëlle's cousin and he made some ridiculous statement, you know how deep and serious his voice is."

Nicholas signed loudly. "Oh really, what did you guys talk about?"

Lacey laughed. "Now that I think back on it, it was kind of humorous. Anael said something to the effect that our family situation could depend upon his offer of help. I was really paying attention to that part because he made this ridiculous offer of marriage promising to give me three million dollars up front."

Abruptly Nicholas interrupted her. "What did you say?"

She laughed. "Of course, I didn't take him serious."

Nicholas loudly cleared his throat. "Look Lacey, don't forget about tomorrow I'll pick you up. Don't worry about getting Art and London a gift Maëlle and I have taken care of that and we put your name on the present as well. Don't worry, it ain't cheap. And it more than shows our family's wish for a happy union between Art and London," he replied. "I've got to go. Don't forget I'm picking you up tomorrow, bye."

The line clicked off.

Chapter 34

Bitter Pill

The Palm Event Center located in Pleasanton had to be the perfect place to hold a wedding. Lacey thought as she walked around the ballroom admiring the ice sculpture; it took her breath away.

Lacey looked all around, and she hoped she would have something as grand as this when she got married. Weddings made her happy.She looked up as the bride walked her way and smiled joyously.

London Maveaux was the pretty half of Mr. and Mrs. Arthur Maveaux.

The just married couple made their way through their reception, greeting each guest personally.

London and Lacey hugged.

"Ahhhh… Lacey thank you very much for coming. You don't know how much this means to me and Art," London said.

"I wouldn't have missed it for the world. You look so radiant and beautiful London."

"Too bad Maëlle and Nicholas had to leave," Art said. "They will miss out on all the fun we have planned."

Lacey drew in a breath. "What?"

A worried frown crossed London's face. "Oh no Lacey, that's right. Nicholas told Art and me to tell you. We saw Nicholas and he said Maëlle wasn't feeling well and that he was taking her home, but not to worry. Quinn is supposed to be arriving soon and he will take you home."

Art pointed. "Oh, and there comes Quinn now," he said waving him over.

Art pulled Quinn into a hearty handshake and the two chitchatted easily.

Silently Lacey stood there.

London leaned over and whispered. "Lacey don't you think Quinn is a hunk, and he's single. You know what they say. Romance can blossom at a wedding," she said patting her hand.

Quinn closed the distance between them. "Congratulations London, you make Art a very happy man."

"Thank you, Quinn," London said, sharing air kisses with him.

Art grinned standing there and he took Lacey's arm. He was beaming like he should get the matchmaker of the year award smiling real big as he made introductions. "By the way Quinn, Nicholas had to leave early. He expects you to give Lacey a ride home."

"No problem Art. Congratulations"

"Well Lacey, I'm leaving you in Quinn's capable hands," Art said grinning.

London and Art walked a short distance away and greeted other guests.

Lacey waited until Art and London were out of earshot and looked anxiously at Quinn. "Okay Quinn let's just avoid each other until it's time to go home. Or unless I manage to find myself another ride home."

Quinn watched her walk away. "Believe me Lacey, you won't find another ride home tonight but me," he hissed under his breath.

###

Hours later, Lacey took one last look around the dwindling crowd of people. There wasn't a familiar face she could finagle to give her a ride home. She spotted Quinn and walked over.

"Alright Quinn I'm ready to go. Where are you parked?" She asked.

Shortly they found where Quinn had parked his BMW 745il and got in.

"Thanks again for taking me home."

"No problem, I'm just glad I was there to help," he said turning on some soft music. He checked the gas hand of his car. "Lacey if you don't mind I need to pull over the first chance I get to get some gas. I'm pretty sure there's a station just off Bernal Road." He said. "You can run in and get us a couple cups of coffee. Do you mind?"

"Sure, I don't mind.

A few minutes later Quinn pulled up in front of the gas station on Bernal. He got out and filled his gas tank. He then moved the car to a waiting area just under some trees while he waited for her to get the coffee.

Lacey walked out of the Bernal Market with two steaming cups of coffee. She looked around and saw that Quinn was waving at her from his car just under some nearby trees.

"Why did you park so far away?"

Quinn smiled wickedly at her. "I just like watching you walk in that dress." He said. "You do that Miss America pageant catwalk strut thing so well. I could look at you all night." His eyes gleamed under the moon light.

Lacey tried not to show her smile as she walked over and handed him his cup of coffee.

"You feel like talking Lacey?" He asked. "The night is so right, and it makes the coffee taste better standing out in the air."

Lacey smiled softly. "Do I detect a man who doesn't want the smell of a strong coffee all over in his nice clean car?"

"No," he lied, *that was the main reason*, he thought and cleared his throat. "It's just the night is so peaceful, and the moonlight is shining so bright."

He said. "And well, I value your opinion and I knew if anyone had the right answer it would be you."

Lacey tossed all logic aside it was a beautiful night. "Okay Quinn, what's on your mind?"

"Do you believe people can change?" He asked. "I mean really change, be a better person and all that?" He took a sip of his coffee.

"Sure, anything's possible I guess," Lacey replied, as she listened to the quietness of the night. The roundness of the full moon against the midnight deep sapphire blue-black sky gave her pause.

She turned around back at him. She was pleasantly surprised. Quinn looked sensitive and handsome in his tuxedo. Quinn seemed consumed by a need to talk and get something off of his chest. Slowly she sipped her coffee and watched him.

Quinn kept silent. As the moments went by he looked sadly at the moon.

Curiously Lacey shot him a puzzled look. "What is it Quinn? What's wrong?" She asked.

"I've been trying to figure out how to fix this mess I seemed to have made between you and me," He whispered. "Remember when we were kids and you used to hang on my every word?"

"That was a longtime ago. And like you said we were kids," She felt the warmth of the coffee cup seep through her.

"Correction I'm still a couple years older than you remember," he chuckled. "But sometimes I wish I could turn back the hands of time to when things were so much simpler and happier for me," he said.

The moment was awkward for Lacey.

"Do you remember that time when I took you and Maëlle trick or treating?"

"Yes, I remember it. Mom said we were not real teenagers yet, so we couldn't go to the Halloween Party at the Community Center, it was only for high school kids."

Quinn shrugged. "I knew how important it was to you to go. And I just wanted to make it happen. And you know what? I found that it really made me happy just watching you two have so much fun that night."

"Wow, I'd almost forgotten. We did have a lot of fun. You were our knight in shining armor that night. You wore the costume. I remember," she beamed. She shrugged that would explain her vision. "Thank you for that night. We had a great time that night, just the three of us," she said. "It was magical and fun, and it was the second-best life of mine just before my high school days."

Quinn hesitated and then in a low hoarse voice. "I wish we could both go back because you had a big old crush on me then and I have always had a crush on you."

Lacey smiled at the memory and then responded quickly back to him. "I did have a crush on you after that Halloween night. You become number one on my list of crushes. I was just a typical young girl with a list of crushes a mile long. They were ever changing every minute of every day."

"Being number one on your crush list was very important to me."

Lacey turned around and stared at him.

"I don't think we should forget the best times of our life." He smiled. "That was the best time of my life Lacey." He looked at her with a deep fascination.

She grew quiet.

"Oh, how lovely your hair looks in the moonlight," He murmured softly reaching out to touch her hair. "Your perfume is so intoxicating. I love the way it smells," he said leaning in closer to her. "Did you know I've always loved the smell of your perfume? He said reaching out and taking her hand and bringing it to his lips. He placed her hand on his chest. "Do you feel the beating of my heart?" He whispered. "Right here is the energy of my life force. It is a force that only beats for you."

Lacey shivered as she felt the warmth of her hand feeling the rising and falling away of Quinn's chest moving under the palm of her hand.

Lacey looked into his eyes and saw heat burning in the depths like lava from a volcano. For some reason she felt drawn to him. The air around her felt dangerous and comforting all at the same time.

Quinn's voice whispered something incomprehensible as his mouth urgently sought hers. His kisses were hungry as he moaned softly.

"Don't Quinn!" She squawked pushing him away. "Take me home, now!"

"What did I do wrong? You were enjoying my kisses. I could tell. What's come over you?"

"Nothing…" She murmured. "It's just not right. I don't want to be leading you on."

"You think there's someone else, but have you asked him if he thinks of you that way?"

"You don't even know who he is?" She folded her arms. "Just take me home. Now, please!"

Agitated and angry Quinn's voice shook. "Yes, I do!" He said. "I'll take you home, alright," he said reaching for her cup of coffee and throwing it away. "I don't allow anyone to drink that shit in my car! Get in!"

Lacey did as she was told and quickly got into Quinn's' car.

Quinn got into the car and started the engine. He eased his BMW 745il onto highway 680 heading towards San Jose.

The moment was tense inside the car.

Finally, Quinn broke the ice and said. "Do you…Do you think he's waiting on you, Lacey? You will never be anything to Kienan but an outlet for him. He's got a child on the way. Did you know that's why you haven't seen him? His baby momma is just one of his many whores," his voice was enraged.

He gripped the steering wheel as his thoughts raced. *I love you for you, can't you see that? There's nothing I wouldn't do for you."* He rubbed his chin and shook his head. *He hoped she couldn't see into his thoughts.Why don't you want me Lacey...Why?*

Quinn's sleek BMW 745il took the over-pass and made the full moon shine luminously bright as they drove in silence.

Minutes went by and Lacey watched as Quinn drove past exit after exit that would have taken them to her house. "Quinn, you can take the next exit. It will take you to my house."

Quinn did not respond. Instead he took the connection to highway 101.

"This really is the long way Quinn. But we can still get there. Did you forget where I live?"

"No!" He said sharply.

Quinn took the Capitol Expressway exit just off highway 101 and then took a right onto Aborn Road and headed past the old Mirassou Winery, they drove past the new fire station and took to the road leading high up in the hills. Higher and higher Quinn's sleek BMW 745il climbed and before Lacey knew it, she had lost track of the right and left turns he took navigating the curvy hillside roads.

All at once his car slowed down in front of a large house with an elegant and very expensive looking townhouse nestled deep in a canyon valley. The homes loomed back just like something designed out of the lifestyles of the rich and famous.

He slowed down and stopped abruptly in front of a distinct town house with an iron gated entry. Parked just out front was a BMW M6. He turned off his car lights.

Remember, I told you about a townhouse Lacey? Well these are the town houses. Take a notice of the house number. Tomorrow, why don't ask your girl Maëlle about it. She can tell you all about it." He murmured softly. "Do you notice anything else Lacey?" Quinn's voice grew stern. "Like that car parked out front?"

"It's just a BMW." Lacey shrugged then looked away.

"No Lacey that's not an ordinary BMW and you know it." He said. "Take a good look at it Lacey I know you notice something very unusual," He said, "Like maybe it's a modified M6."

"So, what, it's M6 with Pimped out chrome details. I heard that there was another one in town just like it," she said.

"Yeah…" Quinn said shaking his head. "But how many have a chrome slide ruler running through a Cadillac Sedan logo?" He said turning to watch her closely. "A miniature Cadillac Sedan, just like his mother had, don't you see it?"

"No! I don't see anything Quinn!" She whined.

"Oh, its dark out, forgive me Lacey, how can I expect you to see anything in this darkness!" Quinn said turning on the high beam lights on his car.

Lacey flinched at the sound of the tenseness in Quinn's voice. She adjusted her eyes to the light. She gasped.

"Do you recognize anything now Lacey?" His voice hissed out. "Do you think Kienan's waiting for you, Lacey?" He smirked. "I've always recognized Kienan for what he is Lacey. A leopard doesn't change his spots. He got another woman pregnant. He practically lives at a whore house. How much more information do you need, before you'll see the truth, Lacey! He doesn't want you" His eyes blazed at her wickedly.

Quinn leaned in closer to her. His breath was warm against her face. His jealousy consumed him. He grabbed her hand and pulled it to his heart. "It's a bitter pill to swallow knowing that the man you thought was your hero is just a man," he paused. "I know I'm not your ideal man. Maybe I'm not in the package you find pleasing to accept. But take me for what I am Lacey, the man who loves you, the man who would do anything for you, love me Lacey or would you rather be alone with a memory of a man like Kienan who doesn't love you?"

Lacey turned her head away. She couldn't deny what she saw. "Take me home Quinn, please just take me home." Her voice shook with a sob.

Minutes later, Quinn pulled up in front of her house.

"You are not invited in Quinn," she venomously said reaching to open the door.

"Oh yeah I'm tired of being a nice guy. You do know Anael won't be renewing his offer to set you up to marry him. In fact, if you don't want your family to lose that home you were raised in you'd better settle for me, Lil Ole Quinn. And real quick. Because if you don't I'll ruin your family. Lacey, and I'll make sure the authorities put Nicholas in jail for all of the stupid, illegal trading stuff he's been doing!"

"What are you talking about?"

"Ask Nicholas where he is supposed to get the money to pay back his loans," he reached over and opened her door. "Get out Lacey and think about what I said."

###

Lacey made it back inside her home and promptly set the alarm system. She hadn't used the alarm system in ages. Not since the last time she and Maëlle had gone to Las Vegas for the weekend and the alarm malfunctioned. Her neighbors had threatened to call the police. She promised them it would never happen again.

"This is just ridiculous," she mumbled under her breath. "I need to just ask Nicholas what is going on. She quickly dialed Nicholas' number. It went straight to his voice mail.

"Nicky, it's Lacey. Call me back," she urgently said before hanging up.

She thought about Maëlle. She recalled Nicholas and Maëlle had left the wedding together. She dialed her number and it went to voice mail. "Hey girlfriend it's me Lacey. Give me a call back. Oh, and if you've seen Nicholas tell him to call me."

She had just hung up the phone when the jarring ring filled the air. "Hello Nicky!"

"No Lacey it's me Grand *mere*. What are you looking for that brother of yours for?"

Lacey paused. "Oh, nothing really, hello Grand *mere* Catherine how are you this evening?"

"I can't complain. How was the wedding?"

"It was nice."

"Good, I never did like those two girls with the city names. Paris London and London Paris. They were just too fast with boys for my taste.

"Grand *mere* Catherine, London's maiden name was Devereaux."

"So."

Lacey knew she was waging a losing battle. "Never mind Grand *mere* Catherine, what you called me for anyway.

"Tomorrow is Sunday and I want you to take me to the Berryessa Flea Market."

Lacey knew this was a command without asking. Besides, she thought it would give her a chance to talk to her grandmother about Nicholas.

"Sure, bright and, early right?"

Chapter 35

Busted

That Sunday morning Lacey arrived early to pick Grand *mere* up and take her to the flea market. She checked her watch. It was now nearing twelve noon. They had been at the flea market for almost three hours. She watched as Grand *mere* Catherine bartered and persuaded an elderly produce vendor to lower his prices.

Lacey was bored and found the flea market only good for giving her a good dose of vitamin D. She glanced again at the tall elderly produce vendor her grandmother was haggling with. The old guy was handsome, and then she recalled where she'd seen him. It was Perry Breaux; he was the brother of Remington Breaux an ex-boyfriend of her grandmother's.

Lacey smiled. No wonder her grandmother had been idly chitchatting with the vendor. She was checking up on Remington.

"Grand *mere* I'm going to go get a cold drink and a Churros at the taco stand. Do you want something?"

"Yes, get me a beef taco and a bottled water and get us a seat at one of their tables, in the shade. I'm about ready to sit a spell just as soon as I'm done here," Grand *mere* Catherine smiled.

Lacey quickly walked over to the taco stand and waited her turn at the walk-up window. "I'd like two super beef tacos, two CHURROS, a cherry ICEE and bottled water please," Lacey said as she leaned into the walk-up window looking at the girl taking her order.

She paid for her food and had just been given her change when another girl pushed her order through the open window. Lacey took a big sip of her ICEE before walking away to find a table in some shade.

The aroma of the beef taco sent her senses reeling. She took a big bite into her taco." "Whew this is good," she murmured taking another bite.

"Lacey don't eat so fast," Grand *mere* scolded sitting down. "Look at all the deals I got today," she exclaimed. "Here give me my taco before you eat that one too."

"Ah, Grand *mere*." Lacey shrugged her shoulders and continued eating. "Those pecans you got look really good. Will you promise to make pecan pralines with some?"

"Yes, but I did want to make a pie with those pecans." She said taking a bite of her taco. "Whew, this taco is good," Grand *mere* said. "It's a good thing I sat down when I did." She took a sip of water. "Coming to the flea market was just what I needed. I'm having loads of fun, aren't you?"

"Sure, Grand *mere,* especially the food. Oh, by the way both the Churros are mine. Hands off okay?"

"Oh, Lacey you wouldn't deny your grandmother one Churros for herself? The taco stand is just there," she pointed. "You could walk over and buy another one."

"If you will recall, you didn't ask for one, remember?"

"Lacey I can't believe you can be so selfish." Grand *mere* looked away. Her expression looked grim. "Oh my God!"

"What?"

"Kienan..." Grand *mere* whispered out frantically. "He's right over there staring at us with that pregnant woman."

Lacey gasped. This could not be happening. Kienan strolled

leisurely toward them with the woman named Lucy Mondragon in tow.

Lacey leaned over and whispered. "Well Grand *mere*, now maybe you'll see why I have not been so receptive to all your Kienan is *a good man talk*."

Grand *mere* Catherine handed Lacey a napkin. "Here Lacey wipe your mouth. We have company," she said, in a regal tone.

"Kienan, over here," Grand *mere* Catherine waved her hand cheerfully in the air to get his attention. "It's good to see you."

The moment was tense.

A deep expression of disappointment creased Grand *mere*'s brow as she regarded Kienan. He used to be a worthy man in her eyes.

Kienan approached slowly with a very pregnant Lucy Mondragon by his side.

Grand *mere* Catherine's thoughts raced. With a quiet reserve she watched the couple approach. She'd been wrong before, but maybe if they got close enough, she could see into their eyes. She always felt the eyes were the window to the heart.

"Kienan it's good to see you," Grand *mere* called out, with an easiness in her voice. "Please introduce me to your friend."

Before he could say a word, Grand *mere* Catherine looked at the woman by his side. "Oh, honey you're going to go into labor at any moment!"

Lacey tried not to stare.

"Hello Grand *mere* Catherine, Lacey…" Kienan said with a nod. 'May I introduce you both to… Ah… Lucy Mondragon?"

"Hi, Lacey, oh and by the way I'm Kienan's fiancée now. He keeps forgetting."

Lacey pushed back her hair and took a sip of her drink and remained calm. "Hi Lucy. Well it looks like congratulations are in order, for the two of you." She put on a fake smile and was glad she'd paid attention to Maëlle's homework assignments for her acting classes.

The atmosphere was tense and silent.

Grand *mere* Catherine didn't hold her tongue. Her expression was grim and her voice cold as she glanced back at Kienan. "Fiancée huh? Well, well…Mr. Kienan you are a man who can keep secrets."

Kienan cleared his throat loudly. "Huh."

"So, Ms. Mondragon, you're out here walking the flea market trying to pop that baby?" Grand *mere* Catherine asked.

"Yes," Lucy said. "As you can see I'm certainly not in a shopping mood today. As a matter of fact, I really need to use the ladies room, it's just over there. If you guys will excuse."

Lacey shrugged rising from the table. She didn't even look up at him. "I really need to get myself another beef taco and Grand *mere* wants a Churros…Bye Kienan," she said abruptly making her exit.

Grand *mere* Catherine's eyes locked with Kienan's. Her voice was taut with anger."I'm so disappointed in you Kienan, you got a girl pregnant and you've kept it secret all this time?" She paused and then continued. "Have you ever considered a lie can be exposed to show the truth?"

"I don't know what you mean?" Kienan shrugged.

"Your lies, all this time I had you over to our house to fit things so that you and Lacey could be thrown together, and you had a baby due. All this time I told her Quinn was no good for her and all this time you were a wolf in sheep's clothing."

"Look Grand *mere*…What was I supposed to do, when Lucy came to me and told me she was pregnant with my baby. I had to do the right thing." Kienan shrugged and put his hands in his pocket. "It's killing me up inside what this is doing too Lacey."

"You should have been an honest man with Lacey, with me, with our family!" she breathed out. "At least you should have come by the house and had a bowl of gator gumbo with me. Ain't *nothing* we couldn't have talked about and solved over a bowl of my gator gumbo."

"You are so right," Kienan muttered as a fleeting sad expression came across his face.

Grand *mere* Catherine wrung her hands and breathed out slowly as she calmed herself. "Jesus, what a mess you've made Kienan." She sighed heavily. "But what's done is done. If the baby is yours you must take care of it," she breathed slowly. "But if it ain't that's another man's headache. So, when are you planning to have the genetic testing done, as soon as the baby is born?"

"What?" Kienan said with a surprised expression.

"Kienan your blank expression tells me you don't understand the situation. We old timers can do the math. Lucy is about to drop her baby any day now, which lets me know she got pregnant nine months ago.Where were you at nine months ago Kienan? Start adding up the months, you Geek King. I thought math was one of your strong subjects," she shook her head. "Do I have to do all of your thinking for you?"

Kienan's brain started thinking and then he cracked a smile. "Possibly," he said staring at her astounded.

Grand *mere* clasped her arm in his. "You know Kienan, I saw something just like this on this TV show one day, a man had been told he was the father of this child by this girl, but the man became suspicious because the cable guy kept coming over to fix the cable TV, only it wasn't broken, the man had said. So, the man put a private investigator on the two of them. Then he took the baby and got himself a genetic test one day while the woman was out playing around. And guess what? The man found out the baby wasn't his," she giggled. "Yep you should not wait on these things too long." She hesitated. "I think the law might say something like if you marry her and you let the baby reach two years old without doing the genetic test thing, the baby is yours for life," she said with a nod. "But don't quote me on that because the State of California laws change every time some new politician gets elected."

Kienan threw back his head and laughed.

Grand *mere* Catherine took a deep breath. "Yes, a lie can be exposed to reveal the truth."

Suddenly Kienan swooped Grand *mere* Catherine into a warm embrace. "That's why I love you so much Grand *mere* Kat! You always know exactly what to say."

Kienan cleared his throat as he pulled out of her embrace. The old lady was smart he thought. And he loved her like she was his own grandmother. No matter what he was going through right now he had neglected her, the family and most of all Lacey. "Look Grand *mere Kat*, if you need anything you just call me, I'll be there."

Grand *mere* Catherine smiled. "I always knew you were a very smart man Kienan."

Kienan chuckled lightly and rubbed his hand across his brow and breathed out slowly.

"So, what do you want a boy or a girl?" Grand *mere* Catherine asked curiously.

Kienan cupped his chin in his hand and shrugged. He scratched his head. "I really need to get going Grand *mere* Kat. I've got a lot of thinking to do."

He turned and walked away towards the ladies' restroom just as Lucy wobbled out.

Grand *mere* Catherine's voice called out sincerely. "Don't forget to invite us to the wedding." She called out so that Lucy could hear her.

Chapter 36

F *ace facts!*

Days later Maëlle returned Lacey's call.

"Hello Lacey, it's me Maëlle."

"Hi, there finally returning my calls.

"Actually Lacey, I'm on my cell phone and I was just pulling into your driveway. Can I come in? We need to talk."

"Sure."

Lacey walked to her front door and let Maëlle in.

"I need a drink before I tell you what has been going on. Let me at the good stuff," Maëlle said.

Lacey watched as she walked over and grabbed two glasses and poured from the Black label scotch bottle.

"Whew, hold on a minute, I never said I wanted a glass."

"Trust me Lacey you're going to need ole Johnny's help to digest what I'm about to tell you," Maëlle said handing her a glass.

Slowly Maëlle filled Lacey in on Nicholas' little investment problem.

As Maëlle talked. Lacey felt like her stomach twisted into knots. Slowly she sipped her drink and felt it relax her.

Finally, Maëlle sighed out heavily. "Gamblers gamble all the time trying to hit it big. Nicholas thought he had a sure thing, getting in on the investment at the ground floor. That's why I told my cousin Anael about the problem and he was willing to marry you and give you the money to fix Nicholas' mess. But then Quinn found out about it. And well…"

"Why are you telling me this now?"

"Because I don't know where Anael is and Nicholas is angry at me because he said I should have talked to him first about my cousin Anael's plans," Maëlle's voice was filed with anguish. "Then once Quinn found out about Anael and that he had proposed to you he got real mad. And he told Nicholas he wouldn't give him one dime of the half a million that he needed to keep his project going," she paused. "Not unless he got to sleep with you first, she choked back a sob. "And right now, I just feel so bad about everything," Maëlle sobbed out stopping short of telling her about her affair with Quinn.

Lacey blinked in astonishment at what Maëlle had told her.

Chapter 37

❧

ator Gumbo...

GSometimes the reality of life could be funny Lacey thought as she took the path that veered to the back of the house. She slowly walked up the deck of the back porch as quietly as she could, lifting her feet gently. She made her way to the back door trying not to make a sound.

The kitchen was the most unique part of the house. With its Rustic old world charm the many cabinets had faces that looked worn and weathered and added to the character of the kitchen.The cabinets had been specially designed by her father Louis.

Her grandmother stood over the stove stirring a pot with her back towards the door. "Come on into the kitchen Lacey, I heard you when your foot hit the first step." She said without turning around.

Lacey knew from years of experience her grandmother had eyes in the back of her head. "Hello Grand *mere* Catherine."

"Get back in there! You get back in that pot! You hear!" Grand *mere* Catherine yelled beating it with her spoon. "That gator tails trying to jump out of my pot," she said giggling.

"Grand *mere* Catherine remind me not to stand too close to you in a lighting storm," Lacey laughed. "By the way where is mom?"

"The Casino whores have all gone up to give their one-armed boyfriends their hard-earned money," she hesitated. Your Aunt Elise gave your mother some money."

Lacey looked up with a surprised expression. Money didn't grow on trees she knew. "Grand *mere* Catherine, if Aunt Elise was giving away money to throw away in a slot machine. Why didn't you go?"

"You know why," Grand *mere* Catherine said but kept her eyes on an envelope, she had in her hand. "I wanted to talk about it and a few other things,"

Lacey eyed the envelope curiously and noticed it was from the bank. "What's that letter about?"

Grand *mere* Catherine's expression was perplexed. "This is nothing, just some junk mail," she said putting it in her apron pocket, and then taking a turn around the kitchen busying herself cleaning off an imaginary speck of dirt from the counter. "I need to talk to you about something."

"Go on, I'm listening."

Grand *mere* Catherine stopped turned and glanced up. Her voice grew soft. "I think your brother has gotten himself into a big mess. But that's not my main concern Lacey, I'm worried about you. You've been real quite since that day you saw Kienan with that girl Lucy."

"I'm been worried about Nicholas, I heard talk that he may be in trouble with some business investment."

Grand *mere* Catherine's face grew taunt with anger. "Nicholas' ass needs to go to jail, if he's done something wrong."

Lacey's voice was hoarse with anguish. "Grand *mere* Catherine, you don't mean that."

"Does it surprise you that I feel that way Lacey?" She took a deep breath. "Your brother has been selfish and self-centered from the day he was born. Let him clean up his own mess for once. Besides, his father is going to help him."

Lacey looked up. "Grand *mere* Catherine have you seen daddy too? I know you said the dead watches the living. I saw daddy the night us five friends all went to the concert."

Grand *mere* Catherine turned and gave Lacey a strange look. "Really sweetie, you saw you father, at the concert? You didn't tell your old Grand *mere*, she said in her Cajun drawl.

All at once a light seemed to flash behind Grand *mere* Catherine's eyes. "Some big shit is about to happen now, if you ask me."

Lacey let out a deep sigh. "Oh, Grand *mere* what are we going to do?"

"Have a seat Lacey you need a bowl of my Gator Gumbo. Ain't anything Gator Gumbo can't fix?"

Chapter 38

Lucy **Mondragon**

Lucy's heels clicked across the hardwood floor as she paced around the room. The condo was decorated with warm lavish colors and an antique décor that spoke volumes about her taste.

Nervously Lucy walked over to the sofa where Kienan sat.

"Don't you like it? It's a chance to own your own home."

"But our baby should be living in her father's home." She paused. "And when are we going to get married Kienan?"

She tried to remain cool. Her baby girl had been born well over three weeks ago. Kienan hadn't looked at the baby once. "Why won't you even look at her? The way you're acting now is just plain ridiculous. For Christ's sakes she's your baby Kienan!" Lucy yelled angrily.

Kienan just sat there in silence and stared back at her. He'd long since got over the anger he felt at what Lucy had done to his life. Now he just felt sorry for her. "Maybe I should be the one asking you questions Lucy," he said coldly.

Lucy Mondragon was beautiful, and she knew it. She was the kind of woman that knew how to manipulate a man.

"Oh Kienan… I didn't mean to yell, forgive me," she cooed warmly closing the distance between them on the sofa. She pushed her body closer to his.

He wasn't responding. Lucy tried harder. She licked her lips and gave him her sad puppy face. She watched him attentively as she did. "My breasts are full and swollen with milk," she said. "You know I hear some men have fantasies about drinking breast milk. You could try it for yourself."

Kienan shook his head sadly. "You're sick Lucy, grow up. You're somebody's mother now. He moved away from her.

Lucy Mondragon looked frighten.

Kienan stood up and walked over and stared out of the window. "Lucy I never touched you before and I'm not going to touch you now."

"What is wrong Kienan?"

Kienan breathed out slowly. "Lucy I'm going to ask you one more time is there anything you want to tell me?"

Lucy shook her head. "No."

Kienan reached over and opened his brief case and retrieved an envelope from it. "You might want to change your mind after you open this."

"Whew! I'm feeling so tired right now. Look Kienan, maybe I could read this letter of yours later. It will be time for our daughter's feeding soon." Lucy said with all the dignity she could muster.

Kienan's eyebrows rose as he looked at her. "You have pumped milk in the refrigerator. The nanny can take care of her."

Lucy huffed out. "What's that letter about? Do you have my nanny spying on me?"

"Don't be stupid Lucy, just open the envelope."

Quietly she did as she was told.

"Oh my God!" Lucy grimaced.

Kienan looked directly at her. "So, Lucy do you want to tell me why you lied to me about the baby being mine?"

"Who the hell do you think you are Kienan? When did you have my baby tested?"

"And who the hell do you think you are, blackmailing me all these months?" Kienan yelled.

Lucy gasped. "My baby hasn't been out of my sight. These tests are fake."

"The hospital took care of the genetic testing a few hours after she was born." He looked at her with contempt. "Why did you lie to me Lucy? Why did you want to try and destroy me?"

Lucy Mondragon looked frighten. "The hospital could have tested the wrong baby."

Kienan tried to ignore her. "Come on Lucy you're more intelligent than that. Besides don't you think I would investigate thoroughly? He swallowed hard. "Did you do this because you knew I was in love with Lacey and you hated her for it? Or did you just want to hurt both of us"

Lucy grew silent.

"That's not how this all started," She breathed out slowly. "Being Miss San Jose doesn't make you rich overnight you know." Lucy shrugged. "I'm poor you're rich, that's really how this all got started. I needed money and I figured you would give it to me and take care of my baby."

Kienan looked at her questionably. "You know how I think this all started. I think the father of your baby started this. He told you to go after me, right?"

Lucy sat back on the couch and folded her hands. "Well…No that's not true. Maybe my own father told me to get pregnant by a rich man."

"Your father is rich. I don't think he would say that. In fact, I think he would have wanted a big wedding for you with all the glitz."

Lucy shrugged. "That was then, now my parents are broke. My father's business partner stole everything and ran off to Mexico with his mistress. And me, well I'm just a scared pregnant single mother with a new baby girl to raise all by herself," she sighed heavily.

Kienan was silent as he studied her. "So, tell me about your daughter's real father Lucy?"

"Why should I?" Lucy's voice shook with tears. "It won't get your precious Lacey back. Why don't you just stay with me and the baby? We could be a family you know."

Kienan studied her. "Well I could just dig a pit for you and your baby's father to fall into. Like say for instance I just happen to drop a line or two in the local gossip column. And let the news hit that a certain prior local beauty queen doesn't know who her baby's daddy is. The paper will run amuck desperately pleading for anyone to come forth with information."

Lucy didn't wait for him to finish. She choked out. "Her real father would not claim her, even if his life depended on it," she breathed out. "I can't believe you would do something like that Kienan. You've always been a gentleman. I was just trying to make sure my baby was taken care of," she said, lowering her head. "I'm sorry Kienan I really didn't mean to hurt you," she muttered. "I just thought a baby would make you happy and make you want to settle down."

Kienan felt sorry for Lucy. He shook his head thinking about what she had just said.

Lucy brushed at a tear running down her face. "I guess you want me to move out now," she said.

He shrugged. "No, this condo is yours."

She gasped. "What, after everything I've done to you. You're giving me the condo?"

"No," he said.

Lucy shrugged. "What then?"

"You're going to tell me the name of your baby's father. But I have a pretty good idea who it is already," he said. "Anyway, your daughter's real father is going to be paying me back for the condo, the money I've given to you and taking care of his baby."

Lucy studied him. "You're pretty sure of that aren't you? I mean you think you can get my baby's father to take care of her?" She wiped her tear stained check. "I don't think you know what you're up against.

Her father won't acknowledge her."

"Lucy let me assure you I just need you to say his name. I have a pretty good guess already. Don't worry, I'll take care of the rest," he assured her.

"That's the reason why I wanted you, to be my baby's father Kienan." She said with hopeful trusting eyes "You always were and always will be a protector of women. You remind me of that Kinsman redeemer in that bible story; you know the one, Boaz." She smiled.

"Lucy," Kienan scolded softly. "Please just tell me his name."

Embarrassed Lucy hung her head sorrowfully. "I'm ashamed," she whispered. "It could be either of two men," regret was heavy in her voice. "James...James Fairway or Quinn Rolandis, I dated both of them, at the same time."

Kienan nodded his head and smiled softly. He figured out as much. He also knew James Fairway was sterile. He couldn't have children.

Chapter 39

Pearl La Cour *& Horace Sherlock Garrison*

Pearl La Cour woke up at four o'clock that morning and gently got out of bed. She smiled softly watching Horace sleeping. He snored softly, as she put on her robe and tiptoed over to Horace's desk across the room. She was determined to open the important mail she brought from home with her. One letter looked very important. It was from The Golden California Bank and Trust.

She silently turned on the desk light and took the envelope in her hands and opened it. She read the letter.

"Oh my God…Oh my God!" Pearl cried in anguish.

Instantly Horace jolted awake and sprinted across the room. "Pearl! Pearl! What is it!

###

At noon that morning, Horace and Pearl walked arm and arm out of The Golden California Bank on First and San Fernando Street in Downtown San Jose.

Abruptly Pearl La Cour stopped and turned and stared at the man standing beside her. The slight gray at his temples made him look distinguished. "Thank you so much Horace, I don't know what I would have done if you hadn't come along."

Pearl stood there smiling at the tall man with a commanding presence. She let her fingers touch the collar of his jacket. She loved the way Horace could always make himself look impeccably dressed, when the situation called for it.

Anyone watching the mature couple knew they were in love.

Horace Sherlock Garrison knew Pearl would have never confided in him what had been in the letter from the bank earlier that morning, if he had not been with her. He would have done anything for her. But he knew the type of woman Pearl was. She was proud. She would have never asked him for a cent. He kissed her softly on the cheek.

"You know I am happy to take care of anything that concerns you Pearl."

As they walked past the parking garage Pearl stopped abruptly.

"Horace the car is parked at this garage," she said raising a quizzical brow.

"Pearl, my love I know where I parked the car. The Fountain restaurant is just there," he pointed. "I'm starved let's have breakfast."

"But Horace its lunchtime," Pearl replied.

"Pearl my love if you want lunch you can have lunch. You can have whatever you like. But me I want a good plate of grits, potatoes, ham and eggs to give me strength because today is the day, we've got to handle some serious business, and before we do that, I'm having breakfast," he winked back at her.

Pearl understood what Horace meant. She nodded her head in agreement. "You are right Horace Sherlock Garrison we need to have our strength about us."

###

Horace and Pearl ate and drank strong black coffee and sat in the window of at the Fountain Restaurant for nearly three hours.

When they first sat down, they laid out the course of action for that night. Now they sat and chitchatted about nothing and drank more coffee.

Horace sighed and looked out of the window. "What started out as a perfect day looks like it will end with a big storm rolling in tonight." His warm almond shaped eyes held Pearl's. "See those clouds rolling in the distance?" He pointed. "Maybe we should postpone…"

Pearl interrupted. "Those clouds are miles away. We are not postponing what must be done, today. Besides, we can take care of it just as soon as I get a return call."

She thought for a moment and studied Horace. Was he getting cold feet? Was the role she expected him to play too much for him? She wondered.

As if he could read her mind, "No Pearl I'm not getting cold feet. I understand my role in this, and I am here to play out my part to the fullest," he smiled. "Now come on let's go to my house and get changed. We want to be ready no matter what storm blows through."

###

Later that evening it poured rain as a storm blew in from the north.

The sudden flash of bright lights in his rear-view mirror startled him. He had forgotten he had agreed to meet his mother here. He wiped the tears from his face and cleared his throat.

Nicholas watched as the old familiar truck pulled alongside his BMW. He slowly rolled down his window.

Horace leaned his gray head out of the window and smiled gently.

"Hey Nicholas, rainy night out isn't it? I hope you haven't been waiting too long?"

Nicholas smiled back. Lately his feelings toward Horace were softening. "Hey Horace. No, I just got here," he grinned and nodded. "It is a bad night isn't it?"

Horace smiled back. "Yeah, look son lets all get into the house. It's warm there," he said opening the door of Nicholas' car.

The way Horace talked to him made Nicholas feel warm inside and filled him with a sense of wonder as he stared back into his eyes. "Sure," Nicholas said.

Pearl grabbed Nicholas' arm as they walked into the house together.

The first thing Nicholas noticed when he walked up the brick path to enter Horace Sherlock Garrison's home was that the bright porch lights seemed to welcome him as he drew near. He stepped over the threshold and a crystal chandelier spun a vortex of light in the foyer. The house looked like the ones he had seen thumbing through his mother's *Old Southern Homes* Magazine.

"Come on Nicholas Horace's office is right down this hall," Pearl said leading the way.

"Oh, Pearl I'll go and brew us that pot of tea you started earlier in the kitchen," Horace hesitated. "Unless, you want me to be present while you talk with Nicholas?"

Pearl turned and gave Horace a knowing nod. They both knew now was the time to tell him. "That will be fine Horace, it will give me and Nicholas a chance to talk. You bring the tea in when it's ready."

Nicholas stood there and studied the way his mother and Horace looked at each other. They had something special between them. He wondered why he had never seen it before.

Once in Horace's office alone with his mother Pearl, Nicholas watched her pace the floor. He knew she found out about the money he'd borrowed against the house. Today was his day of reckoning.

Nervously he thought of something to say. "Look mom if this is about the money, I got on the house I'll pay it back. I swear. My investments will more than…"

"Now is not the time to talk about your investment Nicholas," Pearl sternly replied and then choked back a sob. "Your heritage is what I wanted to talk to you about first Nicholas."

"My heritage? Okay mom what is it you're trying to say?"

Pearl drew in a quick breath. "It's a mess Nicholas and I'm not talking about what you did with the house with that money loan," she said. "I'm talking about the mess I made of my life and yours." She sniffed back tears.

Nicholas walked over and retrieved a box of tissue from a table. "Can't be as bad as what I've done." He tried to smile to cheer her up.

"I had hoped that over the years maybe your father Louis had talked with you about something… Maybe me for instance," she asked and dabbed at her nose with the tissue Nicholas had offered.

Nicholas shrugged. "What do you mean?"

"Oh, it's just as well. Louis said he would never tell you. He'd leave it up to me," she shook her head sadly.

Nicholas felt sorry for his mother. Something big was troubling her.

Pearl breathed out slowly. "I…I have a secret."

"Who doesn't?" Nicholas shook his head.

Pearl continued. "You know your father Louis was a wonderful man. A wonderful man…"

The moment was tense.

Nicholas cleared his throat.

Pearl continued. "Your father was smart too," she said trying to buy herself some time. "Did you know your fingertips can activate the drawers in Louis' old desk?"

Nicholas gasped his eyes darted to look back at his mother. "You knew about that mother?"

Pearl cleared her throat. Her nervousness subsided.She looked closely at him. "I don't know why I'm telling you all of this. I guess I just hope to prolong what I really want to say," she said. "I'm so sorry for laying this all on you this way. Your father had a secret or two and so did I. Well I had one secret and that was you. Nicholas I was pregnant with you when I married Louis and he knew…"

Nicholas stared straight ahead not daring to look at his mother. He rubbed his face. "I think you're trying to say Louis wasn't my father. I guess I kind of knew."

"I suspected you knew," Pearl said. "Children can always tell when something is just different." She hesitated. "You weren't Louis' biological son."

Nicholas closed his eyes. He always knew it. He could just tell. Now hearing it from his mother hurt. He felt the tears form in his eyes.

Pearls words tumbled out nervously. "But Louis loved you like you were his own…"

The tears rolled down her face.

Pearl looked up into her son's face. "Nicholas please try to understand. I was just a baby myself when I got pregnant with you. I was too young," she hung her head. "My parents threaten to take you away from me.And the man I loved. Well he was just a boy himself. He was with me when you were born, and we put his name on your real birth certificate."

"What? I can't believe it. The only birth certificate I ever saw had Louis' name on it," Nicholas said his voice was flat.

"It's all true," Pearl said. "Horace and I were only fifteen when you were conceived. And Louis was older. He had inherited pretty much the whole town where we lived so I guess someone alerted him when I had you. Anyway, all of a sudden, Horace's father got a job in Berkley California and his parents took him away. When they moved away you and I were left all alone. I was so scared Nicholas. I did what I thought was right for both of us." Her words tumbled out in broken sobs. "Louis said he loved me… He said if I didn't marry him people might try and take you away from me because I was so young," she sobbed out slowly. "So, Nicholas I did what I thought was best, so that I could keep you, I married Louis La Cour."

Nicholas eyed his mother for a moment. He remembered how overpowering his father Louis La Cour's personality could be especially when Louis wanted things done his way.

Pearl swallowed hard. "Louis was very clever. He fixed everything he even made you a second birth certificate to show he was your father. But I hid the original. It was mine. My parents and Horace's may have taken your father away from me. But they couldn't take my proof that Horace was your father."

Nicholas wiped his face with his hands. "So many things make sense now," he paused and lowered his tone. "He couldn't be mad at her. Pearl was just a child herself when all of this happened to her."

Pearl cried hard. It took time to compose herself.

Finally, Pearl breathed out slowly and told her story as her tears flowed. All that Nicholas really remembered was hearing his mother sob. "Nicholas can you forgive me for not telling you any of this. But you see, I promised Louis I wouldn't because he said he wanted to do it when the time was right. I felt I owed him that since he stepped up and became my husband and your father. And he kept his word," she sobbed. "Please forgive me Nicholas. I was young…I was too young… I made a mistake that could have ruined both our lives. I did what I thought was right," she sobbed. "Please forgive me. I swear I thought only of you." She started crying again.

Nicholas opened his eyes and turned to stare at his mother. Watching her cry broke something deep inside of him. "Don't cry mommy, please don't cry." He said pulling his mother into his arms and crying with her.

Several minutes' later Pearl pulled back and studied Nicholas' face.

"I always knew mamma," Nicholas said. "You were right I just always had a feeling. Not that my father… I mean Louis ever did anything or said anything… I just knew."

Pearl hung her head.

Nicholas cleared his throat. "Mom you said Dad… I mean Louis had secrets too. You told me yours please… I've got to know. What was his? What was dad's secret?"

Pearl blinked several times her face sobered. "Once when I was feeling really bad about having you so young and the secret surrounding your birth Louis told me not to be angry at myself because everyone had secrets. Everyone made mistakes. Then he told me that he had had a child by a girl when he was in college. We were both only human," Pearl shrugged and then continued.

A frown creased Nicholas' brow. "My father Louis had an affair with a young woman he went to college with?"

"Yes," Pearl said. "And they had a child."

Nicholas rubbed his brow and breathed out slowly."Whew! Man! Talk about some drama," he said. "So, mom what do I have a sister? Or a brother? How old are they?"

Pearl shook her head. "That, I don't know, Nicholas. Louis never told me. But I suspect your Grand *mere* Catherine knows. She knows everything."

Nicholas stared across the room at a gold framed gilded mirror. "Mom, one more thing, Horace is my father, right?"

Pearl shrugged. "Didn't you ever look hard in the mirror Nicholas? You look just like him."

"Now that I'm staring at my face in the mirror, I can see the resemblance," Nicholas shook his head. "Damn, I look so much like Horace. Hell, I'm pretty good looking," he said rubbing his chin. "I can't believe I never noticed before."

Pearl and Nicholas laughed together.

Then Nicholas hesitated. "Mom I've got to ask you one more thing."

"Sure Nicholas."

"The money I borrowed you said we'd talk about it later. What happened? How am I ever going to raise the half million dollars I need to pay back."

Pearl shrugged and gazed across the room.

Nicholas' eyes followed her gaze. He watched Horace carefully as he walked into the room with the tea tray and put it down.

Pearl took a deep breath and asked anxiously."Well Nicholas why don't you ask Horace how he parlayed that money that you owed into a financial win for the both of you. You might want to talk to your real father about how you plan to pay him back?"

Nicholas turned and eyed Horace. This was his heritage. This was his real father.

The tension in Horace's face was real. "Can I get you a cup of tea son?"

"No dad but I think I'd like to give you a thank you hug for saving my ass. Now I know why you were always nice to me all of these years."

Nicholas and Horace embraced warmly. "Well Nicholas you might not want to thank me after you learn how I plan for you to pay back the money."

"No problem Horace, but since you and mom laid a lot on me today, I hope the two of you won't mind if I skip out on having a cup of tea. I've got a lot on my mind right now."

"No problem Nicholas, I understand and I'm sure you mother does too," Horace said never taking his eyes off of his son.

Nicholas reached out and hugged Horace again and then pulled his mother into an embrace. "Mom I want you and Horace to be happy. I just need a little alone time to digest all of this if you don't mind."

"Sure, Nicholas you take all the time you need son," Pearl said. "Come, Horace and I will walk you to your car."

A few minutes later Pearl and Horace watched Nicholas' car until it drove out of sight.

Chapter 40

The Grandmothers Knows...

The next hour flew like a blur, as Nicholas headed to his family's home. His sister Lacey was standing on the back porch when he made his way around the back.

"Nicholas, where have you been?" Lacey called out.

"Oh shit!" Nicholas exclaimed walking closing the distance between them. "Lacey you won't believe what I've been through these last few weeks or what I just heard a while ago," he said choosing his words carefully. "But this evening I got a bomb dropped on me like you wouldn't believe," he exclaimed.

"Shhhhh Nicky keep your voice down."

Nicholas laughed out. "Hump, I'm happy and confused right now. Oh, by the way Lacey you need to get a hold of Kienan and give him another chance. Some of the things going on in his life right now ain't his fault," he chuckled. "Talk about that Lucy Mondragon now there's a woman who can keep a secret. Hell, what am I saying? Lucy ain't the only woman that can keep a secret our mother and your grandmother are some of the best secret keeping women in this whole wide world!"

"Nicky, I told you to keep it down," Lacey whispered.

Instantly the kitchen door opened. "Nicholas, I thought I heard you out here. Boy get yourself into this kitchen."

Lacey leaned over and whispered in a disapproving voice. "I tried to tell you to keep it down. Grand *mere* Catherine's got company."

"Who?"

"Wait and see," Lacey said nudging Nicholas toward the kitchen door.

"Nicholas where is my grandson Quinn Darnell Rosolado Rolandis? Quinn's grandmother Ina asked with a heavy Spanish accent, "Where you find you, you find him," she said in broken English.

"Damn!" Nicholas sighed.

"Nicholas you know I don't allow no cursing, now sit down at the table."

Lacey shot Nicholas a glance that said kill me now. She leaned over and whispered. "Well Nicky, these two old girls have been whispering together like crazy, for the last few hours. I wonder what they've got to say. This really is a strange day."

Nicholas looked between the two elderly old women and just knew. They didn't have to say a word.

"Sorry Grand *mere* Catherine, no can do. I'm supposed to be someplace else right now. And Lacey is too. He said suddenly grabbing his sister's hand.

"Come on Lacey we got somewhere we should be."

Lacey thought for a moment. "No, I don't Nicky."

"Trust me Lacey you do! Don't worry I'll drive you."

###

By the time they made it to Kienan house Lacey was dumbfounded. "Nicky you must have lost your mind, Kienan and I are not on speaking terms."

Nicholas nodded. "Yeah, I'm kind of, sort of a little responsible for that," he mumbled low.

"What?" Lacey asked guilelessly.

"Well the thing is I had my eyes opened to the real truth. You and Kienan were meant to be together. Somehow me and my grand schemes got in the way of that," Nicholas shyly grinning. "Do you want me to try and tell you all about it?"

Lacey shook her head. "For some reason Nicholas now is not the time."

"I agree," he said pulling into the driveway and honking his horn loudly. But there was no need. Kienan stood on the side waiting anxiously.

Kienan opened Lacey's car door and she looked into his gray eyes. The pain she saw in them ran deep and it gave her the answers she sought.

"Lacey, I'm couldn't believe it when Nicholas phoned and said he was bringing you over."

"Yeah it caught me by surprise too. What is this?" She asked as he placed a plain brown paper bag in her hand.

"I didn't have time to really get you something to say how sorry I was for everything, so I rushed down to the Seven Eleven and bought you a bag of your favorite."

Lacey reached into the brown paper bag and all her anger against him instantly dissolved. "You brought me a bag of Hersey kisses," she cried joyfully.

Kienan's eyes watered with tears. "My Lacey…My beautiful Lacey please forgive me. I was wrong the way I broke up with you in college. I was wrong for not explaining to you about everything that's been happening." His voice shook.

Her eyes beamed with tears. "I know Nicky told me on the way over here that Lucy's baby wasn't yours and that she had lied to you on purpose to break us up," her words tumbled out. "Oh Kienan, I've been wrong too."

The two lovers stood there under the moonlight and stared back at each other.

Suddenly Lacey quickly rushed into Kienan's arms and leaned her head against his chest.

Nicholas chuckled watching them from his car. "Now you two are getting somewhere."

Kienan hugged Lacey tight. "I've just been wrong. I'll always be wrong as long as I'm without you," he murmured softly. "I need you in my life for the rest of my life Lacey."

He nuzzled her neck and kissed her. "I'm going to hold you tight like this until you forgive me."

"You know I can't resist when you talk to me like that. You're forgiven," she said losing the battle to resist him. His brazen kiss proved to her beyond a doubt how much she meant to him.

They devoured each other with their insatiable need for each other.

"I love you Lacey, I always have," Kienan said as he kissed her.

"You'd better," she said playfully.

Nicholas gunned his engine. "Well I guess my work here is done. I'll see you two later," he said backing his car out of the driveway and driving away from the curb.

Finally, Kienan broke the silence. "Lacey would you like to go inside?"

"Kienan I thought you'd never ask."

They held each other tight as they walked inside and closed the door.

Chapter 41

At just past ten o'clock, the next night miles away in Oakland, Nicholas watched the soft light mist that seemed more like fog than rain, as he leaned over the railing of the boat pier at Jack London square. He blew out a long breath watching the lone boat coming in. It seemed strange that it had been the only one he'd seen for hours as he stood there. The boat that slowly pulled in front of him was beautiful. He turned his head to see the name written on the back of it.

A tinkling sound like crystal bells filled the air. "Believe in Angels, what a name for a yacht," a heavy Irish accent voice called out.

Nicholas looked up quickly. He murmured under his breath. "Another bum."

The old man closed the distance between them and joined Nicholas leaning against the railing.

For some reason the old man didn't make Nicholas feel uneasy. He stood there beside him for several minutes in silence.

The old man lifted his hand reaching into his jacket. His ghostly hand glowed in the dark night.

Nicholas turned his head to keep from staring.

The old man cleared his throat. "When a man gets older, he gets smarter and wiser, don't you think?" The old man cleared his throat. "There's no need for you to respond son, I'm just speaking out loud to no one in particular."

Nicholas was glad that it was dark. He could not see the old man's face. His words caused him to think. He spoke out loud without realizing it. "Some men get smarter. Others keep on making the same stupid mistakes; I know I'm one of them."

The old man shrugged. "No…No I think you may be too hard on yourself, son. You look like a man that's done a good deed lately. Want to tell me about it?"

The old man was easy to talk to, Nicholas cleared his throat and continued. "Yeah maybe you're right. Yesterday I did get my sister back with this Geeky best friend of mine who's been in love with her since forever," he grinned. "And I know she's been in love with him forever too."

The old man chuckled softly, "See my son; I can tell a man who's done a good deed or two."

Nicholas breathed slowly, "Perhaps…"

"Tell me what is wrong my son?"

The old man felt safe to be around. He made Nicholas believe in miracles. Nicholas smiled softly, "I guess I just can't get over my family? My family kept secrets."

The old man stared ahead. "Huh, sounds to me like somebody got the courage to tell you about their secrets. That took a lot of strength to do that," he said. "You know this life doesn't come with an instruction book. Maybe your family kept secrets from you because they loved you."

"Maybe," Nicholas breathed out.

The old man's manners were gentle, kind and regal. "Men are weak my son. It doesn't mean your father didn't love you because he didn't tell you he was your true father. Maybe he didn't tell you because he was scared. Women have all the strength. In mind, soul and heart," he said." He clasped his hands together almost like he was praying.

"Be open to forgiving others for the mistakes they made. In the end it's all just really about the love

"Are you praying?"

"Forgiveness is real," the old man said.

Nicholas pulled his jacket closer. It was really cold out to night. "Yeah, I suppose, I could tell my mother was being truthful when she told me who my real father was. And I do look just like Horace the man who is my biological father. But Louis, he was my father, the one that raised me and is listed on my birth certificate. Well he and I we just never seemed to get along," he paused. "In fact, I was arguing with him hours before he passed away. And I remembered what he kept saying. *Take care of your sister Lacey she doesn't know and keep her safe.* At first it didn't make sense and then when I saw my Grand *mere* Catherine and Mrs. Ina sitting in the kitchen I knew, and everything made sense."

"It's never too late to ask the ones you love for forgiveness." He said. "Never turn your back on your family. They are all that you have. No matter what secrets they hold or that they've told you. They were probably only thinking of you when they told them." The old man shrugged. "Son never be afraid to protect the females in the family predators and vermin. Too bad *Jack London* didn't do a damn thing about the rat population in his day."

Nicholas frowned. He was certain now the old man had to be crazy.

The night was eerie quiet.

Nicholas stood there lost in his thoughts. After several minutes he checked his watch and stepped back from the railing. "And then all at once he remembered the old man had mentioned Louis not being his true father before he'd even told him his story. How had he known, he wondered and turned to look back at the old man

All at once loud violent gun shoots pierced the air.

"They are shooting at us. Duck for cover my son," the old man yelled. "Tell *Jack London* to get his gun."

Nicholas jumped and dived low. He lay crouched down on the

ground.The old man laid right beside him. He wasn't slow on his feet.

Nicholas found himself staring back at deep emerald pools of green. Green eyes studied him. "Are you okay son?"

Nicholas stared back trying to remember where he'd seen those familiar green eyes before. Quickly he pulled himself up. He was amazed at how fast the old man followed his lead.

"Watch out, there's a rat right over there," the old man declared. His teeth were glistening white, "This town is overrun by rats. But then again, it's overrun by gun fire too. Maybe somebody was just shooting at a rat."

Nicholas just stared back at him in disbelief.

"Rats don't just crawl in back alleys and gutters you know.Rats are everywhere!" The old man shook his head, "Some rats even have human bodies, did you know? Vermin are everywhere. Sometimes they stick closer than a brother and that's the worse rat of them all."

Nicholas looked on in silence.

"Be careful son and know your friends. They are never the most honest and sincerest until they are betraying us." The old man said as he pointed. "Look there's a rat there!"

Nicholas looked where he pointed. When he turned back the old man was gone.

Nicholas felt like he could really use a drink.

###

At just past midnight night Nicholas sat in Sam's place at the bar. He had been lucky he found a seat.

Sam's place was packed tight that night.

He waited patiently for Quinn to come over. He checked in the mirror in front of him. He saw Quinn behind him talking to a man.

The two exchanged looks through the mirror.

His cell phone humming vibration and flashing blue light signaled an incoming call.

He checked the number. It was his sister, Lacey.

"Hello," Nicholas yelled into the phone.

"Hi Nicky, it's me Lacey. I was worried about you. Where are you?"

"Lacey don't worry, I'm fine," he replied. "Are you still at Kienan's?"

"Yes, I want to thank you Nicky for getting me and Kienan back together."

"That's what big brothers are for," he said.

"Oh, Nicky we are all going to have Sunday brunch at home. Please be there okay? And stop and get Grand *mere* her favorite bottle of wine," Lacey said.

"Lacey you think you are slick.I know you are asking me to bring the wine to make sure I'm there but no worries I wouldn't miss being there."

"Good, then I'll see you tomorrow. Good-bye Nicky," Lacey said and hung up.

When Nicholas hung up, he looked up and caught Quinn staring back at him. He hoped Quinn hadn't heard who he was talking to.

Suddenly he stared back at Quinn astonished as flickering orbs of light appeared again.

Quinn saw Nicholas staring and quickly came over with a bottle in hand.

"What's wrong with you Nicholas? What are you staring at?" Quinn's voice shouted. He tossed back his drink.

Nicholas took another swallow of bourbon. This time the warm liquid made him feel a little strange. He stared back into the mirror. All at once a shiver ran down his spine. He stared as smoky white misty orbs of light shifted rapidly before his eyes.

Nicholas rubbed his eyes and blinked hard several times trying to focus. The images disappeared. He gazed back at the mirror again. He saw a blue light flashing brightly in the mirror right next to his drink.

His cell phone humming vibration and flashing blue light signaled an incoming call.

He checked the number it was his sister, Lacey again.

"Hello," Nicholas yelled into the phone. "Lacey let me call you back, I can't hear a thing."

Nicholas quickly looked up. He caught Quinn staring back at him.

He was astonished. The flickering orbs of light appeared again. This time they surrounded Quinn. Startled, he was sure he gasped out loud.

Quinn saw Nicholas staring and quickly came over with a bottle in hand.

"What's wrong with you Nicholas? What are you staring at?" Quinn's voice shouted. He tossed back his drink.

Nicholas watched Quinn pour another glass.

Quinn's eyes darted nervously. "Stop staring at me like that Nicholas!"

Nicholas averted his eyes and tried to think of something to say. "Sam said to always keep the bottle out of sight Quinn."

Quinn swayed then took the bar seat next to Nicholas. "So, what, Sam ain't the boss of me."

The two exchanged looks.

"To what extent do I owe you the pleasure of my company, Nicholas? Did you bring that little whore playing hard to get sister of yours here for me to fuck? You know I ain't going to give you one cent of my money to help you with your little problem."

"Just shut up Quinn, you're drunk!"

"No, you shut up Nicholas! You're the one with the money problem and I've got the money," Quinn let out a sinister chuckle. "And once I've I fucked that stupid bitch of a sister of yours maybe I will give you some of my money, and maybe I'll let you watch just like I did with me and Luscious."

"Shut up Quinn. I won't ever let you degrade Lacey."

The two exchanged looks.

"Dammit Nicholas, why have you suddenly changed?" he downed another drink. "You promised me Lacey was mine! And I can't even get to first base with her."

Quinn chuckled lightly. "Get out of my way Nicholas. I'm going to go find your sister and fuck her right now. I'll make your sister sorry for making me feel like shit! And you can't stop me!"

Nicholas rose with determination.

Quinn chuckled. "You want to fight me Nicholas? Because I sure as hell want to kick your ass," he exclaimed lunging.

Nicholas ducked quickly and shot out a quick left. It made contact immediately with Quinn's jaw. Quinn went crashing to the floor.

"You Gator back bastard!" Quinn yelled as he crawled out of Nicholas' distance.

People moved hurriedly out of the way.

A redhead woman laughed out loudly. "Quinn you look like a real man crawling around on your knees."

"You look just like a woman giving head." A blond woman yelled laughing.

"Fuck you Jellie-Ann. You can't laugh at nobody. What kind of fucking mother names their kid Jellie-Ann?" Quinn burst out laughing.

All at once Rémi Mae kicked Quinn in the rear. "Somebody should just break the bastard's neck."

"Rémi Mae you ought to be ashamed at yourself for kicking a man when he's down," someone laughed out behind her.

A chorus of laughter followed.

A cold stern voice sliced the air, "Nicholas and Quinn what the hell are you two doing fighting in my place?" Sam bellowed making his way forward. "You two have been best friends for years. What's gotten into you?"

Quinn's voice trembled, "He started it," he cried out like a spoiled child crying to his parent.

Nicholas looked up at Sam, "I'm so sorry Sam."

Quinn took advantage of Nicholas' distraction and swung out with fury.

Nicholas blocked Quinn's blow. Powered with his left and sent Quinn flying.

Sam's voice sliced the air. "Quinn and Nicholas stop fighting in my place now!"

Nicholas took a step back.

"Quinn, get up off my floor," Sam said. "You two take this shit outside!"

Nicholas slowly walked toward the door as Quinn followed.

A woman touched his shoulder, "Hey Nicholas you come back and see old Rémi Mae any time. Rémi Mae likes a man who's big and strong and knows how to whoop Quinn's ass."

Outside in the cold night air Nicholas' head seemed clearer.

For the first time Nicholas realized he was more mature than Quinn. He never noticed it before. He shook his head. "Look Quinn man I'm sorry for those things I said back there. Sam's right. We've been friends for too long. We both need to apologize," he said. "I've just been having one crazy night."

Quinn rubbed his jaw. "You know the trouble with you Nicholas," he said. "You had too much. A father who loved you…You had everything. My father never acknowledged me. And still you're just spoiled and selfish," he said ruthlessly.

Quinn's revelation was a news flash for Nicholas. He'd never seen this side of Quinn before. Plus, he realized Quinn still didn't know. "Look Quinn, I never knew that. Man, I'm sorry to hear it. For what it's worth, I'm proud of you Quinn, you and all that you've accomplished."

Quinn swallowed hard at his words. Nicholas' revelation caught him off guard. "I appreciate…Thanks Nicholas."

The soft humming noise of Nicholas' cell phone quickly filled the air.

Nicholas looked at the display on his phone and glanced up at Quinn. "Let me answer this Quinn, its Lacey calling again."

At the sound of Lacey's name Quinn's ears perked up. "Sure, go ahead," Quinn said.

"Hello Lacey? What's that?I can't hear you. There is some crazy gibberish coming through your cell phone right now." Nicholas nervously said. "Lacey don't cry. I'm okay I swear. I'll be home soon." He paused. "Please don't cry."

Quinn watched Nicholas out of the corner of his eye.

Nicholas swallowed hard. "I can't understand you Lacey, too much gibberish on this line. Look, just know I love you. I'll call you back later and check on you. When I have a better connection," he yelled. "I love you Lacey; I'm hanging up now."

Nicholas stood there and studied Quinn and rubbed his brow. Earlier he'd seen something flash in Quinn's eyes.

Quinn studied Nicholas. "So…Where is Lacey?"

"I don't know Quinn I couldn't understand a word she was saying." Nicholas hoped Quinn couldn't see the lie he told.

Nicholas turned and looked at Quinn. The streetlight shone in Quinn's face revealing truths Nicholas had been too blind to see. He could see the resemblance. At that moment the shadows from the streetlight were playing tricks on his eyes. In the darkened night Nicholas focused his eyes and shuddered. It looked like a man was standing next to Quinn. And then all at once the man vanished in front of his eyes.

Rattled, Nicholas suddenly sucked in a deep breath.

"What are you staring at Nicholas?" Quinn whispered.

"I swear a man was standing next to you Quinn."

Quinn shrugged. "Stop it Nicholas, you and I both just had too much to drink."

Nicholas rubbed his face and thought. He'd come to a hurdle and everything flashed before his eyes. The deep greens eyes of his father Louis kept flashing back at him and then he recalled the knowing look Grand *mere* Catherine and Mrs. Ina gave him. Mrs. Ina was Quinn's grandmother. And then he remembered what his father Louis kept saying over and over to him. You are the one I raised to be responsible, like me Nicholas. And then it was as if Nicholas heard his father Louis' voice.

"You see that boy over there," Louis said to Nicholas. "One day you will understand why he is always over here at your home and why I keep the three of you close."

Then suddenly Nicholas said."It's over Quinn!" he exclaimed. "You can't have Lacey because Lacey is your sister. That's why the three of us have been raised together like brothers and sister. Because that is what we are."

Quinn's twisted smile grew faint."What…What are you talking about Nicholas? That's ridiculous."

All at once Nicholas gasped as his eyes caught sight of Louis' ghost. "Didn't you see him Quinn? Look its Louis!"

Scared Quinn stepped away from Nicholas a short distance. His eyes held a deep concern. "Nicholas we've been friends for far too long. I'm not arguing with you anymore tonight," Quinn said clearing his throat. "I think you and I both had too much to drink."

"No Quinn I swear, there's a man standing behind you."

Quinn looked beside him. There was no one standing there. "I'm out of here Nicholas," he said turning to walk away.

Chapter 42

❧

I promised always...

Hours later, Nicholas stood there overlooking the Pacific Ocean. It always calmed him. He remembered an old Cherokee prayer that said you could wash your spirit clean if you prayed by the ocean. He hoped it was true. He just finished saying a prayer. He looked around. He stood alone. He looked to his right and he could see the outline of Golden Gate Fields.

His thoughts were clear now. In a few hours' dawn would break. He felt it was time he headed home and cleaned up his life.

He walked back to his BMW and started the engine. The bright display lights of his cell phone flashed boldly. He'd missed eight calls. All of them were from his grandmother. He knew he'd better call her back or he might live to regret it.

He gunned his engine and made his way down Buchanan Street and on to Gilman Street and eased on to highway 80. The connection to highway 880 loomed in front of him.

In just under thirty minutes he approached the Alvarado Niles Canyon Road exit in Fremont. It was the short cut home. He quickly made the connection.

Before he knew it the twisting, mountainous road ascended higher.

The Oak, Sycamore and Eucalyptus trees took on an eerie effect in the moonlight.The forest land grew dense and thick as a soft rain began to fall. It grew misty in seconds. Deep pockets of foggy mist circled around him.

Nicholas felt strange. He felt like something was chasing him. But nothing was behind him. He checked his mirror again. No car was in sight. He shook his head trying to clear his thoughts.

Suddenly out of nowhere the car lights loomed in his rear-view mirror. Nicholas glanced back. He accelerated. The car behind him did the same. He looked down at his speedometer. It read ninety. All at once the car behind him got real close.

Nicholas glanced back again. The car was right on his tail.

The road ahead took a sharp right turn. Nicholas took it with ease. The car behind him didn't miss a beat.

The road up ahead climbed higher.Nicholas pushed his gas pedal, the speedometer read 100. He was sure to lose the car now.

Even doing 100 the car was gaining on him. He looked back. The car was still on his tail. He sped up faster.

Suddenly as Nicholas drove higher the foggy mist turned into white thick clouds around him.

The atmosphere grew strange.

The landscape unraveled into a blur and everywhere looked like a dream. He checked his mirror. The car lights behind him had disappeared. Good thing he knew the road, he thought. Just ahead was a turn.

He felt like he was dreaming; only he was driving. The fog seemed like a cloud. Nicholas slowed down more as he descended off the mountain.

He checked his mirror. The car lights behind him had disappeared. He smiled. He was glad.

Slowly Nicholas breathed out a sigh of relief. His heart was beating fast. He could not believe this was happening to him. He needed to call someone. He pressed the phone feature on his blue tooth phone and he pressed the button.

"Call Kienan Egan," Nicholas called out trying to keep his voice cool.

It answered on the second ring.

"Hello," Kienan said groggily turning on the light beside his bed.

All at once the car came back out of nowhere and was on his bumper. "Kienan!"

"Hello Nicholas, what's the matter?"

"Some guy is chasing me, and I don't know why."

"Where are you?"

"Somewhere at the top of Niles Canyon."

"Hang on I'll call the cops on my other line," Kienan commanded.

At that moment something caught Nicholas' attention out of the corner of his eye.

Nicholas tilted his head and looked at the empty passenger seat beside him. He gasped as a brilliant white orb light descended from thin air. The light settled into the seat beside him.

Suddenly the mystical light descended into an apparition. The light became like a human form.

Nicholas' teeth chattered "What the…!"

"I am proud of you my son!"

"Dad? How did you get here?"

"I promised your mother I would love you always," the apparition that was Louis replied. "Now look at me my son!"

Nicholas didn't want to take his eyes off the road. He looked up suddenly and slammed on his brakes.

"I said look at me my son!" Louis' voice commanded.

"Holy shit!" Nicholas yelled hysterical.

"Nicholas! Nicholas!" Kienan screamed into the receiver.

Chapter 43

Someplace over the rainbow...

It had rained hard since Lacey had come to the emergency room at *Alexian Brothers Hospital.* She couldn't stand not knowing if Nicholas would be alright.Lacey nudged herself awake and slipped her hand into the arm next to her.

She looked up and her eyes met Kienan's. "Thanks again for being here." She mumbled softly.

He smiled back. "You know I couldn't leave you."

Lacey turned and focused her eyes across from her. Her mother Pearl sat with her head lying on Horace Garrison shoulder fast asleep and her Grand *mere* Catherine was on Horace's other shoulder, all three were still asleep.

The double doors of the emergency room flew open and a young doctor strolled through. His name tag read Dr. J Santana. His face showed no indication of his patient's injuries. He walked directly over to Pearl.

"Mrs. La Cour…Mrs. La Cour," Dr. Santana said clearing his throat. "Your son is going to be fine. He has a broken arm, a cracked rib, and some head trauma, from his head hitting the windshield. And because of that we want to watch him. He was lucky, as if he had an angel watching over him."

Pearl rose anxiously. "Can we please see him now?" Her panic-stricken face echoed the sadness in her heart.

"Yes, you can go in and see him," Dr. Santana looked between the gathering before him. "If you don't mind, just three of you at a time."

Hours later it seemed like time took forever Lacey thought. But it was finally her time to see Nicholas. She reached back and grabbed Kienan's hand.

"You're family too. You are going with me," she smiled gently.

"Sure," Kienan assured her. He hugged her lightly.

Minutes later, Lacey looked back at her brother sleeping quietly.

Lacey wept openly. "I love you Nicholas, you gator back butthead, don't ever scare me like that again and please, whatever you do, don't die and leave me…Please don't leave me," she pleaded sobbing openly.

Slowly Nicholas opened his eyes. "Hey, is that you half angel? I ain't dead yet," Nicholas whispered faintly. "And what did I tell you about calling me gator back? You know I'm sensitive about my birthmark," his smile was faint.

Lacey looked back at him. "Oh Nicky."

"Where's the Geek King Kienan?"

"I'm right here," Kienan said.

"Move in a little closer so I can see you, man. These nurses have got all this bandage stuff over my head because of the cut I got on my forehead, like a couple stitches needs a big bandage like this," Nicholas said.

Kienan placed his hand on Nicholas' arm. "I'm so glad you're going to be alright Nicholas."

"Yeah, but I'm going to have a scar on my forehead from the gash. Anyway, thanks man. Now you and Lacey pull up a chair, I've got a story to tell you."

"Nicky you should get some rest," Lacey replied.

"No, I've got to tell you this story," and then Nicholas repeated what had happened to him on the top of Niles Canyon Road.

###

After visiting with Nicholas, Lacey and Kienan walked out of his hospital room and headed for the elevator.

"Lacey and Kienan come here," Grand *mere* Catherine softly called.

Lacey closed the distance between them. "Where are Mom and Horace?"

"Horace took your mother home," Grand *mere* hesitated. "There's something I have to tell you. Quinn is here in the ICU."

All at once a little gray-haired old lady walked up to them.

Grand *mere* Catherine turned and looked at Kienan. "This is Quinn's grandmother, Mrs. Ina Rosolado."

Ina Rosolado walked over her eyes filled with tears. "Today is a very sad," she said in her broken English.

Her voice shook.

Grand *mere* Catherine turned her attention. "Kienan I have a favor to ask again. Would you be so kind and go down to the cafeteria and get two old ladies a strong cup of coffee?"

"Sure," Kienan said

She watched as he walked away.

Ina Rosolado eyes brimmed with tears. "Lacey...Lacey please my child needs you," she choked out. "I promised Quinn I would bring you to him. He asked to see you," her eyes softly pleaded. "I... I beg of you. Do this for me."

Lacey's heart broke watching Ina Rosolado cry. "Sure Mrs. Rosolado I will come."

-

-

-

Minutes later, Lacey stood silently by Quinn's hospital bed.

The stark white interior of the room looked just like Nicholas' room.

Her eyes followed the lines of tubing connecting Quinn to the numerous life supporting machines. She listened to the soft rhythmic bleeping of the monitoring machine and watched as Quinn laid there in the hospital bed, looking as if he was just sleeping.

Lacey moved closer to his bedside and her fingers went out to touch his hand. His touch was indifferent and unfeeling. No warmth or human feelings flowed.But he was alive. She could feel the pulse in his hand.

All at once she felt herself gasp as she felt like Quinn's internal being was trying to make a connection with her mind.

Quinn's lips never moved. Nor did any facial expression creep across his face.

Lacey stood there looking down at Quinn as if she was stuck to the spot by some invisible force.

"I've been waiting for you to come, Lacey." Quinn spoke to her mind soul to soul. Lacey watched again, checking to see if Quinn's lips were moving. They never did. Nor did his eyes ever open.

Then mysteriously Quinn continued to talk to her. "Continents don't exist in the mind. That's why I can talk to you. There is no distance or barrier between two close souls."

Quickly Lacey looked around the room to look for grandmother. She stood right next to Quinn's grandmother. "Grand *mere* did you hear something."

"That's just the soul man talking," she said. "Be quiet and listen Lacey."

The room was eerie and quiet.

"Only you can hear me Lacey," Quinn's voice said again. Lacey looked down at Quinn his eyes were still closed, and he still looked like he was in a comatose state.

"Come closer Lacey I need you to do something for me," Quinn's voice said again.

Lacey wasn't afraid. She didn't know why.She leaned in closer to Quinn's bedside and stared down at him. She looked attentively at him as if waiting for him to speak again.

"I didn't want to believe it when Nichols told me that we were brother and sister. I guess by now you know my love spell on you didn't work on you. Our blood lines were too close."

Lacey spoke in her mind and felt her words easily being understood by Quinn."Now that I've thought about it more, you always did seem like my brother Quinn," she couldn't believe they were communicating like this. She wondered if she had a gift like Grand *mere* Catherine. "Where are you Quinn? Why are you telling me this? Why don't you wake up?" She asked him with her mind.

"Please don't ask so many questions," he said again speaking with his mind. "Don't you understand? Louis loved Nicholas as his son. I could never take that place. So, I tried to kill Nicholas. That is why I'm in this place. I hurt myself trying to hurt him. The love spell and a few other things that I've done have backfired."

And then Lacey thought back to something her grandmother had said. "Grand *mere* Catherine said something bad was about to happen. Maybe she can help you Quinn."

"This is the best thing to happen to me. So that I don't do it again," his voice seemed to echo faintly. "I…never learned what I was supposed to learn on this earth. You know how to forgive; therefore, I must go back. In fact, I'll have to go back in a minute."

"Where is this place?" She felt her mind ask.

"Oh, somewhere over the rainbow I call it a holding place, sort of like the sea of heaven. It's where the souls live." Quinn's mind spoke back to her as he caringly said. "They let me keep my favorite memory." His mind seemed to smile back at her. "I bet you don't know what that is."

"No, Quinn, I don't. What is it?" Lacey's mind quickly spoke back to him.

"The one when you danced with me. You taught me how to slow dance, remember? It was the day Kienan had to miss practice. You wanted to practice so you let me practice with you. I held you close, and we slow danced. It's my best memory."

Lacey could feel the sting of tears. She remembered that day. She'd only practice with Quinn so that she could get better and know the steps when Kienan got back. Her motive was purely selfish. She never knew how much that day meant to Quinn.

"Oh Quinn, just wake up and go home. We can all be friends again like we used to." Lacey's mind told him.

"I've already told you I can't. But I need to ask you a favor. I've been just waiting for you to come."

"What?"

"Lucy's daughter is mine. Please watch out for your niece. When the time comes, love her like she was your own." Quinn's mind spoke again.

"I," she hesitated. "I will," she gazed bewildered.

"Thanks," his voice was a whisper. "Lacey there's something else I need you do to. I need you to say that poem…*The miss me poem.*"

Lacey looked down sadly at Quinn. She couldn't believe he understand what he was asking. "Maybe you'd like another poem something else, huh Quinn?" She smiled. "We just need to hope you'll get better Quinn."

"No, no…" His mind assured her. "It has to be the *miss me poem.* Please say it for me Lacey." His mind pleaded with her.

"You want to hear the miss me poem?" Lacey's mind said back to him.

"Yes. Please say it to me out loud, right now." Quinn's mind said.

Lacey drew in a deep breath and with tears in her eyes she recited the poem.

When I come to the end of the road
and the sun has set for me
I want no rites in a gloom filled room
Why cry for a soul set free
Miss me a little—but not too long
and not with your head bowed low
Remember the love that once was shared
Miss me—but let me go
For this is a journey we all must take
and each must go alone
It is all part of the Master's plan
a step on the road to Home
When you are lonely and sick at heart
Go to a Friend we know
And bury your sorrows in doing good deeds
Miss me—but let me go.[1]

By the end of the poem Lacey reached out to touch Quinn's face. He felt strange.

"Quinn…" Slowly a soft cry escaped her lips and her voice shook uncontrollably.

[1]*Author Unknown[1]*

Chapter 44

I ain't that kind...

Six weeks later Brunch served that Sunday afternoon, was supposed to be a simple quite family affair.

"Grand *mere* Catherine there is nothing French, Cajun or Creole about that brewing apparatus you've got sitting on the stove. In fact, I think it resembles a ...."

"Hush Kienan, you want some homemade Muscadine wine or what?"

"Yeah, we do and I for one would love for you to make me another Red Bean Omelet with Alligator sausage," Kienan said.

"I'll take another one too," Horace Garrison said raising his hand. "That is, if you don't mind."

Grand *mere* Catherine smiled playfully. "Well Pearl it looks like you've got yourself a hit with your new recipe Red Bean Omelets with Alligator sausage."

Pearl grinned. "Well it's a good thing I made extra," she said passing the tray."

Nicholas rattled out a whistle and sucked in a deep breath. "Whew man! That's some good Gator Gumbo right there."

"This is just perfect all the family around," Lacey said.

"Let me see your engagement ring again Lacey," her mother Pearl said.

Horace Garrison coughed loudly. "Oh no, Pearl is ring sizing again. Looks like I'll be on my way back to the jewelry store."

Everyone at the table laughed.

"Poor Horace," Grand *mere* Catherine said.

Instantly the doorbell chimed.

"The door is open come in," Nicholas yelled. "It's probably Maëlle, I promised her at our couples counseling class that I would invite her over. We are slowly working our problems out."

Maëlle walked in with a shocked look on her face. "Hi everybody, look who I found standing on the front porch.

Lucy Mondragon took a step from behind her, holding her baby in her arms."

"What the hell?" Nicholas replied with a disbelieving look.

"Hello, everyone, I'm attorney Toto Dubois," he said gripping his leather briefcase.

A hushed quiet descended on the room.

Attorney Toto Dubois cleared his throat, thankful everyone held their comments about his name. "Well I guess I should tell everyone why I'm here.It seems Miss Lucy Mondragon has a proposition. In fact, she believes that since this little girl is actually a La Cour niece, you fine folks won't object to her relinquishing custody to you. That is unless you want this child to be raised in an orphanage, or worst yet, put into the California foster care system."

Lacey stood up. "Lucy you wouldn't do that, not to your own child. What kind of mother are you?"

"Well sister, I ain't the kind you think I am," Lucy said tilting her head coquettishly to one side. "Besides Lacey, didn't you promise Quinn you'd take care of his brat for him?"

Stunned Lacey stared back at her in surprise. "How did you know that?"

Lucy walked over and placed the sleeping baby in Lacey's arms.

"Because that old wizard of love, told me himself," she said flatly. "You got to hand it to Quinn, he's one hell of a seducer."

Lacey looked up at Kienan.

He looked suspicious back at her. "My gut tells me there is more you want to share Lucy," Kienan said firmly. "Who's the guy behind you?"

Lucy took a step back and said apologetically. "Oh yeah, this is Attorney Dubois. Please tell everyone why we are here."

The attorney took the papers out of his briefcase. "As you will see one Quinn Darnell Rosolado Rolandis, and one Lucy Lynn Mondragon," and the attorney read the relinquishment documents.

Finally, attorney Dubois loudly cleared his throat and said. "And one Lacey Kadira Catherine La Cour and one Mr. Kienan Maitland Egan are hereby named as parents, and legal guardians of Miss Kadira Marie Catherine Ina Rosolado Rolandis La Cour Egan."

"Hump! Quinn better had put my name in there somewhere," Grand *mere* Catherine replied. "No offense Pearl but it looks like Quinn left your name out."

With a quiet sadness for the child she held in her arms, Lacey leveled a steady gaze. "Lucy, why did you agree to do this, just give up your baby?" her voice shook.

Kienan sat there and watched in stunned silence, he watched Lacey's shoulders slump and he roses and put his arms around her. "It's okay Lacey, here let me help you with the baby. I'm here for both of you," he said hugging her and the baby close.

"I just can't believe a mother would give away her own baby," she sobbed out.

"For the money of course," Lucy said putting her hands on her hips. She seemed unfazed by what she was doing. "Besides Lacey, everybody can't have a good man like you do. Quinn knew I wouldn't make a good mother," she said with frankness. "If Quinn isn't sticking around to raise his kid why should I?"

Kienan gave Lucy a deadly glare. "How can you talk about the dead like that Lucy? Do you have no respect?"

Lucy laughed out. "Quinn isn't dead. Unless you called being whisked off to a hospital in Mexico as dead. His grandmother took his butt out of the country. Why do you think she begged you to tell him goodbye?"

"Lucy you're a sad twisted bitch," Maëlle snorted.

"And we both know you know exactly what a twisted bitch looks like Maëlle," Lucy laughed out.

Maëlle jokingly waved her hand. "Be gone my fellow twisted witch! Be gone! And take your Toto Dubois, your attorney friend too!"

Lucy shrugged her shoulders, turned and took her leave as attorney Toto Dubois followed closely behind.

Everyone listened as the front door closed soundly behind them.

"Whew! I'm glad Lucy the witch has left," Lacey replied.

"And Toto too!" Grand *mere* Catherine roared with laughter. "Okay then that means Kienan you need to go over that attorney's documents with that Geek King brain of yours and make sure every dot is dotted and every box that matters to us is taken care of."

"I'll check it out," Kienan promised with a smile, and then gave her a knowing look.

Epilogue

*S*ix months later, The Wedding...

   "Grand *mere* Catherine, please doesn't give her that. You're spoiling her rotten and she'll mess up her dress."

"Oh, hush up Lacey. That's what great grandmothers do. Spoil the younglings and then give then back to their parents."

"Mom!"

"Quiet Lacey," Pearl said helping Lacey put on her veil. "Today is your wedding day. Your guests are waiting in the ballroom for the reception," Pearl said shaking her head.

"Okay Mom but please make sure Grand *mere* doesn't give Lil Kitty any more sweets," Lacey replied.

Lacey watched her grandmother playing with her daughter. All at once she whispered. "I'm so lucky. I have a daughter and a husband now," she exclaimed. "You know Mom and Grand *mere* it's strange how things work themselves out. Who would have thought Lucy would just up and give me her daughter?"

Pearl shrugged. "Okay you want the truth. I thought she would. The first time she called the house looking for you."

Grand *mere* Catherine wiped Kitty's face. "To tell you both the truth, I think it was Louis' doing. I believe your father came back, as an

Angel, of course. But he came back and made everything right. He had to make sure his granddaughter Lil Kitty as alright."

"Um hum!" Pearl cleared her throat. "I agree with your grandmother," she smiled. "Look you too. Have you forgotten we got a crowd of people waiting at a wedding?"

Lacey checked her earrings and headed toward the door.

"Lacey I've been looking for you." She said pulling her away. "That cousin of yours, Acadia, she had better not get married before I do." She leaned over and whispered, "She scratched my arm trying to get your bouquet. It's a good thing I elbowed her good, or I never would have caught the bouquet."

Lacey shook her head and laughed out, "Oh Maëlle, what am I going to do with you."

A shrilled high-pitched Cajun drawl filled the air. "Lacey you know you are my favorite niece. Introduce your Cousin Rufus to that pretty friend of yours, Paris. I think they'd make a wonderful couple," her aunt Mimi yelled.

"But Momma I like Kienan's Cousin Bella de Burgh better," Rufus muttered.

"Hush up Rufus, that girl Bella is a little touched in the head," Mimi whispered.

Maëlle grabbed Lacey's hand and pulled her away. "What am I going to do while you spend three weeks on your honeymoon? Oh, I have an idea.Why don't I go to New Orleans for a few days with you, before your flight to the Caribbean? I've always wanted to go to Frenchmen Street and hear Miss Sophie Lee and the Three Muses."

Lacey sighed, "No Maëlle, because then it wouldn't be a honeymoon. We'll be back before you know it."

Kienan walked briskly over. "There's my favorite wife." He took her in his arms and kissed her.

"I better be your only wife," Lacey eyed him laughing.

"Hey, Kienan, my cousin Father Anael is still mad at you for taking his woman," Maëlle said.

"Maëlle, tell Anael Paschar he's a Priest. He doesn't seem to know it," Kienan laughed out kissing his bride.

Her mother and Horace walked over.

Pearl's voice rung out cheerfully, "See how handsome my new son-in-law Horace is." She softly said. "And he made me a Grand *mere* already too."

"Horace Garrison, watch out for my mother, while we're on honeymoon," Lacey smiled.

"You know it," Horace said giving her a hug.

"Hey Lacey and Kienan," Nicholas' voice sliced through the air. He walked over and patted Kienan on the shoulder. He leaned over and pulled them together into a hug. "Hey Kienan, want to be the best man at my wedding?"

Kienan smiled big at his new brother in law, "I think Horace and your mother may beat you getting married."

"Yeah, you could be right about that, Maëlle and I are still in couple counseling," Nicholas said. "So Kienan, I knew you had that Irish heritage thing going on with that African American thing, but you could have warned me about that uncle of yours."

"Uncle Séamus is harmless."

Nicholas shrugged, "You know Kienan, if your Uncle didn't have brown eyes, I'd swear I saw him before. In fact, if you put green eyes on him, I'd swear he was a homeless guy I saw once."

Kienan stared wide eyed back at him, "Ah, he did have a twin brother that died. They looked the same in every way, except Uncle Ceallagh had green eyes."

Nicholas laughed out nervously."Whew! Stop spooking me man. Thank God your uncles didn't have bright golden red hair."

Kienan hesitated, "The fact is that when Uncle Séamus and Ceallagh were young men they both had bright red hair."

Nicholas looked thunderstruck. "I've got to go find Maëlle. I'll talk to you later Kienan.

A deep thick Spanish accent sliced the air, "Folks can I get you all in a photo?" The photographer called.

Three hours later the limo driver pulled away from the curb in front of the Fairmont Hotel.

Lacey sighed, "I'm so glad that's over with."

"Come here," he said. Kienan's voice sent shivers down Lacey's spine. As he pulled her close, "We're finally alone."

"You are the stuff my daydreams are made of. You are so deliciously wicked, Kienan Maitland Egan!"She breathed out smiling down at her husband.

Kienan stared back looking at the woman he loved. "Lacey, I promise to try to always be the ideal man you were looking for. I know all about that ideal husband stuff you told Father Anael back at Mrs. Oshun. He told me. I almost punched that Priest in the face when he told me he was your ideal man."

"You care…You really care about me," she softly smiled.

Kienan pulled her close and kissed her slow and tender. "I love you…Always have and always will."

He ran his hands brazenly over her body. His kisses grew demanding and frantic. "I could touch you forever."

Lacey murmured soft and low. She angled her head to the side. "Kienan," she choked out. "You'd better stop that, or we'll never make it to the airport."

"Oh, I'll promise to be finished by the time we get to the airport," he whispered.

⸙

It's Here Book II!

**Lovers,
Players
&
REVENGE!**
A
Geek,
An Angel series
Book 2

Coming Winter 2019

Winter

2019

Dear Gentle Readers

Dear Gentle Readers

Dear Gentle Readers, Fans, Family and Friends,
In an effort to provide you with the most honest information about me. I confess I am a self-published author. That's right, I am committed to writing a story, a novel every chance I get (hopefully I will put out two to three books a year). Even though I have a whacked-out, frenetic, hectic schedule as do many others. I persevere. I am committed to writing my stories.

With that said, I'd like to make a request of you my gentle readers, followers, friends, and family. I appreciate that you read my books. And I need you to please leave a review of my book, with your site.

I will be truthful if you do. Your kindness to me in reviewing my books would go a long way in helping me continue my self-publishing journey.

Again, thank you for your time, it is greatly appreciated. Your kindness to me in reviewing my books would go a long way in helping me continue my self-publishing journey.

Thank you for all that you do. I truly appreciate you!
Sincerely,
J. A. Jackson
Email: jerreecejackson@gmail.com

Thank You Myra !

✦

"It takes someone strong to make someone strong."

Books by J. A. Jackson

Books by J. A. Jackson
A Geek an Angel Series
The Deceiver
The Proposition
The Grand Hotel
Lovers, Players, & The Seducer
Lovers, Players, Revenge
The Mistress of Desire
& The Orchid Lover
The Mistress of Desire
& The Orchid Lover Book II
When A Taker Dreams
Diamond at Midnight

About the Author

About the Author J.A. JACKSON

J.A. JACKSON is an author who lives in an enchanted little house she calls home in the Northern California foothills with her husband and Big Sally an American scent hound. She fell in love with writing as a small child. She spent over ten years working in the non-profit sector where she wrote grants, press releases and contributed many stories to their newsletter. She was their Newsletter editor for over ten years. She loves growing roses, a good pot of hot tea, chocolate, magical stories, suspense stories, ghost stories, and reading Jane Austen again and again in her past time. Please write her at P.O. Box 612751 San Jose, CA 95161.

Pseudonym: J. A. Jackson

You can connect with me on:

- http://jerreeceannjackson.blogspot.com
- https://twitter.com/jerreece
- https://www.facebook.com/JerreeceJackson/?ref=bookmarks

Subscribe to my newsletter:

- https://mailchi.mp/ddf9555be2a4/theauthorjajackson